T0171036

Also by David Lozell Martin

Tethered

The Crying Heart Tattoo

Final Harbor

The Beginning of Sorrows

Lie to Me

Bring Me Children

Tap, Tap

Cul-de-Sac

Pelikan

Crazy Love

FACING

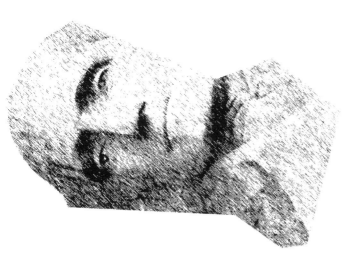

Simon & Schuster

RUSHMORE

David Lozell Martin

NEW YORK LONDON TORONTO SYDNEY

SIMON & SCHUSTER
Rockefeller Center
1230 Avenue of the Americas
New York, NY 10020

This book is a work of fiction. Names, characters, places, and incidents
either are products of the author's imagination or are used fictitiously.
Any resemblance to actual events or locales or persons, living or dead,
is entirely coincidental.

Copyright © 2005 by David Martin
All rights reserved,
including the right of reproduction
in whole or in part in any form.

SIMON & SCHUSTER and colophon are registered trademarks
of Simon & Schuster, Inc.

For information about special discounts for bulk purchases,
please contact Simon & Schuster Special Sales:
1-800-456-6798 or business@simonandschuster.com.

DESIGNED BY PAUL DIPPOLITO

Manufactured in the United States of America

10   9   8   7   6   5   4   3   2   1

Library of Congress Cataloging-in-Publication Data
   Martin, David Lozell.
      Facing Rushmore / David Lozell Martin.
         p.   cm.
      1. Mount Rushmore National Memorial (S.D.)—Fiction.
   2. Government investigators—Fiction. 3. Indian activists—Fiction.
   4. South Dakota—Fiction. 5. Land tenure—Fiction. I. Title.

PS3563.A72329F33 2005
813'.54—dc22   2005051589
978-1-4516-5648-0

To David Rosenthal

The past is not dead. In fact, it's not even past.
—WILLIAM FAULKNER

Part I

Cracking the Arch

1

"DANCE. I DANCE, CHARLIE. If you want to put that down as my occupation, go ahead, it's all I do, it's all I've done for sixteen years, since I was seventeen. I didn't go to college, didn't even finish high school. I never married. I danced. During the day I danced with other dancers, at night I danced alone."

"How'd you end up in Tennessee, isn't that where all this started?"

"Three months ago the grandfather asked me to move to Tennessee."

"Did he tell you why?"

"He gave me money to rent an apartment, he gave me money to live on, he asked me to wait, but he didn't tell me why, no."

"You move from Montana to Tennessee without knowing why?"

"Yes, because the grandfather asked me to. The apartment I found in Nashville, there was no place to dance outside, so I danced in my apartment until the woman below me complained. I would watch the window for her car to leave, then I'd dance while she was gone. I know all the dances, Charlie. I wanted to ask you—in prison will I be allowed to dance?"

"You think you're going to prison?"

"Don't you?"

"It depends on how much of what you're telling me checks out."

"And how much is just me being crazy."

"What's the grandfather's name?"

"I won't tell you that."

"When I cut you down, you said you'd tell me everything."

"No, I said I'd tell you the truth."

"How about the woman you were traveling with, the prostitute, what's her name?"

"Elena. I was never told her last name, I'm not sure if she had one."

"And she came with the grandfather to your apartment in Tennessee?"

"Yes. At three A.M. She had fish eyes."

"What does that mean, fish eyes?"

"At the outside corner of each eye, two black lines intersected, one that had been drawn above her eye and one from below. These intersecting lines looked like the tail of a fish, the two fish facing each other across the bridge of her nose."

"What did he say about her, about why she was there?"

"The grandfather introduced her as God's whore, he said her mother sent her to see the ghost dance."

2

I TOLD THE GRANDFATHER that dancing at three A.M. would make the neighbor below me pound on her ceiling with a broomstick, but you have to understand, Charlie, I would be ashamed not to do what he asked.

When I was sixteen and living alone in a trailer, when I was incorrigible and drunk and had dropped out of school, the grandfather came to me. I figured he had been sent to deliver a lecture about staying in school and bettering myself, this lecture I had heard many times from the apple Indians, those who are red on the outside but white inside, and from European teachers, from Christian ministers.

I invited the grandfather into my old trailer, a hunter's trailer without power or water, and out of respect for his age offered him a chair and then I put on my Indian face. It's the face I wore when you first began questioning me, a good face to show during grandfather lectures and government interrogations.

The grandfather asked if I knew how to read. I said I did. He told me, "We Indians believe in the words a man speaks looking us in the eye. But the Europeans will tell one thing to your eye and then write another thing on paper and then it is the written word they swear by. So it is good you can read what they write. Each morning I walk to the library and read yesterday's *Jew York Times*. You can trust the Jews to write the truth, they are a tribe."

I think you will meet the grandfather before this is over, he is negotiating on our behalf, and when you see his face you will see how old it is, how dark, creased by ravines, and I believe you will trust him.

The grandfather delivered a lecture brand-new to my ears, saying it was good I quit school, good I refused job training, good I would not work for wages, good I spent all my time hunting and fishing and riding horses. The European ways must be rejected, he told me. Especially their poison. I had beer bottles everywhere on the floor, lined up and leaned over.

The grandfather explained that tolerance to alcohol increases with a people's exposure to alcohol. He said that the ethnic group that has used alcohol the longest will have the lowest rates of cirrhosis, dementia, public drunkenness. He said he was thinking of the Jews again, who have been drinking wine for thousands of years and have a low incidence of alcoholism. But for a people newly exposed to alcohol, it is poison to them. Europeans knew this intuitively, which is why they gave us alcoholism along with other diseases for which we had no tolerance. He said I could not be a ghost dancer if I kept drinking alcohol, it would disrespect our ancestors to ask for their resurrection while I was drunk.

You asked me, Charlie, why the little whore's mother wanted her to see ghost dancing, why I have spent so many years ghost dancing. Let me tell you.

In 1889, the Paiute medicine man Wavoka had a vision during a solar eclipse, and in this vision Wavoka saw the new world rolled up and, underneath, the old world revealed as it once was, with fish in our rivers and lakes, game in our forests, and buffalo, not Europeans, by the millions on our land. In this old world, occupied only by Indians and by those we call our friends, we would be reunited with our resurrected ancestors. All this would be brought about without violence, without war, without killing.

The promise of ghost dancing required two things of the Indians. One was rejection of everything European: their culture, their money, their jobs, their religion, their alcohol. Their law, too. The grandfather asked me many times how can you trust a legal system that says if a man has committed a crime but you can't prove it, then that man is not guilty.

The second thing required of the Indians was ghost dancing.

Ghost dancing is unlike our other dances. It is slow and without instruments, not even the drum, and women are permitted to ghost dance. We move in a circle following the sun while singing softly our resurrection chants.

In 1890, ghost dancing appealed to the defeated Indians of the American West. Many whites called ghost dancing the messiah craze; it was said Jesus had given up on the whites and was coming this time to the Indians.

Why did ghost dancing frighten your ancestors? Think of it, Charlie. You have defeated a proud and fierce people. They have become compliant. They line up for Army beef and stay drunk. But then, because of some crazy dance, these former warriors sober up, no longer tame. Now these Indians are keeping their own counsel, rejecting everything European. And they dance, Charlie. I think maybe it reminds you of those long hot nights on the plantation when you heard jungle music from the slave quarters.

No, of course, your ancestors didn't own slaves, I know that, Charlie. They were innocent.

When the great Sioux medicine man Tatanka-lyotanka, the one you call Sitting Bull, began ghost dancing, the Europeans became even more frightened. He was an old man but he had been at Greasy Grass, what you call the Little Bighorn. For the sin of ghost dancing, Tatanka-lyotanka, sixty years old, was arrested and killed while resisting arrest. Shot in the back by tribal policemen.

Trying to stamp out the ghost dancing messiah craze, the U.S. Army rounded up Indians at Wounded Knee Creek. Five hundred Army troops with four rapid-fire Hotchkiss guns surrounded four hundred Indians, men and women and children and babies in their mother's arms, many of the Indians without blankets or food. The Army was so afraid of ghost dancing that even the Indian women were disarmed of cooking knives and sewing awls. While the Indians were being disarmed, a shot went off and the Army opened fire. When women and children fled into the ravines, they were chased down and shot in the head, in the back. Twenty of the soldiers were awarded Congressional Medals of Honor for shooting women and killing babies held in their mothers' arms.

The chief they called Big Foot died at Wounded Knee as he rose from his sickbed. And now at gas stations and drugstores in the western states you Europeans buy postcards with the picture of Big Foot's frozen body. I don't know what you do with such a profane image. I think you must take it home and gloat.

The Indian dead at Wounded Knee were left where they lay for three days in the snow, more than three hundred murder victims. When a hired burial party finally arrived, four starving babies were found still alive, wrapped in their dead mothers' blankets. The grandfather said this again reminded him of the Jews and how a few of them were on occasion found alive in Nazi burial pits.

White curiosity seekers came to Wounded Knee to snatch up souvenirs. Indian babies whose parents had been killed were adopted by white families but the Indian babies were said to be like certain wild animals, cute while young but unmanageable when mature.

With the Europeans' grisly sense of history, they called this massacre the Battle of Wounded Knee. Not even the Nazis were so indiscreet as to call Auschwitz a battle. It is dangerous to make the comparison, but six million Jews were killed by the Nazis, more than ten million Indians killed by Europeans in the conquest of the Americas.

If the Nazis had won the war they might have put up monuments to the Final Solution. The Europeans, who did win in America, put up a memorial marking the jumping-off spot for settlers, explorers, prospectors, soldiers, and others who were heading west to complete the genocide of Indians—and that memorial is the Gateway Arch in St. Louis, and that's why the whore and I cracked its ribs.

The grandfather brought her to me in Tennessee. At his request, I showed Elena the ghost dance. After a few minutes, before the downstairs neighbor began complaining, the grandfather said, "You can stop now. The promise of ghost dancing has come about."

I asked him, "If I walk outside, will all the apartments and houses be empty of Europeans, will the roads be empty of their cars?"

He said in good time. "God's whore will explain everything."

She was too young, Charlie, just a teenager. And I couldn't imagine her being interested in ghost dancing, she spoke into a cell phone and chewed gum and played with her hair. She was little, maybe a hundred pounds. Dressed in a short red skirt and tight white T-shirt and wearing knee-high white boots. An underage whore. Her face was made up with thick red lipstick and blue marks painted like diamonds and stars. Her eyes were strangest of all. Yes, those fish eyes. She had outlined them with thick black streaks. Yes, I know. I've already told you this. It is our way. We handed down our history by repeating its stories. Which is why you never hear an Indian say, "You already told me that." When her eyes crossed, which they did frequently, these two fish looked as if they were staring at each other past the bridge of her nose. Her voice was high and chirpy and frequently profane on the phone.

The grandfather asked me to take her to California, where she would meet with her mother.

"My mother is a fucking saint," she got off the phone long enough to say.

Irony? I don't know, Charlie. All of this was being laid on me without warning, a couple hours before dawn, the grandfather saying he wouldn't be going with us, he'd be returning by Greyhound, and that the whore and I should leave immediately because there were people who would try to stop us from reaching California and we needed to get a head start. I filled a garbage bag with my things.

Her car was a big black ten-year-old Thunderbird, which she had left running in the apartment complex parking lot. The little whore got in the driver's side while I took shotgun, throwing my garbage bag in the backseat and telling her, "I don't have any money."

She was adjusting the phone book she sat on to see over the steering wheel, then looked at me as if she hadn't understood what I'd said. I was mesmerized by her fish eyes, which at the moment were fully crossed, making me think I should volunteer to drive.

I rubbed my thumb against my fingertips to indicate money and told her again I didn't have any.

She laughed, turning to study the gear shift as if this was the first time she'd used it. She finally dropped that big V8 in Drive and took off with tires squealing, barely missing parked cars, straddling the center white line, and when she remembered about headlights, she took her crossed eyes off the road to find the right knob.

I grabbed the wheel and turned us out of the path of an oncoming car, which blared its horn. She looked up at the road, slapped my hand off the steering wheel and laughed again, shouting and swearing. . . . Charlie, it was the damnedest thing.

3

"IF THIS WASN'T ALL PLOTTED out beforehand, as you say it wasn't, then I don't understand. Someone asks you to go to California from Tennessee and you throw a few things in a garbage bag and take off, just like that?"

"I didn't have a suitcase."

"You know that's not what I meant."

"Ask me what you want to know."

"Why did you go with this teenager, this stranger, to help her destroy the St. Louis Arch?"

"I wasn't aware that's where we were going. I wasn't aware that's what we would end up doing. All I knew at the beginning was that the grandfather had made a wise decision, taking Greyhound back home, because the little whore drove like a crazy person. Acted crazy, too. Kept playing with the radio. Sang along with the songs, except it wasn't really singing. She chirped and keened. Always laughing. She'd point to a cow and laugh like a cow was the funniest thing she'd ever seen in her life. As exhausted as I was, I stayed awake, petrified, as she drove us across Tennessee, heading for Memphis, or so I thought at the time. I asked her to stop. I needed the toilet and I also wanted to drive before she killed us both. But every time I spoke to her, she would look at me with those spooky fish eyes, listen carefully, and then nod and laugh as if I had just told a joke.

"At one point, halfway between Nashville and Memphis, she stopped the Thunderbird right on the pavement—on the *interstate,* Charlie—and took out a map. I was telling her to pull off the road. She kept smiling. I reached my foot over to hit the accelerator and used my left hand to steer us onto the shoulder. Just then, a semi went screaming by, blowing his air horn. The little whore powers down her window, leans halfway out, and *waves* to him with both arms and gives him the finger. I told her I was going to drive. But she stayed in the driver's seat, on that big phone book, studying the map. Then she took off again, north at the next interchange."

"Heading for that Kentucky motel where you say you killed the man."

"Yes. But I didn't know that's where we were headed, I didn't know she had an appointment with the Viking. Her driving was even hairier on the two-lane roads, she kept drifting off the pavement. The ditches in that part of Tennessee are deep. They get a lot of heavy rains. Finally she stopped at a gas station. I hit the can at the run. When I got back she was standing behind the Thunderbird talking on her cell phone. Seeing her in the cold morning light I got a dose of reality."

"Because?"

"Because I realize that this little girl with her short-short skirt and tight shirt and the way she was made up looks like a junior high kid playing grown-up hooker and I'm going to get caught with this Lolita and have my red ass seriously in a sling. I tell her *Hurry up* and get in the car.

"I got behind the wheel and asked her if she had filled the tank. She said yes and told me to go. She said she's in a hurry, let's go already, talking to me like I was an idiot. As I'm pulling away, a little Iranian dude came out of the station, hollering at us. Elena told me, go, go. I knew then she hadn't paid. You can add that to our crime sheet. A tank's worth of stolen gasoline. She's a whore and a gas thief."

"Where was this?"

"I don't know exactly. An hour or so south of the motel. I headed north, watching behind us for cops. The whore kept studying her maps. She directed me, pointing right, pointing left, finally to the motel, which was just over the Kentucky border."

"I've talked with the manager of that motel."

"I know you have, Charlie."

"No crime was reported for the day you were there. Two weeks ago, right? On the eleventh."

"Someone cleaned up after us."

"Who?"

"I don't know. At first I thought the Viking was one of yours."

"FBI?"

"Someone from the federal government, yes. FBI, CIA, BATF, BIA, I don't know, there's a whole alphabet to choose from."

"The CIA can't operate domestically."

"If you say so, Charlie."

"If neither of you had any money, how'd you get a room?"

"She had a key. Room Twelve. Unlocked it and waltzed right in the room. I got my garbage bag and her suitcase, followed her."

"He wasn't there at that point?"

"No. I didn't know the Viking even existed at that point."

"So you're in the motel room with the girl."

"So I'm in a cheap motel room with a whore, yes. A situation I am not unfamiliar with, how about you, Charlie?"

"How about me what?"

"Do you frequent whores?"

"I'm married."

"I'm right-handed, but that's not what I asked you."

"No, I don't have sex with prostitutes."

"You stopped when you got married?"

"The truth is, I've never been to a prostitute."

"Never? Not even when you were a young man, not even when you were on a drunk or out with—"

"Never, no."

"I know you're shitting me. But I understand. The videotape is running and you don't want it on your FBI record, I understand."

"You can believe what you want to believe, but I have never been with a prostitute."

"Not even one time?"

"Not even one time. What are you doing? Sit back down."

"I was just going to shake your hand. You're the first—"

"Stay in your chair, that was our agreement."

"Or else the local cowboys watching behind that glass will rush in here and beat the shit out of me."

"Something like that. Okay, so you're in the room with the young prostitute."

"She pulled off her T-shirt, wearing a white lacy bra, and now I'm giving myself serious lectures about not thinking what I was thinking. She puts her suitcase on the bed and proceeds to strip and soon enough she's walking around naked except for those knee-high white boots."

"Did you have sex with her?"

"You want I should describe her naked body?"

—

"Charlie?"

"Did you have sex with her?"

"She had narrow hips and a little ass, all of which contributed to her underage look, but then again she had really nice tits. Stuck straight out. Big brown nipples. And a bush."

"Did you have sex with her?"

"Wow. Single-minded on that issue, aren't you? No I didn't have sex with her, Charlie."

"Because you feared she was underage?"

"No, because I didn't have any money. Actually, Charlie, at that point I was more interested in sleep than sex. I was waiting for her to stop fooling around with her suitcase and take it off the bed so I could lie down and sleep, when *bang-bang-bang*, there's someone at the door."

"The man you describe as a Nordic type."

"A Viking, yes. Except at the time I figure it's the motel manager wanting to know how the hell we got into this room without paying, or maybe it's a cop who's after us for skipping out on the gas—whoever it is, it's not good news, because they're going to come in here and find me, an Indian, with an underage girl and that ain't good, Charlie, even if the girl is a professional, that ain't good."

"What did you do?"

"I'm looking at the whore for some direction, she's the one who brought us here, but she runs into the bathroom with her suitcase and shuts the door behind her. So I'm left to face whoever's kicking the door and hollering to be let in. I see no way around it. But before I go to the door, I slip a folding knife from my front pocket and open the blade."

"Describe it."

"The blade was about four inches long, the knife eight inches overall."

"If you didn't know who it was, why did you arm yourself?"

"Exactly because I didn't know who it was. Maybe the whore was meeting a john. Or her pimp."

"Or maybe it was the law."

"Whatever. I locked the blade in place and put the knife, blade first, into my back pocket. I opened the door and there's the Viking, a big white slab of a man, taller than I am and broader, his head the size of a bowling ball that sits on those broad shoulders without benefit of a neck, long blond hair pulled back and knotted, his eyes that terrible blue—devil eyes I call them, when they're that blue and that cold. He looks angry, ferocious, a chained dog wanting to get at me like I was the one been tormenting him. Adding to the unreality of this situation, he's dressed like a villain in an apocalyptic movie, long black duster that goes to the ground, black leather pants, dark red shirt that's tucked in but unbuttoned to showcase a V-section of his torso, his curly-haired chest, blond and ripped. Black boots. Hooked nose. About my age."

"What did he say?"

"He asks me who the hell I am."

"And you said?"

"For the first few seconds, I didn't say anything. This big storm trooper frightened me. I wouldn't run from him and, if a fight started, I'd do my best, but big angry white guys have always frightened me. The football coach was like that. He wanted me to play on the line, referred to me as the big buck. He had a terrible temper. I've met ranchers like that, and cowboys and cops. I don't know what makes them so pissed off, what puts the blood in their blue eyes. You have eyes like that. I haven't seen them angry yet but, yeah, those icy blue eyes. Light brown hair. Blond as a kid?"

"Yes."

"Hell, Charlie, you could be the Viking's brother. If you beefed up. The sight of an Indian doesn't piss you off?"

"No."

"You been around Indians much?"

"I wrote a paper about Wounded Knee Two, that's why I was called in here."

"In your version of Wounded Knee Two, who was at fault?"

"There was plenty of fault to go around."

"Amen."

"Did the man ask for Elena?"

"First thing the Viking says, he says, 'Listen, Nanook, you speakum the English 'cause I asked you a goddamn question, who are you and what are you doing here?' I wasn't surprised the name-calling started already but that was the first time anyone referred to me as Nanook. Then he asked where Elena was. 'Where's the whore?' is how he put it. Before I can answer, she steps out of the bathroom, the Viking and I both staring at her. If it wasn't such a tense situation, I would've fallen down laughing. Her face was freshly made up, the fish lines around her eyes even darker than before and the diamonds and dots re-blued, and she had slicked back her hair with some kind of oil. The funniest part, she was wearing a baby-doll nightie that came to her thighs, see-through to show off her boobs—but now she was wearing tiny white sneakers like you'd buy at a kid's shoe store."

"What happened?"

"Let me tell you something first, Charlie. She didn't look twelve or fourteen any longer, she looked early twenties."

"Did the two of them know each other?"

"Put it to you this way, she's smiling the big white teeth for him, he has blue eyes only for her, and I'm obviously three's a crowd. Which is fine by me. I plan to leave and wait in the Thunderbird. She tells him he's early. He says, 'Yeah, so I gather.' He means he got here early enough to catch me in the room. 'What's with Nanook?' She says I'm her escort. The storm trooper laughs and mutters something obscene about having a goddamn Eskimo for an escort. 'He's Sioux,' she tells him. Which doesn't seem to matter one way or the other to the storm trooper who instructs Elena to get rid of me. I'm more than willing to leave but she says, 'No, he stays.' *Get rid of the Eskimo.* She says no again and before he can say yes again, she asks him, 'Did you bring it?'

"This gets the Viking's mind off me and he turns and checks the door before taking out from the deep front pocket of his greatcoat a package about the size and shape of a small loaf of bread, wrapped in brown paper and elaborately taped. Elena puts out her little hands. He tosses it to her. She begins loosening the paper. He tells her it's all there. You know what I was thinking, Charlie?"

"Drugs."

"Bingo. She opens the top of the package and looks in, then she smiles another mile of smiles at him and tells the Viking to sit down. She indicates the bed while she takes a cheap motel chair and positions it against the wall, putting herself on display, crossing her legs and flashing him her cootchie."

"And at this point you're assuming it's a drug deal and that you've been brought in as protection."

"Something like that. The grandfather would never knowingly get involved with drugs, so I figure the little whore somehow duped him with stories of bringing about the promises made by ghost dancing. It's better all around if I leave, even if I have to hitchhike. But when I stand, she calls me by my European name. 'John! Don't go!' She doesn't sound like a little girl, sounds like a woman now. 'Sit,' she says. 'Stay. Please.' The Viking doesn't bother to turn his big head to see if I am going to leave or not, he no longer cares, I might as well be a dog that Elena is trying to get to sit, to stay. I take a chair in the corner. I knew it was stupid for me to stay but stay I did. This whole thing had become dreamlike, starting with being awakened at three A.M. and taking off on a trip to California with a crazy woman I'd never met before."

"Then?"

"She asks the Viking if he knows where it's going to begin."

"Where what's going to begin?"

"I don't have a clue. He starts to speak but then finally remembers me and he does something with his hand. Makes a semicircle in the air, the top half of a circle or the shape of a rainbow."

"The arch."

"Yeah, but again, at the time, I'm clueless. It's obvious that Elena knows what he's referring to. He tells her, 'If you're a good girl you'll get another package when it's done. Now, where is she?' Elena says, 'California.' He says, 'I know she's in California, where in California?'"

"Who were they talking about?"

"I didn't know."

"Elena's mother."

"Yeah, but I didn't know that at the time. She tells him, 'On the California coast.' Which makes him mad. 'I *know* she's on the coast,' he says, '*where* on the coast?' Elena won't say. Then he asks the strangest damn question, he asks, 'How old is she now?'"

"Meaning what? How old was Elena's mother?"

"You got me, Charlie. He leans forward as if to catch her scent and tells her, 'Have you forgotten there are certain individuals who don't want you to make this trip? If something happens to you, we need to know where she is so we can take her to the president.'"

"*The president?*"

"Easy, Charlie."

"You think they were referring to the President of the United States?"

"At the time, yes, I did. Because all of a sudden I'm thinking these aren't drug dealers, they're terrorists. Elena accused the Viking of being one of those certain individuals who didn't want her to make this trip. 'Then why did I bring you that?' he asks, indicating the brown paper package, which Elena has put on the floor by her chair. She laughs. 'To have sex with me?' And he says, 'Let's do it.'"

"So if they're terrorists—"

"Yeah, I'm thinking maybe they're discussing picking up something in California and taking it to the president in Washington, D.C., maybe not Elena's mother for real, that's just code for a bomb."

"What was your role in all this going to be?"

"Exactly. I'm thinking, To be the patsy. You ever see the tape of Lee Harvey Oswald hollering to the press one of the times he was trotted out, hollering that he was being made the patsy? I'm thinking, *Exactly. That's me.*"

"Meanwhile, what are they doing?"

"The Viking stands and takes off his big coat, dropping it to the floor, removes his shirt. His body is perfect and the little whore is grinning at him like she can't wait, playing the whore's role. She pulls off the negligee, he puffs out his chest for her, and I'm thinking I can't imagine two more mismatched people, the big white Viking and the little fish-eyed whore. When I stand to leave, Elena looks past the Viking and pleads with me, uses my full name. The storm trooper has his boots off and turns to me as he unbuckles his big belt. '*John Brown Dog?*' Laughing. He says, 'If I took a name it would be Screaming Eagle or Howling Wolf . . . sure as hell wouldn't be *Brown Dog*.' He drops his leather pants, underneath he's wearing a black thong. Elena keeps begging me to stay. "Please, please." I sit again in my corner chair like the fool that I am. Leaving her sneakers on, Elena gets on the bed, she's not even going to have the decency to put something over them so I don't have to see the actual screwing. As she lies down to be mounted I keep thinking she's not really going to have sex with him, at the last available moment she's going to say she's changed her mind or maybe pull out a pistol and blow his brains onto the wall, something is going to happen to prevent her from fucking him right there in my presence."

"Why were you thinking that? She was a prostitute who'd just been given some sort of payment, why wouldn't she have sex with the man?"

"I don't know."

"Because she was so young?"

"She didn't look so young anymore."

"You had feelings for her?"

"She's a whore, Charlie."

"Did they have sex?"

"They were getting there. The Viking peels down his thong and turns to me. 'Tell you what, Nanook.' He is half erect and, Charlie, he is enormous like a porn star is enormous. A real asshole, too. Tells me, 'If you sit quietly in the corner and don't make a peep while I fuck this whore, when I'm finished I might give you a little reward . . . 'cause I know you got a thing for me, I saw you go all gooey-eyed at the sight of me.' Then he strokes himself hard."

"And you stayed there?"

"I know what you're thinking. I am without dignity."

"For staying there, yes."

"An honest man."

"Go on."

"He's holding both of her wrists in one of his big hands and forces her arms above her head. He reaches down between them with his free hand. She's saying things like 'Oh, yeah, baby, easy baby, you'll be there, baby.' You know, whore talk. Or I guess you don't know. And he keeps asking Elena, 'Where is she? Where on the coast? How old is she?' Elena laughs at him. He grunts and pushes, she tells him, 'Not there, don't put it there.'"

"And you just watched?"

—

"Did she ask you for help?"

"You're making me ashamed of myself, even more than I am already. No, she didn't ask for help. She didn't say, 'Oh great warrior, come rescue me.'"

"But at some point . . ."

"I told them both to stop, yes. He turns his big head to send me his blue-eyed contempt. 'Sit down, Nanook, I'll let you know when it's your turn.' Then he slaps her and then, Charlie, he makes his left hand into a fist that he holds high above her face, warning Elena, 'Either you tell me exactly where you're meeting her on the coast or I will by God pound you until not even an Eskimo will want to fuck you.' Which is when I tell this Viking Nazi storm trooper Aryan Hitler wet dream, 'I am not Inuit, I am Lakota.' Which impresses him not at all. He's annoyed with me, like he would be with a barking dog. 'I don't care if you're fucking Hiawatha P. Squanto, go sit down or I'll beat the shit out of you, too.' He hits her in the face. You know the sound that makes, Charlie, that fist-to-face meaty thud? Elena, the breath goes out of her little body. But all she says is, 'Oh.'"

"And that's when you attacked him?"

—

"John?"

—

"You can have a lawyer whenever you want. I've told you that."

"I believe you. The grandfather always said that Europeans put their words upside down and backward but you're one European I believe."

"I'm not a European."

"Where did your people come from, however many generations back when they first came to America, where did they come from?"

"Go on, how did you attack him?"

"I jumped up on the bed and grabbed his long blond hair and pulled his head back and slit his creamy white throat, is how I attacked him."

4

INDIANS TELL OF GOING RED in the eyes, of becoming so psychotically furious during a fight that we literally see red, everything bathed in red light, and you feel no pain and you fight with ten times the normal strength and it is only later, when the red rage has lifted, that you realize bones have been broken and veins opened. But I was not like this, the killing did not enrage me, and I did not give the death cry, though it was taught to me by the grandfather.

Elena's nose was broken, her right eye already swollen. She sits up covered in blood and looks at me with a focused concentration that makes me worry what she's going to say.

"Scalp him" is what she says. And then she does that thing they do, that strange sound women make with their tongues. *Ululate?* Okay. Whatever it's called, it's spooky and it gets your blood up and it was that sound which finally made me go red in the eyes.

Did I scalp him? No, Charlie, I did not. But I did give the death cry and I did dance for the young whore with fish eyes, and in that small room with the copper smell of blood in our nostrils we made a spectacle of ourselves . . . but, no, I did not scalp him, Charlie.

You know what else I didn't do to that big blond bastard, I didn't break his legs. Have you read that the legs of the soldiers killed with Custer were broken, those we had time to break? We do that so our enemies will hobble in the next world. When the Lakota women found Custer dead on the field, they rammed their awls into his ears to unstop them so that in the next world he could hear and would not ignore the warnings he'd been given in this world, to leave the Indians alone.

The little whore got dressed and called me a great warrior. This is the second time a whore has called me a great warrior—see what you're missing, Charlie, by not patronizing whores?

My first whore— No, Charlie, this won't take long. The grandfather had made arrangements when I turned twenty, when he found out I had not yet been with a woman. He took me to an Indian whore who I thought was very old, though she was probably as old as I am now. She was fat and smelled of deep frying, of lard. Her little house trailer smelled of soiled diapers. I don't know where her babies were, maybe she had put them in a back room and told them to be quiet while she conducted business. The grandfather waited outside in his truck.

Without speaking to me, she walked to her bed and pulled up her skirt. I was shocked by the size of her bare naked suzie, it seemed as big as a football. Neither of us said anything while the transaction was conducted and then she wiped between her legs with a diaper she picked up off the floor.

I know what this sounds like, like one of those sad pathetic stories of someone being introduced to sex in a way that is ugly instead of beautiful as lovemaking should be, but, Charlie, I remember the Indian whore with great affection. She was patient with me and did not criticize my inexperience. Before I left, she said, "You are a great warrior." She spoke without enthusiasm, as if being called a great warrior was part of what I had paid for, but her words wrote themselves on the place where a man keeps his pride.

And now Elena was telling me the same thing.

I was hyped up. I was terrified at what I had done, at the consequences. I was pissed at this crazy teenager for getting me into this trouble. Putting my bloody knife at her soft throat, I demanded the stupidest thing a man can demand of a whore, "Tell me the truth."

5

"TRUTH ABOUT WHAT?"

"Everything, Charlie. What had she told the grandfather, why was the Viking asking her about California, was she a terrorist or a drug dealer or what."

"How'd she answer?"

"She laughed."

"Even though you held a knife at her throat?"

"That's correct. She laughed and then she offered to blow me."

"I find that hard to believe, she could be so casual after seeing you kill a man."

"Yeah. A man who was, at the time I slit his throat, still inside her. Before, when we were acting crazy, she had described what that felt like . . . inside of her. Yes. I told you this little whore was profane, Charlie. What, you don't believe me?"

"No. There's no evidence a crime was committed at that motel, certainly not a murder that involved slitting someone's throat, which would have left a lot of blood."

"What's the point of me telling you all this if you don't believe what I say?"

"Do you want me to *pretend* I believe everything you tell me?"

"I guess not."

"So you left the motel."

"So we left the motel."

"Go on."

"It seems pointless."

"Maybe you'll convince me, go on."

"Her face looked absolutely ruined, from where he'd hit her, and I cleaned my knife and I'm telling her we ain't going to get far and she insisted there was nothing to worry about, *his* people would be along to take care of everything. The body would be removed. The room would be cleaned. And if anybody heard anything or if the manager was suspicious, all that would be taken care of, Elena said."

"Did she say how?"

"No. People paid off, I guess. The package the Viking gave Elena was full of twenties and fifties."

"How much?"

"I don't know, I didn't count it. Thousands."

"So then you left."

"She put on a pair of jeans, white blouse, still wearing those white sneakers. We got our stuff and took off in the whore's Thunderbird, driving a two-lane through the toe of Kentucky, driving toward the Mississippi River. In spite of her terrible facial injuries, the whore won't let me take her to a hospital. I keep checking behind us for cops and my certain demise. A sickness in the stomach rose up in my throat, sick from having killed that man and exhausted from lack of sleep, and, also, for the first day in sixteen years I wasn't dancing.

"We drove past little Kentucky farms where workers were spraying chemicals to create fields so toxic that the farmers won't even walk through them—poisoning their own wells, watching their own children die of cancers, but still chemically soaking their land to boost yields, flooding the market with product, bringing down prices, needing even more chemicals for higher yields for less profit, a system put in place by corporations not to provide cheap groceries but to sell chemicals."

"Is that what this is about, some kind of environmental—"

"Environmental what, Charlie—environmental *nonsense*?"

"Just answer the question."

"What was the question?"

"Did the woman say anything about eco-terrorists?"

"The whore didn't say anything about shit. She was back to her maddeningly happy and manic self, in spite of a broken nose and swollen eye, apparently unconcerned by what happened at the motel, and I have to keep flipping the radio back off as she keeps trying to scan the dial for tunes. Have you ever been with a crazy woman?"

"No. No, I guess not."

"Never been with a whore and never been with a crazy woman—Charlie, you must have money in the bank."

"Where did—"

"Some guys I know, they're, like, addicted to crazy women. Woman cuts up all her man's clothes with a pair of scissors, woman crashes her car into the front of his house, shows up where he works screaming about loving his cock, that kind of shit, and I ask these guys, *Why do you put up with it?*, and they can't exactly explain it but basically they're addicted to the excitement, the novelty, anything to avoid the boredom of life."

"Like you with Elena."

"No, I wasn't with her voluntarily."

"Where'd you go after Kentucky?"

"We pass over to Illinois, Elena back with her maps and directing me this way, that way, until we're traveling the river road along the Mississippi. She was fascinated with the river, trying to get me to stop."

"But you didn't stop."

"No, sir. In spite of what she told me about someone cleaning up the crime scene, I considered us seriously on the lam. She directs me across a bridge spanning the Mississippi and leans out the window to look at the river. She's smiling like a boxer who won at a terrible cost. I ask her, 'Do you realize what would've happened if he'd continued hitting you in the face like that?'"

"What'd she say?"

"She puts a soft hand to the side of my head and asks if a blow job wouldn't make me feel better. I knock her hand away and drive a few more miles until she tells me to pull into a church complex outside Perryville, Missouri."

"What church?"

"The big sign said, 'The National Shrine of Our Lady of the Miraculous Medal.' Elena gets out and goes into one of the church buildings."

"You didn't go in with her?"

"I felt beat up. I melted. I fell asleep."

"Even though you were on the lam?"

"That's right, on the lam but dead to the world. Wake up. It's raining like a son-of-a-bitch, late in the day, no other cars in this huge parking lot, and God's whore apparently still in His church. I was debating going in after her or driving off without her when she came out a different door, Elena walking in the rain, which was falling now in end-of-the-world sheets, holding out her arms and turning slow circles, her head back so the rain could fall on her face. By the time she reached the Thunderbird she was soaked to the skin, her white blouse transparent and I can see that lacy bra she's wearing. Her makeup has run in vertical streaks, blue and black. But the strangest thing is that the wounds, the swollen eye and broken nose, look a lot better. In fact, in my paranoia, I began thinking that the Viking only *faked* hitting her and then, when I wasn't looking, she used theatrical makeup to create the artificial wounds."

"That was possible?"

"No. I saw him hit her. I saw her wounds right afterward. I'm saying, *in my paranoia* I was trying to figure out how her face could possibly be looking better already when it should've been even more swollen, even more discolored. You know how facial wounds are, for a while after the injury they look worse and worse."

"So how could hers be getting better?"

"You're going to get sick of me saying this, Charlie, but I don't know. Maybe she went into the shrine and got healed by some miraculous medal, I just don't know. Also, I realized then that I'd been wrong about her age. She wasn't a teenybopper. I don't know what had fooled me before but now, her face fresh washed by the rain, I could see she was well into her twenties. She insisted on driving and when she got settled behind the wheel, sitting on her phone book, she asked me about the ocean."

"The ocean? Apropos of what?"

"I don't know, out of the blue she asks, have I seen the ocean, is it really as big as they say it is."

"Which ocean?"

"She didn't specify. I told her, yes, oceans are big. Was it salty, she wanted to know. Yes, salty. She opened her mouth and showed me her little pink tongue darting around like a snake's and she said, 'Mmm, salty!'"

"Where'd you go from there?"

"River roads travel up both sides of the Mississippi but Elena had to be on the Illinois side so we crossed the bridge again, Elena steering like a crazy woman, through the town of Chester, the home of Popeye, which she hadn't heard of. I tried to explain to her but—"

"She doesn't know about the ocean, she doesn't know about Popeye?"

"Yeah, crazy. But she knew everything about *Indians*. Said she studied Indians in another lifetime. Crazy whore."

"Which way did you head . . . north?"

"Yeah, we hurried north, raining like a son-of-a-bitch."

"You could've stopped and done a dance to make the sun come out."

"Charlie, what are you, a comedian?"

"No."

"Catholics can swing smoke and sprinkle water and make the high sign before attempting a field goal, but when Indians dance the rain dance, suddenly everyone thinks it's vaudeville."

"Sorry. I was out of line."

—

"John?"

"Fair enough. Elena's driving, I'm drifting off again when she stops the Thunderbird. The road is blocked by a tree blown down in the storm. Looks like neighborhood people chopping and chainsawing the limbs. No highway crew that I can see. Must've just happened. I'm ready to resume sleep but Elena nudges me and indicates this could be trouble."

"Did she say what kind of trouble?"

"No. But I can imagine all kinds. After all, I was a murderer only several hours old, so I go on alert. Has she seen cops? Is this a roadblock? Are the neighborhood people really undercover agents? 'Remember!' she tells me."

"Remember what?"

"She tells me to remember what I must do, go to the California coast and find her mother."

"But she hadn't told you where her mother was, had she?"

"She does now. Her mother is in a castle overlooking the sea."

"A castle, huh?"

"Charlie, I'm telling you what she told me. A castle by the sea. I don't know where that might be or what she means by it. We see a woman walking toward the car. Middle-aged and stocky like a man, wearing a hood over her head for protection from the rain and inside that hood I can see her white face smiling. In her left hand she's holding a hatchet. 'Get ready,' Elena warns me. Get ready for what? The woman is probably coming over to tell us how long it might be before they have the tree removed and we can be on our way. This isn't a police roadblock. Elena begins revving the engine, the woman raising her hand to say hold your horses. I'm about to tell Elena to calm down when I notice the woman glancing back at some men who've stopped working on the tree to stare at us. It seems to me—and I am admittedly deep into paranoia by this time—that the woman was signaling something to the men and that they acknowledged her."

"Signaling to what, attack you?"

"Wait. The woman has just stepped to the driver's door when Elena floors the accelerator, heading for a narrow gap between the top of the fallen tree and the water-filled ditch as people dive out of the way, slipping and falling on the slick pavement. I brace for impact, for the gut-sick sound of running over a body, but the whore makes it through, one jagged tree limb putting a long scratch along the Thunderbird's right flank, all the way to the rear bumper. And behind us the people who'd been working on the tree aren't shaking their fists and shouting and giving us the finger like I thought they would, like they had the right to do, instead they're just standing there watching us speed away."

"Do you think it was an ambush or merely some people removing a downed tree?"

"I could go either way on that, Charlie. Events had overtaken me at that point."

"No one tried to follow you?"

"No. Through a driving rain we drive the river road skirting the east bank of the Mississippi. Elena keeps slowing down at intersections, looking left toward the flooding river. I don't know what she's searching for. I pick up her map. It wasn't from AAA, believe me. It wasn't even in English."

"Did you recognize the language?"

"No."

"Would you recognize Arabic if you saw it written?"

"It looked more like hieroglyphics. Symbols. A little bird here, a pack of dogs there. What I do recognize is a red line showing our route, and when I orient myself where we are on the map I can see that the red line will be taking us off on a little side road and, sure enough, there it is. She hangs a left onto a muddy road."

"She didn't tell you where you were going?"

"No. All I'm thinking is, *Don't get stuck.* She takes the Thunderbird down toward the river and stops in front of an abandoned church. Next to the church is a small cemetery, no more than thirty or so stones surrounded by a waist-high iron fence. The graveyard is under a foot or so of water. The river is also flooding past the church, water halfway up to the first-floor window. I ask her what're we doing here. Outside there's a world of rain with that big river on the run. Instead of answering me, she gets out and hurries down to the Mississippi and jumps in."

"Jumps into the river?"

"That's right."

"Which is flooding?"

"Yes. I'm waiting for her to be swept away but the whore is having a great time. In the river to her waist, she ducks under the water—filthy chocolate water—and comes up laughing. When she gets back to the car she stinks of river water. The remainder of her makeup has washed off, and I swear to God, her swollen eye, the one that was so badly injured that I thought she might be blinded, it's barely puffy, and her supposedly broken nose is back to normal."

"I don't understand how that can be."

"Me either. She takes off all her wet clothes. Elena sitting there in the driver's seat, perched on her phone book, looking at me, and she's totally cross-eyed and totally naked. You ever fuck a cross-eyed girl?"

"Don't ask me those kinds of questions."

"Okay, Charlie. I figure she's going to change into dry clothes but instead she keeps eyeing me the way a woman will, the way a whore does when she asks if you want to party. Staring at me her big dark eyes slowly uncross, which freaks me out, and then she *leaps* catlike over onto me. I thought I was being attacked. Elena slips down to the floor at my feet where she's in position to start working my belt loose. She makes her lips into a saucy pout and gets my zipper down, which is when I grabbed her wrist, small enough that I could encircle it with a finger and thumb. Tiny as she was, she was strong, and she managed to get my dick out—"

"Maybe you weren't trying hard enough to stop her."

"Again, the comedian. I don't know if I want this recorded on an FBI videotape."

"Whatever you feel comfortable telling me."

"They teach you that at FBI school, Charlie—how to win over the guy you're interrogating?"

"Yes."

"Ha! Charlie, be careful, the way you're slinging around the truth—somebody could get hurt."

"I just want to understand. You believe yourself to be fleeing from the scene of a homicide but you take time out to park by the river and receive oral sex?"

"Yes."

"It doesn't calculate."

" 'Calculate'? You don't have a very strong sex drive, do you, Charlie?"

"That's not at issue here, what's at issue here is if you're telling me the truth or stringing me along."

"I gave you a promise, that I would tell you the truth, and I don't think you understand, Charlie, what an insult it is for you to keep implying that I'm a liar."

"So you had oral sex, and then what?"

—

"You're mad now?"

"I could clam up and let you pepper me with questions and just keep giving you my Indian face."

"You're either going to tell me or you're not."

"Charlie, damn it, the problem is, you don't want to hear what I have to tell, you want to hear something that'll be easy for you to believe."

"I want to hear the truth."

"Okay, the truth is, she's down there on the floor sucking my dick and at one point she looked up with eyes that have re-crossed and she says, 'I practiced on cucumbers.' Which strikes me as funny. Hilarious. I'm laughing while I'm getting my dick sucked and then I see a kid unlatching the iron gate to the cemetery and come wading out toward us. Damnedest thing, he's wearing a dark suit, white shirt, like he's just gone to Sunday school at that church then stopped by to visit a grave, which is crazy, the church was obviously abandoned years ago . . . and we're in the middle of a rainstorm, but there he is, wading toward the Thunderbird."

"How old was the boy?"

"Around eight or nine. He's got blue-black river mud all over his face and on his clothes. I pull Elena up off the floor and she sees the kid and gets out of the car, she's still naked, and the two of them are out in the rain, obviously they know each other or know of each other, and the kid is pointing this way and that, giving her directions or instructions and then he starts making that half-circle, rainbow shape."

"The arch again."

"But I didn't know that, did I? At that point the arch hadn't been damaged so it wasn't exactly in the forefront of my mind. I had never been to St. Louis."

"I'm just having a real hard time believing all of this."

"You should be a whole hell of lot nicer to me, because I'm going to explain how the arch got ruined, how it got covered in black, and that information is going to make you a hero in the FBI."

"We'll see."

"Because your guys haven't figured it out yet, have they? I heard that someone was trying to blame the damage on an earthquake. Which doesn't explain why the stainless steel arch is now black, does it? Christ, look at this, I'm bleeding all over the place."

"Do you want to see a doctor?"

"I'd like to have the dressings changed, I'd like to have a clean shirt."

"We can do that. I'll arrange for a doctor to come to your cell. You can catch a meal, grab a nap. I'll have you brought back here in a couple hours, okay?"

"One thing I wanted to tell you."

"What?"

"Suicide isn't part of my culture. It was said that some soldiers at the Little Bighorn were so terrified that they killed themselves before the Indians could. The Indians couldn't understand that. Suicide was shameful, especially for a warrior. Custer had a bullet hole in his temple, he might have shot himself, too. I know that's sacrilege for you to hear."

"What's your point?"

"If I'm found hanging in my cell with a bedsheet knotted around my neck, it wasn't suicide."

"I'll post a guard."

"These South Dakota cowboy cops hate Indians."

"I'll post one of our agents."

"You're a good man."

"I'm doing my job, is all."

6

ROUTE 3, I THINK. A good river road, Charlie. In Southern Illinois it ran by itself next to the Mississippi, ran through rough river towns, but then we're driving away from the river, through heartland towns, Ruma, Red Bud, Waterloo, north toward St. Louis. Miles later, day gone, that great river road becomes just another street in suburban sprawl, power lines crisscrossing overhead and neon on both sides, the traffic stop and go, stop and go. I close my eyes to the ugliness and let the whore risk my life driving cross-eyed through traffic and rain. When I awaken, it's dark and we're alone, stopped in the road, the rain even worse than before.

I look up at what the headlights are trying to illuminate through the rain. McKinley Bridge, it says. Closed.

Elena turns the car around and says she's scared. It's the first time I've heard her admit to that. She taps the map with her fingers. "It said cross at McKinley Bridge! Closed! Ambush!" She whips out her cell phone and starts manically punching numbers.

But the bridge looks to me like it's been closed a long time and not just for us. On the other hand, we're in a wasteland and I can't discount the possibility of an ambush.

Unable to raise anyone on the phone, she drives on. We're across the river from St. Louis, Charlie. We're approaching cities at their worst, East St. Louis and Venice and Madison, Elena looking for a way to cross the river, getting us more and more lost.

This is such a bad idea, I'm thinking. Being here.

Somehow we're back on Route 3 and on one side are great industrial complexes, apparently abandoned, surrounded by chain link and razor wire, final resting places for hulks of rusting machines, the uses of which I cannot imagine, the rain a deluge. On the other side are tenements, burned-out buildings with random windows glowing TV blue, abandoned cars, hardly a street light working. No other cars on the road. You don't want your Thunderbird to flood out on these terrible streets. Africans live here, but it doesn't matter your color, you don't want to break down on this mean stretch of Route 3.

Elena is speeding up, skidding, recovering, and I mean to tell her slow down, don't kill the engine in all this water, but instead I reach over and hold her arm for comfort, as a warning to be careful. Elena takes my hand and brings it to her mouth and kisses my fingers. For the first time since this trip began, I feel like we're in it together.

Up ahead is an urban cemetery surrounded by a ten-foot chainlink fence with razor wire on top and I'm, like, *What's with the fence?*, you know, Charlie—are they trying to keep the dead in? Because what's in there for the living to steal, plastic flowers?

Our headlights catch a guy standing out in the downpour. What the hell's he doing, waiting for us? Using one hand to make that halfcircle, rainbow shape in the air. Arch.

I tell her, *Don't stop.*

But of course she does. This guy has given her the high sign.

He stands there. I have to step out into the deluge to open the back door so he can get in the car.

An African. I don't know, in his twenties. Okay, at this point I'm sufficiently spooked and paranoid and wasted from the events of the day that I start getting as weird as the whore I'm traveling with, because you know what I start thinking, Charlie, that this African kid in our backseat is a zombie. He moves, but he looks like he's dead. His color is all wrong, gray under the black. His eyes are sunken, his mouth hanging open. He's wearing dark dress slacks and a black leather jacket styled like a sports coat and he's got on a white shirt and his clothes are spattered with mud, he's wet through to the skin, he's shivering. He looks small, like he needs blood.

Elena hasn't mastered the concept of pulling over to the side, she just stops in the road when something happens. But now, at this hour, past midnight it must be, and in this torrent of rain, there's no other traffic, I'm not worried about being hit by another car, what I'm worried about is the African in the backseat. How'd he know we'd be coming by here, and what the hell happened to him to make him look like the living dead?

"You're going to be taking a left at the next road," he tells Elena, his voice calm and normal sounding even though his teeth are chattering with the cold. He smells of dog, of dirt. "Go under the viaduct. It'll be flooded in the low spots, so be careful."

The African gives Elena a series of directions, Go right, go two and a half miles, go left, three blocks, then right . . . I don't try to remember the route he's giving but Elena's downloading every word he says.

He says, "John Brown Dog, they're going to try to get you to stop."

Yes, it blows my fucking mind, Charlie. I have no idea how he knew my name but at this point I'm ready for him to sprout wings or disappear in a puff of smoke, I'm bracing for miracles and ruins and rapture.

I asked him, What do you mean they're going to try to stop me. Who?

"Temptations," he says, then leans forward and touches Elena softly on the shoulder. "The whore will be one of them."

She laughed.

He tells me, "The whore won't be wise until she's old, so be careful how she tempts you." I have no idea what he's talking about. "Don't stop," he says. "Not for anything, anyone. Don't get out of the car. No matter what you're offered." Then he tells Elena, "Left at the next road."

She starts the Thunderbird, hangs the left, goes down under a viaduct, taking it slow. Water leaks in the bottom of our doors. When she comes up the other side, she increases her speed.

From the backseat the African says, "Watch out for the dogs."

I don't see any dogs, but no sooner has he spoken than Elena takes a corner and there's a pack of feral city dogs right in the middle of the street. Elena has to hit the brakes, which puts us in a skid and we end up crashing into a mailbox. Add that to the list, Charlie—destruction of United States Postal Service equipment.

We're stopped half on the sidewalk and when I turn around to see if the African is okay, he's gone. The back door is open. The dogs take off after something, the African kid, I guess. They're howling.

Elena doesn't seem surprised or concerned, she backs off the sidewalk and drives away through the rain. The Thunderbird's right headlight must've been damaged in the crash with the mailbox because that light is shining up and out at a crazy angle. The back door's hanging open, but it closes when Elena makes another sharp turn.

We continue past broken houses, burned cars, trash everywhere, wet and floating, taverns have bars on all windows and doors, which I'm used to seeing, but so do the houses, so do the churches. You got to wonder what terrible things are out and about that people here have to lock themselves behind bars while praying to the Lamb of Peace.

Near a racetrack are sex clubs advertising adult couples, strippers, lap dances, escorts, and one windowless concrete-block building with a single neon sign that apparently blinks all night long: SEX.

Another pack of feral city dogs crosses in front of us, some of the smaller ones forced to half-walk, half-swim the flooded street. Once the dogs get up on the sidewalk, a Rottweiler jumps a skinny hound and starts fucking her while the other dogs come sniffing around and get into fights, a Black Lab clamping down on the throat of a soaked Chow who gives up but isn't shown mercy.

Elena appears to be following the route given to her by the zombie. We somehow end up on a narrow side street. We have to go slow because it's so narrow here, more like an alley than a road, in places there's barely enough room for us to squeeze by piles of garbage bags, overturned trash barrels. Right next to this alley, in a covered passageway between two abandoned buildings, a teenage girl, thirty pounds overweight and bare-ass naked except for knee-high rubber boots, is pulling a train, a dozen men waiting in line while the girl, leaned over and spread-legged, grabs a drainpipe to offer up her big white ass, some of the waiting men stroking themselves to keep ready for when it's their turn.

The girl brightly lit by an alley light no one has got around to breaking yet sees us creeping by in the Thunderbird and over her shoulder throws me a cretin's smile.

Elena stops the car.

I ask her what's wrong.

"Get out," she tells me.

"And do what?" I ask her.

"Go fuck that fat white whore," she tells me.

"You're crazy."

"I know you want to."

"That black kid said for us not to stop. Not to stop for anything, he said."

"You got a hard-on, don't you?"

I called her an evil little bitch, which she was, Charlie, she was, but you couldn't insult her, she just grinned and flashed her crossed eyes and suddenly she looked all used up like an old whore.

"I didn't finish your blow job," she says. "You've had a boner ever since. Go on, go fuck her."

I get out; the rain is freezing.

Elena says, "You're going to fuck her good, aren't you?"

"I'm going to put a stop to it."

She laughs, she doesn't believe me.

Coming into the alley, I must've looked intimidating, the big buck, because the men in line start backing away, the fat white whore glancing over her shoulder and nodding to accept me while the man next up steps off to the side and offers a stupid *after you* flourish with both arms, surrendering his place in line.

At the entrance to this covered alley, back out in the rain, the Thunderbird sits idling. Elena honks the horn. We all look. A couple of the men laugh. One of them says something about leaving my woman in the car being a big mistake. The men are a lot older than I am, all of them African except me and one Vietnamese guy last in line.

Elena leans on the horn, keeping up a steady blast and one of the old Africans tells me, "You better get her to stop, that horn'll attract exactly the wrong kind of attention."

I'm about to return to the car and speak to Elena when that wrong kind of attention comes sauntering from the back of the covered alley, half a dozen African warriors in their late teens, early twenties, wearing letter jackets and black hoods and colored doo-rags.

The men who'd been in line all scatter out the other end of the alley, out into the rain; a couple of them in passing kick the Thunderbird for spoiling their alley fun and now it's just me and the fat whore facing six Africans.

I should go. I can probably make the car before they catch me.

The alley whore finally lets go of her drain pipe, sees the situation, and boosts up on a garbage can to await the outcome. She's pulled a yellow raincoat around her shoulders, her heavy breasts looking cold and dead and her dullard expression saying she doesn't care who wins the coming fight because one way or the other she's fucked.

I turn for the Thunderbird but Elena has come into the alley and is standing near me. Now we're fucked, too.

"Get back to the car," I whisper, ready to make a run for it with her, but then I'm hit hard in the side of the head with a full can of beer. The blow makes me lurch. I grab Elena to keep from falling and the Africans cheer the good strong throw hitting its target. By the time I regain my senses, they are around us.

"Yo, Tonto, what the fuck you doing off the reservation?"

So it begins. I wait for them to call me Cochise and Shitting Bull and redskin.

Elena keeps close. Although she isn't dressed provocatively, is wearing jeans and that white blouse, she is soaked through, attracting their worst attention.

Another African asks what I'm doing with this little cross-eyed bitch.

I want to tell them that we should be war brothers, united against the Europeans who took the Indians' land and took the Africans *from* their land, but I can imagine the derision my message will receive and derision is what I deserve because I'm on their territory now and I came into this alley against good advice.

The Africans try to get a better look at *my* whore, reaching for Elena as she holds tightly to my shirt and keeps close.

I can feel warm blood on the right side of my head but there's no pain, not yet. Long black arms push me one way and then the other. I am called more names. I see no weapons and wonder if I will make things worse by taking the big folding knife from my pocket.

"Call on the shape shadows," Elena says, speaking from close behind me as one of the Africans grabs her shoulders and pulls her away.

She laughs at them, curses them, then gets away and tells me again to call on the shape shadows.

"They're in the Badlands," I say, surprising the Africans who apparently thought I could not speak or would do so only in movie-Indian grunts.

The grandfather explained shape shadows to me by saying they were bad spirits gone good. You ever known a good man to go bad, Charlie? A good man who never missed a day's work, never struck his wife, loved his children, never gambled or whored around—and then one day he snaps and leaves his wife and kids, gambles away all their money, goes on a month-long drunk, takes up with whores, goes bad and stays bad? A lot of people got an uncle like that. The grandfather says that the reverse happens among devil spirits, for some reason some of them go good. And if you know how, you can conjure these bad spirits gone good. The grandfather taught me that dance.

But they're in the Badlands, not East St. Louis. For sins committed in life, these spirits are doomed in death to wander the Badlands. They're murderers, Charlie—and child molesters, cowards, turncoats, suicides, women who strangled their sleeping babies and men who cheated their best friends. And if you go to the Badlands and if you know the dance, you can put out a call among the shape shadows: Any of you bad spirits who want to go good, come now and join me, fight alongside me.

The little whore, so close I can smell her river water and curry, keeps urging me to conjure the shape shadows until I finally holler at her, They're in the Badlands, they're a thousand miles away.

The Africans all laugh.

Elena tells me it's not about traveling distance, it's about opening doors. She said she came from farther away than the Badlands, came here not by covering miles but by opening doors. She said I could reach the Badlands by opening a door. *By dancing.*

The Africans think this is all funny, and then they really break up when Elena tells me in her high chirpy voice, "You are the great ghost dancer, you can dance up the shape shadows."

The Africans shout for me to dance, they stomp around and make what they think are Indian sounds, hitting their palms to their mouths and howling.

"John Brown Dog!" Elena urges me. "Dance."

Hearing this, the Africans give each other spurious Indian names, Black Cock and Big Horse. They're so racked by laughter that I think they might just let us go in appreciation of our entertainment.

But then one of them hits me with something on the right side of my head near where the beer can landed, and two start pulling at Elena's clothes. She's no longer laughing; she says, They're going to hurt me, John.

I begin dancing. Which surprises the Africans enough that they leave Elena alone to form a circle around me, clapping their hands and hooting and aping my steps.

But this does not distract me, Charlie, because I am a dancer, all I do is dance.

When I begin chanting, the Africans chant too, in mockery of me. One of them finds a piece of iron and a stick, and begins pounding on a metal garbage lid. They're laughing, but I'm thinking this is good, what they're doing, because dancing for shape shadows, unlike ghost dancing, requires a strong drumbeat.

They howl and chant and dance, making jokes about being on the warpath and not realizing they are helping me conjure shape shadows, because we are alike, these Africans and me. We have rhythm. We are good dancers. And we have a sense of personal dignity not understood by the Europeans who think Africans are jive, and Indians childlike. You will not see an Indian or an African dressed in pastel Bermuda shorts and wearing black socks and a T-shirt that says something idiotic. The European doesn't mind looking stupid but the Indian and the African would rather look good losing than look bad winning. When word came at Greasy Grass that Custer's men were attacking the big village, many of the Indian warriors, who had been up all night dancing, did not rush into battle. They went to their tents to grease their hair and put on their war shirts; it was critical for them, for their sense of personal dignity, to look good going into a fight.

I look good dancing, I am becoming mesmerized. Although I know the dance for shape shadows, I have never danced it in earnest like this, have never truly tried to conjure shape shadows from the Badlands.

God's whore is standing next to the fat white whore still sitting up on that garbage can . . . they're not watching me and the Africans, they are looking out the alley into the rain.

Because in the street . . . shadows are gathering.

I dance. I am aware of what's happening, Charlie—I've tapped into a spiritual power your world doesn't know. Of course you don't believe me, Charlie, I can see disbelief in those cold blue eyes, but I've promised to tell you the truth.

Nine shapes and shadows, thin and tall, devoid of light, some down on all fours like wolves and some standing tall like NBA centers. They mill, twisting around one another until you can't tell which is which.

The six Africans come together and set themselves, they are braves.

I keep dancing and chanting.

When some critical mass is reached, the shape shadows come rushing. They run through the rain, heading for this covered passage where I keep dancing and chanting and conjuring as the Africans take weapons from under their clothing, filling their hands with guns and knives, their hearts with resolve.

Here, finally, is what makes the Africans break:

As the shape shadows run, the ones that are men lean down like ice skaters swinging their arms side to side, until their hands touch the pavement and they begin running on all fours like spirit wolves, while the shape shadows that began as wolves take great bounds with their front legs and leap higher and higher until they are upright and running on two legs like men. Wolves or men, they howl, an ancient eerie sound that fills the night. I name them—"*Shape shadows!*"— and I dance their music.

The shape shadows chase the Africans, who are not stupid and run for their lives.

Elena pulls me toward the Thunderbird. The retarded white whore looks to where the shape shadows and Africans have disappeared out the back of the alley and throws wide her arms, whining for everyone to come back and show her that trick one more time.

In the car, wasted, I put my head on the dash and would weep if I wasn't such an Indian.

Elena drives faster and faster through the rain until she reaches an interstate crossing a bridge over the Mississippi River. She shouts for me to raise my head and look, look!

Even in this downpour I see it clearly, brightly lit and hundreds of feet in the air, dominating the St. Louis riverside—a gigantic silver ribbon in the shape of a rainbow.

7

"THIS WOULD BE THE EARLY A.M. hours of June twelfth, approximately when the arch was damaged."

"Charlie, you cold-blooded son-of-a-bitch."

"What do you mean?"

"I'm telling you about magic here, showing you the spirit world. What if someone took an Indian from the West in the early 1800s and brought him back east to show him the Europeans gathering in the millions, showed him their superior technology, the guns and the plows, showed him how fucking ruthless the Europeans were in making and breaking deals to get what they want, and said, All this is coming your way, you poor sorry son-of-a-bitch, because all you got to stop them is a bunch of proud and contentious tribes . . . don't you think that Indian would be impressed, would think, *Wow, we are so fucked.* So now I'm trying to explain what's coming your way, Charlie. Big medicine. Spirit medicine. But you don't say *Wow*. All you want to know is what time of morning it was. For crying out loud, Charlie, I'm going to make you famous in the F. B. I., you're the one who's going to explain how the arch was ruined, how it turned black, so how's about some enthusiasm here."

"Go on."

—

"*Go on.*"

"Elena and I are driving through the deluge, heading for the silver rainbow, for that semicircle shape that everyone's been making."

"Strictly speaking, the arch isn't a rainbow shape or a semicircle, it's a catenary curve, the shape formed by a chain hanging from its endpoints. Arches following the catenary curve are the most structurally sound of all arches."

"Charlie!"

"Ever since the arch was damaged, we've all been researching it."

"It's a good thing that curve, that cantebury—"

"Catenary."

"Good thing it's structurally sound because when you see the St. Louis Gateway Arch, it seems impossible, too tall, too thin at top. Just back from the shore of the Mississippi River. How tall, Charlie?"

"Six hundred and thirty feet of polished stainless steel."

"Not polished anymore, is it?"

"No, now it's black."

"But when Elena and I got there, it was silver and bright, lit by banks of spotlights, a beacon in the rain. Finally we're on the road that leads past the park surrounding the arch. Amazingly, this time Elena actually pulls off the highway. But she parks illegally, up on the sidewalk. A foolish thing to do. We could be ticketed, a check could be run, it could be discovered that we're on the lam for a murder in a motel room in Kentucky.

"Elena asks me what I think about the arch and I told her that the grandfather hated it. The grandfather said it required an especially self-righteous and European mind-set for a people to erect a memorial to the jumping-off point for their campaign to commit genocide. He said that if the Germans had won the war, they might have built this kind of memorial to commemorate places where the Jews were loaded into cattle cars for their journeys to concentration camps."

"You already told me that."

"Did I tell you what the grandfather explained to me, that in terms of numbers, the Europeans in America were the greatest killers in human history? The Germans exterminated six million Jews, but the Europeans killed more than seven million in what became the United States, reducing the Indian population from eight million when the Europeans arrived to two hundred and fifty thousand by 1900. And that's just in your United States. Include all of the Americas, and the number of Indians directly murdered by Europeans is ten million, plus another seventy million killed indirectly by starvation and disease and displacement. Charlie! Ninety million Indians lived in the Americas when your people arrived! You got rid of 90 percent. The Germans did it more quickly, killed their six million in less than a decade. But in total numbers, the Europeans in the Americas were the worst in history. And in terms of self-righteousness, the Europeans in America were bigger hypocrites, claiming manifest destiny and their intentions to civilize the heathen Indians and bring them to God's word. What do you think God's word was, Charlie? I think it might have been two words. 'Die, redskin!' "

"What do you want me to say?"

"Martin Luther King, Jr., said that the arc of the moral universe bends toward justice—but where is the justice for Indians? There was an attempt to atone for the sin of the Holocaust—the Germans were defeated and the Jews got their own land. There was an attempt to atone for the sin of slavery—more U.S. whites were killed in the Civil War than in all other wars combined. But the European invasion of the Americas, the biggest land grab in history and the most massive genocide, no one's ever atoned for it. Until now, Charlie. Ghost dancing—"

"We need to stay focused on what happened to the arch."

"You don't want to hear the old complaints. The grandfather warned me not to bother telling Europeans what really happened, that extermination orders were sent from Washington to the armies in the West. He said, 'Their ears are stopped up, which is why they didn't hear those planes heading for the World Trade Center, the Pentagon.'

"The first Europeans coming to America brought war dogs that were fed Indian babies, babies snatched from their mothers' arms and tossed in the air for the dogs to catch and eat. But that was four hundred years ago, right, Charlie? Ancient history. U.S. soldiers killed Indian women and cut off their genitals, stretched them into hatbands or carried them on sticks for townspeople to see, to laugh about—and the children of those soldiers are alive today."

"What do you mean?"

"Figure it out. Whites were mutilating Indians in the 1890s. A young soldier in the 1890s would be in his forties or fifties during World War I; say he gets married to a young wife, has babies, some of those World War I babies are still alive today. Do your numbers, Charlie."

"It's a stretch."

"You know what you're giving me right now, you're giving me I'm-tired-of-hearing-about-it. All you want to hear about is your precious arch, what turned it black."

"Yes, that's what I want you to tell me."

"Fine. Good. We're parked there on the sidewalk, me and the whore. She climbs over into the backseat and opens her suitcase. While changing clothes, putting on a short pleated skirt, a beaded blouse, still wearing her white sneakers, she asks me what I know about Mount Rushmore."

"Mount Rushmore?"

"We'll be getting there, don't worry. Elena said if the four presidents on Rushmore were made into full figures corresponding in scale to the size of their carved heads, they would be four hundred and sixty-five feet tall. The arch in St. Louis is so big, those presidents could hold hands and walk under it. She opens a door to the storm. Where're you off to, I ask. She says, 'Let's go fuck that awful arch.'"

"Which meant . . . ?"

"I don't know but I go with her to find out. We take off in the rain. The closer we come to the arch, the more impossible it seems. The legs are triangular, thick when they go into the ground but getting narrower as they rise."

"Equilateral triangles."

"What?"

"The arch's legs are equilateral triangles, standing as far apart as the arch is high, six hundred and thirty feet, each leg fifty-four feet to a side where it goes into the ground but, like you say, narrowing as the arch rises until, at the top, it's only seventeen feet wide."

"A thin ribbon at top is what it looked like to me. Polished. Clouds above and *below*. The entrances to the underground museum are closed but no fence or barrier keeps us back from the arch itself, too mighty to need protection, its steel is stainless and cannot be marred, but God's whore apparently intends to fuck it down. The arch is glistening in the rain, rain flowing down the top side of the triangle so fast that when Elena puts her hand on the stainless steel, the sheeting water explodes all around her touch. She puts both hands on the shining wet steel, creating a cascade that shoots everywhere, and throws back her head, opening her mouth to swallow it."

"What're you doing while she's—"

"I'm standing there watching. She's making sounds from deep in her throat. She bends forward and puts the top of her head against the arch, creating a third cascade between those made by her hands, and howls."

"Howls?"

"Like something good is hurting her, energy transferred from rainwater washing down a thousand tons of stainless steel to give its energy to her."

"You've lost me. You think she was getting energy from rainwater off the arch?"

"Wait. She turns around and puts her back against the arch, waterfalls sprouting all around the outline of her body. She motions for me. When I'm standing right next to her, she reaches down and lifts her skirt, pulls her white underpants to one side and starts singing about a man in a boat."

"What?"

"She unzips me and brings me out and holds me in her fist, speaking loudly to be heard over the rain. 'This is what you want!' Yes it's what I want. She asks if this is what I wanted ever since I met her, since I saw her naked in that motel room, is this what I wanted from that other whore in the alley, is this what I want from God's whore right now. Yes, I answer to all her questions, it's what I wanted before and it's what I want now.

"When she puts me at the right place, I push in, Elena wet inside and out. 'Easy, John,' she tells me. 'Go easy, you'll be there.' And when I go easy to get there, she ululates—see, Charlie, I remember—and puts her head back. The sheeting rainwater covers her face and splashes over mine. We can hardly breathe. She puts one leg up and around me, drawing me closer as I go deeper. I smell her like the river as I push farther into her, Elena now with both legs around me so that she is no longer in touch with the ground but is sandwiched between me and the arch as if this is a three-way and she's the one in the middle."

"Go on, what did you do then?"

"We fucked grunting."

"I meant afterward."

"You want to skip the best part?"

"I want to know—"

"She takes me by my straight black wet hair, turns my head, and whispers dirty things into my ear, about other women, about how I feel fucking her, telling me that the hem of her underpants is stretched across her clit so that each time I go in and out of her that hem seesaws back and forth across her clit, Elena pledging to me, as a good whore will, that she has never been fucked like this, that this is why she was put on earth. Since you've never been with a whore, Charlie, let me fill you in. A good whore is like a good movie, forcing you to suspend disbelief. You know in your heart of hearts she doesn't really consider you the best fuck she's ever had, just as you know the people up there on the screen aren't really mad at each other, killing each other, but good movies and good whores are so convincing that you believe them. Hell, Charlie, if you married a good whore you could suspend disbelief for years. I don't say this lightly, and I've been with many whores, but this was the most convincing piece of ass I've ever had in my life. If God was going to have a whore, Elena is exactly the one He'd have. She was the perfect fuck.

"I feel her shuddering like she's shivering to stay warm and I feel her squeezing like a hand down there, and she says she can feel me pumping into her and flooding her and we stay together, in coitus against one leg of the arch, and then she pushes me away and tells me to dance. You're sneering."

"No—"

"Yes, you are, but it doesn't matter that you don't believe me because before this interrogation is over I'm going to prove to you what we did to the arch."

"How're you going to prove it?"

"By dancing. The way I danced in that East St. Louis alley, the way I danced around the arch, dancing to conjure shape shadows. They came up from the river, Charlie. Up from the flooding Mississippi, swollen over its banks, a hundred black shape shadows rushing the far leg of that catenary curve, monkeying up the arch like King Kongs, a thousand more emerging from the brown river to climb the arch and stain its stainless steel black, to make it torque under an unbearable moral weight, groaning and twisting until Elena and I can hear its ribs breaking."

8

WE DROVE THAT NIGHT to Hannibal, stayed in a motel butted up against a hillside overlooking the Mississippi, Elena paying in cash from the package the Viking gave her. The night manager was a skinny little guy who got all cat twitchy from having to check in a young whore paying cash and a big Indian with a garbage bag as his suitcase.

I awoke late the next morning with that overpowering dread you get coming out of a drunk blackout when you can't remember what you did the night before. There was blood on my pillow.

Elena was in the bathroom, I could hear her singing, apparently unfazed by yesterday's mayhem.

I had to take a leak but I could wait, I'm Indian. Kept thinking about breakfast. Hadn't eaten yesterday. The whore carried bottled water in her Thunderbird but no food.

What the hell's she doing in there? I go over and knock on the door. Yo, Elena, I gotta take a leak.

She opens the door giggling and covering her mouth. "You're leaking?"

Yeah, very funny, now if you don't mind, I have to—

Then I caught a good look at her face. She'd drawn in those fish eyes again, really heavy black lines and looking at me with her eyes totally crossed. I don't know if she went cross-eyed on purpose, at will, or if her eyes wandered on their own, but when they crossed like that it was mesmerizing. She'd also reapplied various blue diamonds and blue dots. I'm thinking, This should be interesting when we go out for breakfast. At least she was dressed normally, blue slacks and green top.

The weird thing was, her face had healed completely from the injuries the Viking gave her. Second weird thing, she looked like she was my age, not even in her twenties, much less her teens. How could I have been so wrong when I first met her, about her being underage?

In the bathroom after peeing I washed my face in cool water, which felt good, and slicked back my hair with both hands. I didn't want Elena smelling me and thinking it's true what she's heard about Indians stinking up the place, but I was starving and opted for breakfast first, shower later.

I came out and dressed. She stood there watching me, big smile on her spooky little face.

"Ready to eat?" I asked.

She said, "You snore!" Laughing like snoring was hilarious. "You sound like a big bear."

"In the old old days," I tell her, beginning a story the grandfather told me, "when the people lived in caves and were more like prey than hunters, a large cat specialized in stalking the people, sniffing them out in caves at night, creeping in and carrying them off. In certain families in certain caves, some men would snore so loudly that they sounded, as you say, like big bears. At the mouths of these caves the predator cat would listen and decide to go elsewhere, not wanting to tangle with bears. The snoring men protected their families and passed along their genes, which is why we have snoring men today. In those old days, snoring men were prized and women tussled with each other for the right to sleep close to them. But today women complain of the very snoring that kept the ancestors alive."

Instead of commenting on my old story, she began chattering

about how we'll have a great time together, traveling to California to see her mother. "You'll like her," Elena promised. "Everything I know about Indians, I learned in class, but she's Indian for real. She's everything that's good. Not like me, huh, John!"

No, not like you, you spooky bitch.

"And on the way, guess what, John, we'll tell each other stories!"

I said, "Yeah, it's been a riot so far."

She said I was funny.

I felt many things at that moment, but funny was not one of them.

The whore hugs me as if we're lovers, which technically we are.

I pat her on the back, yeah, yeah, let's go get breakfast.

Although it's not raining, the threat is everywhere, in the ominous sky and as a smell of rain on the air. I head for the Thunderbird but Elena indicates that a restaurant is within walking distance. How she knows this, I have no idea.

Crossing the parking lot, I see a maid entering one of the rooms and think of the motel in Kentucky where a maid is entering that room and soon will be screaming about a murdered man, and later the motel manager will tell cops he remembers seeing a white girl with an Indian in tow, a big buck—and they drove off in a black Thunderbird. Whether or not the manager saw the Viking I killed, who knows?

Walking toward the river, Elena tries to hold my hand (I don't let her) as she fishes out her cell phone and punches in a number, chatting away in some awful Valley girl talk about how, last night, she got, like, fucked while up against the St. Louis Arch, dude . . . difficult for me to accept this profane space cadet as my spiritual companion but of course it's not for us to know where angels live.

She told me I had a golden mouth.

"You looked in my mouth while I was sleeping?"

"Paha Sapa!"

Indian talk, Charlie. Black Hills. Although I believe our people called them Khe Sapa, which would be Black Mountains. After the Europeans gave us the Black Hills by treaty, they took them away again when gold was discovered. And my mouth is full of gold, which might have come from the Black Hills, that's what Elena was referring to. The year after my dental work was done, a hawk-eyed government accountant closed that particular generosity in Indian health care—no more Indian gold for Indians! I'm surprised the government didn't make me give back the gold that was already in my mouth, you Europeans are such Indian givers!

We eat in a restaurant a few blocks up from the Mississippi River. The food is good and comes in great quantities, the coffee hot and strong and constantly refilled. I eat and eat. The whore only plays with her food, more interested in watching the big brown river out the window. When I finish my plate, she hands me hers.

"You're not hungry?"

She shrugs.

People were staring at us. I get that a lot, especially when I'm away from the reservation, away from where Europeans are accustomed to seeing Indians—and especially because I am full-blood Lakota all the way back to the beginning, no *wasichu* in the woodpile. No white in the woodpile, Charlie. Which is why I'm so dark. People have told me I look like Indians in photographs taken in the 1800s, dark Indians with brooding faces, faces black like African faces. But the effect, being stared at, was intensified this particular morning because I was with a little whore who had her face made up like a carnival.

A six-year-old boy wearing a plastic cowboy hat stops at our table. His parents are fascinated with Elena but the little boy has eyes only for me. I think if he calls me chief or puts up his palm and says, "How!" I might take my egg-stained fork and shove it into one of his sky-blue eyes.

His mother leads the son away before I can blind him.

Elena asks me what's wrong.

"That Injun blood ain't in me for nothing."

You know where that's from, Charlie? A line from *Tom Sawyer.* Written by America's most beloved author. *Tom Sawyer* was required reading at my school. The villain is Injun Joe. Everything bad he does is because of the Indian blood in him. I think maybe that's why people in Hannibal, Missouri, were staring at me, they've read *The Adventures of Tom Sawyer* and fear I'm going to slit their nostrils, the way Injun Joe planned to torture the widow lady. You should read the book again, Charlie, it's very instructive on the ways of the Indian.

After breakfast we walk through the old part of town. Passing Mark Twain's Boyhood Home, I spit on its clapboard. It's one thing for Clemens to make fun of the high and the mighty but he was also withering toward the poor and defenseless. He called Indians a "silent, sneaking, treacherous looking race." That was in *Roughing It,* Charlie.

The Mississippi was high and wide, fast and brown. We walk parallel to it for some time and then go down to the riverbank where, according to signs, we're not supposed to be. Elena is crouching, has her hand in the river. With her eyes closed she seems at peace, being restored by a spiritual transfusion, river to woman, I don't pretend to understand.

I'll be damned if she didn't come up with a frog. Gets me laughing, Elena holding this big-ass frog with both of her little hands, as if she's just performed a wonderment.

It was a good trick, I tell her.

"A miracle frog," she says.

I tell her, "It's no miracle and that frog ain't better than any other frog, it's just a frog."

She says, "Maybe you don't understand frogs."

She's balancing it now on her two upturned palms. I reach down and touch it, expecting it to jump, but the big old bullfrog doesn't move. When I nudge it harder, the frog gives a heave and hunches its shoulders like a Frenchman but stays planted solid as a church.

"You don't understand frogs," she says again.

"If you kiss that frog, it'll turn into a prince."

She puts her hands closer to the water, whereupon the frog jumps into the Mississippi River.

Elena stands and looks pleased with herself, telling me she already has kissed a prince.

"Me?"

"No, not you, John Brown Dog," she says, taking out her phone and punching in a number.

"Put that away and tell me where we're going from here."

"Storm Lake," she says, ignoring me and speaking into the phone. "Yeah, I just told him."

9

"STORM LAKE IS IN IOWA, Charlie. That's where we were headed. What's the name of that committee investigating what happened to the arch?"

"The Blaine Committee."

"Have you talked to them yet?"

"About what?"

"What do you mean, 'About what'? About what I told you, how the arch got damaged, why it was blackened."

"I haven't made my report yet, no."

"Don't you have an obligation to warn your people what's coming their way?"

"What exactly is coming our way?"

"I'm going to prove it to you before this is over."

"So you say. What part of Iowa is Storm Lake in?"

"Northwest."

"Strange, isn't it, if you're heading for California that you would be going to northwest Iowa?"

"You're right. We weren't taking a direct route. There were certain stops we had to make first."

"Wounded Knee."

"Obviously. That's where you found me, cut me down, let me bleed all over you."

"Can we jump ahead to Wounded Knee, or did anything of significance happen in Iowa?"

"Charlie, you want to skip Iowa? Ah, I know the feeling well. We drove through Ottumwa and Oskaloosa and other towns with Indian names. That's another difference between the European genocide of the Indians and the Nazi genocide of the Jews. If they'd won the war, the Nazis wouldn't have given any of their towns Jewish names, wouldn't have named their soccer teams the Rabbis. But in America, you Europeans were rabid about getting rid of us and then named your towns after us, called your ball teams the Chiefs and the Braves, taught your kids bogus Indian rites on Boy Scout camping trips. I think you liked the idea of us but hated our reality. Once in a sportsman catalog I saw an Indian head, made of plastic but life-size and looking real, with a real-feather war bonnet, that could be mounted on your wall just like a deer head. What are Indians to make of that, Charlie? Should we take it as a compliment?"

"We need to wrap this up. Did anything of significance happen between the time you left Hannibal and the time I found you in Wounded Knee?"

"Significance, significance. The whore shared with me her theory that corn, not humans, was the dominant species in Iowa, that corn somehow convinced the humans to plant it, cultivate it, harvest it, year after year. In Iowa, corn is worshiped, she said. Corn is king. I told her in South Dakota there's a corn palace. She said, 'Aha!' Like that proved her point. I also told her that all the corn she sees is sterile. The hybrid corn they grow in Iowa has good yield but the seed it produces won't grow a new plant next year, you have to buy brand-new seed each spring. Elena said this was a good trick. She said that's how the promise of ghost dancing would be fulfilled. Like hybrid corn, Europeans won't produce seed for new crops. 'No more people born.'"

"Wait a second, what's that?"

"You weren't listening, were you? Soon as Iowa and corn got mentioned, your eyes glazed over."

"What did she mean about no more people being born?"

"I didn't question her about it at the time. She said a lot of crazy things I didn't question. And also my soul was leaking out a little with each mile of Iowa and I wasn't up for detailed discussions regarding the fate of the world. I wanted to get into South Dakota, which is bleak but not bleak like twelve million acres of Iowa corn. I wondered about the leaking souls of the farmers who worshiped that corn king. They ride tractors across fields that extend beyond the horizon and when they reach the arbitrary end of one row of corn, do they turn around and ride back to the other horizon? You don't think that would make you look out upon the world with mad eyes? When we stop for gas, people stare at us. They don't sneak looks, they stand there and stare. I buy a newspaper but the only news is of corn futures, nothing about a throat-slashing murder in a motel in Kentucky. I took my turn driving the black Thunderbird, Elena sitting with her head out the open window like a dog reading our slipstream. We travel like this a hundred miles in silence, then the whore sits back in her seat, breathless and teary from the wind."

"John—"

"You said you wanted to hear anything of significance that happened in Iowa."

"I don't want to hear about every time you stopped for gas."

"Here's something significant. Out of the blue, she begins talking about Hiawatha. And Minnehaha, Laughing Water, Hiawatha's starlight, moonlight, firelight. After the maize was planted, green and shining, Hiawatha told his wife, Minnehaha, that she would bless the fields by drawing a magic circle around them, protecting them from destruction. She would do this by stripping off all her clothes and walking around the fields. In the night, when all is silence. Hiawatha speaking to Minnehaha. In the night, when all is darkness, when the Spirit of Sleep, Nepahwin—"

"Come on, stop screwing around."

"I was laughing my ass off. Hiawatha and Minnehaha are not real, I tell her, they were made up by a European. Based on real Indian stories, she insists. Then Elena informs me very sternly that the Indian stories in Hiawatha were researched by an Ojibway Indian woman whose name was The Woman of the Sound Which the Stars Make Rushing Through the Sky."

"Is this going somewhere?"

"It's how we passed the time of Iowa. Elena claimed she knew every word of *The Song of Hiawatha*. I tell her that's impossible, it's too long. 'Every word of it is in my memory bank,' she says. 'I think of you as Hiawatha and me as Minnehaha, your starlight—' Which gets me laughing again. She starts reciting. 'By the shores of Gitche Gumee, by the shining Big-Sea-Water . . .' I tell her to stop, she's going to make me wet my pants, but then I begin enjoying her singsong voice, speaking the *poem* beautifully, speaking words as if beating on a drum, a constant tom-tom recitation that reminds me of ghost dancing, and I'm thinking, *Hell, maybe she does know the whole thing*. 'Then, upon one knee uprising, / Hiawatha aimed an arrow; / Scarce a twig moved with his motion, / Scarce a leaf was stirred or rustled, / But the wary roebuck started, / Stamped with all his hoofs together, / Listened with one foot uplifted, / Leaped as if to meet the arrow; / Ah! the singing, fatal arrow—'"

"That's enough."

"Charlie, she taught it to me. 'But the heart of Hiawatha / Throbbed and shouted and exulted, / As he bore the red deer homeward, / And Iagoo and Nokomis / Hailed his coming with applauses. / From the red deer's hide Nokomis / Made a cloak for Hiawatha, / From the red deer's flesh Nokomis / Made a banquet to his honor. / All the village came and feasted, / All the guests praised Hiawatha, / Called him Strong-Heart, Soan-ge-taha! / Called him Loon-Heart, Mahn-go-taysee!' Where are you going?"

"We're finished."

"What are you charging me with?"

"Wasting my time."

"You want proof, Charlie?"

"Proof of what?"

"Get ready to be amazed."

10

WATCH THIS, CHARLIE. Film it. And when I'm done you can take the videotape back to Washington, amaze your friends, get yourself made a hero in the FBI. But to conjure a shape shadow, I'm going to have to dance. And if I stand and start dancing, I want you to tell the cowboy cops on the other side of the glass not to come tumbling in here and beat the shit out of me. Because I know how dancing Indians scare them, piss them off. Charlie, this isn't powwow dancing, this is old-time strong medicine big spirit dancing.

Okay, Charlie, if you say so, if you think that'll hold them. Give me a drumbeat. Just beat on the desk there . . . like this, I'll show you.

I understand. You don't want to be caught on FBI video tom-tomming for an Indian—but you're making this difficult for me. I'll keep time myself. Here goes.

—

Watch those two uncovered lights, Charlie. I'm bringing them in through the lights.

—

Watch those two fluorescent tubes, I'm going to conjure shape shadows into those tubes for you to take back to Washington.

—

You'll be able to run all the tests you want, match these shape shadows with the black stains on the arch, you'll know I'm telling the truth.

—

Not yet, Charlie, but keep watching those tubes, I'm about to rock your world.

—

Reposition the camera, Charlie, point it up at the lights.

—

No, don't stop me now, they're coming, Charlie.

—

Do you see, do you see?

—

Charlie! Look what they're doing to me. Charlie! I'm not resisting! Charlie, do you see, I'm not resisting!

11

"JOHN BROWN DOG? Are you awake? Man, I'm sorry."

"I saw you trying to pull them off me."

"When the lights went out, they panicked. They thought you were trying to escape, that you had attacked me."

"Cowboys and Indians, Charlie."

"As soon as the doctor says you can be moved, get out of bed, I'm transferring you to another jurisdiction."

"The important thing is, you saw the shape shadows, didn't you?"

"Yes."

"You believe me now?"

"Yes."

"You're going to make a big splash back in Washington."

"When you're well enough to travel, I want you to come back with me."

"To conjure shape shadows for the Blaine Committee?"

"To tell the committee what you've told me."

"It's better coming from you. People in Washington don't have a good track record of listening to Indians. You're different, Charlie. In fact, I give you a new name. *Listens to Indians*. Do you have those fluorescent tubes in a safe place?"

"Yes. The videotapes of our sessions, too. Taking everything back to Washington with me."

"Your federal government might not believe in magic, but when they compare what's in those tubes with what's staining the arch, they'll believe in the scientific analysis that matches the two substances."

"Like you said, it's going to rock our world."

"Here's something else that'll make you a hero—tell them if they want to remove the black stains from the arch, use raw milk."

"Raw milk?"

"I've been reading that they're finding it impossible to remove the black."

"That's right. They've been trying to scrape it off, using chemicals, trying to blowtorch it off. Anything strong enough to remove the stain is also strong enough to damage the steel."

"Use unpasteurized, unrefrigerated, fresh cow's milk."

"How do you know?"

"The grandfather told me."

"At Wounded Knee?"

"Yes."

"Had you been there before?"

"No. When Elena and I left Iowa and drove west across South Dakota, I knew where she was taking me, I can read a map. It was hot that day. Too dry, she kept saying. I stopped at a convenience store and bought a little spray bottle, the kind you use to mist plants, and I filled it with water and showed Elena how she could sit there and spray a fine mist on her face. Even though the car was air-conditioned, the temperature across South Dakota was more than a hundred and it was hot in that black Thunderbird."

"She was okay then, with the spray bottle?"

"Delighted, squeaking with joy, misting herself, misting me. Man, it was hot. Barren land. No cars. I convinced Elena to stay off the interstates as much as we could, in case the cops were looking for us, and, driving across South Dakota, I wondered if the world had ended and we were the only ones left. Elena asked if the people in South Dakota go crazy a lot. I said they must. She wanted to know what bad things they had done that they had to live here. Things in a previous life, I told her. We drove a lonely road toward Wounded Knee. We finally come to a small village of two-bedroom brick houses close together on low hills. The houses are government built—built to the standard of bleak sameness. The yards are filled with trash. Broken cars are scattered everywhere. I know what Europeans think driving through these reservation villages: *Dirty Indians.* Children are running around and many young men greet one another, as if the whole village is one big family reunion. There are no stores, only houses and one post office which is constructed like a tiny fortress of gray stone with slit windows and no flag flying. I am happy to see that the Europeans can't keep a post office opened here, not at this sacred site, not at Wounded Knee. On the road a hand-painted sign says, STOP KILLING OUR CHILDREN. I think it's a good sign for Indians to post at their villages, even though this particular sign is urging drivers to slow down.

"We stop at a dusty parking area where there's another hand-printed sign about the size of a four-by-eight sheet of plywood. On both sides is the history of the Wounded Knee Massacre. It happened in the ravines near here. But where's the shrine?

"There's a lone Indian selling dream catchers spread out on the hood of his pickup. He comes over and calls me brother and puts a hand on my arm. He is a skinny Indian, dark and in his forties, wearing a ball cap advertising reliable caskets. 'Where is the shrine?' I ask him. 'Where is the visitor center? Where are the guided tours?' You've been there, haven't you, Charlie?"

"Yes."

"The skinny Indian tells me they used to have a church, a community center, but in '73 the federals burned them down with tracer bullets. Have you been to Oklahoma City?"

"No."

"In Oklahoma City, a crazy bomber killed a hundred and sixty-eight people, including nineteen children. And now in Oklahoma City they have a memorial on what they call sacred soil. There's a survivor tree. There's a field of one hundred and sixty-eight empty chairs, nineteen of them small chairs for the children. More than twice that number were killed at Wounded Knee. And not by a crazy bomber. At Wounded Knee, children were intentionally killed by the troops of the United States of America, who shot men and women and children in the back and received Congressional Medals of Honor for doing so. Where are the empty chairs for the victims of Wounded Knee?"

"It was a different time."

"You can't use the passage of time to wipe clean *all* your sins."

"Did you know you were going to participate in the sun dance at Wounded Knee?"

"Not until Elena tells the skinny Indian there at the sign that I am the man who will be honored at the sun dance. I didn't know a sun dance was even being planned, much less that I was going to be honored at it—but Elena knew. She said, referring to me, '*This* is the man who has been ghost dancing for sixteen years. This is John Brown Dog. He brings powerful medicine. *This* is the one you've been waiting for.'"

"Are you the leader of this movement, this new ghost dance movement?"

"You said it, Charlie, not me."

"That doesn't answer my question."

"Yes, it does."

"So you went from there to the sun dance?"

"To my surprise, the skinny Indian says, 'We've been waiting for you. The lodge has been built, all the preparations have been made.' He embraces me and tells me his name, White Belly, and speaks Lakota in my ear."

"What did he say?"

"For me to know, Charlie. He gathers up his dream catchers from the hood of the truck and opens the cab with great ceremony, waving Elena and me to get in. Driving into the back country, he seems very happy. The location of the sun dance is hidden away, but once we get there it is the center of the world. White Belly jumps out of his truck and rushes ahead to tell them I have arrived. Surprising me even more, the grandfather is there. I know the sun dance ceremony, he taught it to me. As White Belly said, the lodge had already been built. I was taken off to be purified, to be painted with white hailstones, to be made ready."

"And even though you knew what was coming, you were willing?"

"Willing? I think 'willing' is not the right word. Was your Christ willing to be crucified? He asked if there was any way for the cup to be passed from Him. I didn't ask if there was any way for me to avoid the sun dance, if that's what you mean. But then again, I am Lakota. When my ancestors were being tortured, they would ridicule their torturers and suggest ways for making the torture more painful."

"Your ancestors were masochists."

"Don't make me laugh, Charlie, it hurts my bruised ribs. In preparation of the sun dance, the drums are beating and, on the way to the smoke lodge, a strange thing, Charlie, my legs begin to move of their own accord, lifting one foot and then the other. It's good to be dancing again. Indians gather around me as I dance, as I take off my shirt and chant. They say my medicine is powerful, they say I am the spiritual one."

"I was such an idiot. I saw you hanging there and thought someone had been torturing you."

"I know."

"I thought they had tortured you and left you for dead."

"I know."

"How long had you been hanging before I cut you down?"

"Long enough to see the future."

"What did you see?"

"I saw how the promise of ghost dancing will be fulfilled, how all the Europeans will be removed and all the buffalo returned without war or violence or anyone being killed."

"How?"

"I tell you this now, Charlie, so that when it comes about, your people will honor you and believe your words, will know that Listens to Indians speaks the truth. It's what the whore was trying to tell me: no woman anywhere on earth will ever get pregnant again."

"Starting when?"

"When the new world passes away and the old world is reborn."

"John. Please. The mumbo-jumbo is making my head hurt. Can you tell me when as in a *date?*"

"No. But after all the women who are then pregnant give birth, no more babies will be born. In twenty years, no children will exist anywhere on earth. In a hundred or so years, after the last human dies of old age, the earth will be bare of people and the animals will return in their former numbers and diversity. A population of six billion people will be reduced to zero without any violence."

"No Indians either?"

"Certain Indians will be taken to a safe place and Indian couples will have babies, a population will be maintained but in isolation so that the Europeans can't snatch them up to experiment on them to find out why they're having babies when no one else is. At the right time, Indians will be returned just as ghost dancing promised. Certain other populations will be maintained in isolation also—Pygmies and the Inuit and others who lived for thousands of years in harmony with nature, before the European conquests. Do you believe me?"

"No. But I didn't believe you about shape shadows either."

"What I'm telling you isn't like the coming of the Messiah, you won't have to wait thousands of years to find out if it's true. I don't know an actual date but the grandfather told me that the new world is aging by the day and the old world is getting ready to be reborn. You can alert Washington now, before the crisis is widely known, and that way the government will remember your warning and will believe you and everything you tell them about Indians."

"Where were you headed after Wounded Knee?"

"Mount Rushmore."

"I thought so. I can read a map, too. Did you intend to do to Rushmore what you did to the arch?"

"Yes, Charlie, that *is* our intention."

"You know I'll alert the Bureau. We'll put an army around Rushmore."

"How does an army shoot a shadow?"

"You won't get close enough to conjure them."

"Don't you remember what Elena said? It's not a matter of distance, it's a matter of opening the right door."

"I know the Black Hills are sacred to you. I know that whole story, but . . ."

"But what, Charlie? It's old news?"

"Yes, it's old news. Get over it."

"We've never gotten over it, that's why we kept dancing."

"Just so you know where I stand. I am *personally* going to do everything in my power to stop you. Those presidents are my heritage and I'm proud of them and I don't want them defaced."

"The grandfather has an offer that will save your country."

"What is it?"

"He'll want to tell you directly."

"Where can I meet him?"

"He'll be at Rushmore."

"When?"

"Charlie, go to Washington. Tell them about the arch, tell them what you saw in the interrogation room, give them the tubes, convince your government that the promise of ghost dancing is about to be fulfilled. Make your government take Indians seriously. When you've done that, when you're ready to talk, the grandfather will be there, waiting."

Part II

Defacing Rushmore

12

IT WAS AN AMBUSH. They took up firing positions and put Charlie Hart in the center of the room. He was given a straight-backed wooden chair. A fucking ambush. Hart should've known. When he landed at Dulles, his boss was waiting unhappily and refused to speak to him on the way in.

Which is not the way Hart imagined it on the plane ride back to Washington; he'd had visions of being greeted as a hero just like John Brown Dog predicted. He was bringing convincing evidence of what had happened to the arch two weeks ago, the nation's biggest news story, the St. Louis Memorial Arch damaged and blackened, closed down and rendered unsafe. Scaring the shit out of the citizenry even more, no one from the government or any number of private engineering consultants had been able to determine the nature or origin of the substance that had blackened the arch's stainless-steel skin. People naturally suspected terrorism, but the Department of Homeland Security had issued a statement saying terrorism was not thought to be the cause of the damage. What, then? Some sources speculated that it was a freak oxidation of the stainless steel and maybe the structural damage was the result of an equally freak earthquake. The public wasn't buying these explanations, and even people in the know, including experts who had examined the arch and reported back to the government, were genuinely baffled.

The president formed a committee to investigate, headed by Congressman Paul Blaine. Blaine's selection was a smart move. Putting the president's political enemy in charge of writing the final report blunted criticism that the administration was hiding information or trying to sugarcoat the results of the investigation.

On the drive in from Dulles, Hart tried again to sort out what had happened back in South Dakota, in that interrogation room with John Brown Dog. Hart—who didn't believe in the supernatural, not UFOs or angels—had seen shape shadows. It was upsetting and exciting and life-changing and now Hart felt like a convert who wanted to tell everyone he met that it's true, all that stuff we ridicule, ghosts and spirits and a supernatural world coinciding and colliding with our normal world. It's really true, he saw what he saw.

He wanted to tell his wife, he wanted to try explaining it to his eight-year-old daughter. Another thing Hart wanted to tell his wife, along with confirmation of the supernatural, was that they were lucky they'd already had their daughter, lucky they hadn't kept putting it off, because according to John Brown Dog, at some point there would be no more children.

Hart hadn't put this in his report for two reasons. First, he didn't believe it. Something had been conjured in that interrogation room but Hart didn't accept that whatever it was could stop the human race from continuing. Second, he was worried the announcement of the human race dying out would discredit everything else he'd written. He still had an obligation to pass along the threat, regardless of how he viewed it, but he decided to deliver this particular bombshell in person.

Six people surrounded him in Blaine's office. No one offered introductions. Hart was shown in, led to his chair, and given coffee, and then everyone just stared at him as he fumbled with his papers and spilled the coffee and placed the four-foot cardboard box containing the two fluorescent tubes on the floor.

He felt sweaty. His scalp itched. When he moved and his suit jacket opened, he could smell his underarms.

The first shot came from one of the congressman's assistants whom Hart had never met but knew by name, Peter Berg. "Special Agent Hart, I wonder if you appreciate the implications of this report you've sent in."

In spite of his intention not to turn left, then right, to face every person who asked him a question, Hart did twist to face Berg. "What implications do you mean?"

Berg sneered. His dark hair was shiny and combed straight back, his eyes hooded. He was about Hart's age, thirty, and wore an expensive tailored suit. He shot the cuffs of his white shirt to show off gold cufflinks and said, "There's already enough misinformation and speculation about the arch to cause widespread mistrust, not only of Congressman Blaine's committee but also of the federal government overall, and now the FBI, in the person of you, is saying that *spirits* caused the damage? Are you an idiot?"

Congressman Paul Blaine laughed dryly from behind his massive desk. "As a lawyer," he said to Hart, "I would advise you not to answer Peter's inquiry as to whether or not you are an idiot."

"No, sir."

Blaine was known to keep the meanest goddamn staff in Congress. His people were slashers, vicious as dogs and just as loyal. Blaine's persona was that of a nice guy, considerate, empathetic, gentle. When someone complained to him of an outrage one of his staff members committed, Blaine winced as if pained to hear such a thing—but then he went back and complimented the staffer for having a killer instinct. It was an old gig, good cop and bad cop, but it had served Blaine well.

The congressman gave Hart a practiced look of kindly concern. "I think what Peter means," Blaine said softly, "is that if we were to have entered your report in the public record, the ridicule and outcry would've crippled our committee's efforts to find the real cause of the damage to the arch."

"Congressman, I reported what John Brown Dog told me."

"No, Mr. Hart, you did more than that, you endorsed the Indian's assertions. But I think we can get beyond that. I think, I hope, Agent Hart, that we can achieve a meeting of the minds."

"Yes, sir."

Blaine smiled. He was from central casting, a tall white-haired New England patrician with light blue eyes and a tight mouth. He had a flaw, however: charismatic one-on-one, effective working in small groups, known as a brilliant political strategist, utterly ruthless when necessary, Paul Blaine couldn't give a speech to save his life. Stand him in front of a crowd and he turned to jelly: stuttering, panic-stricken, and useless. His other political talents enabled him to get repeatedly elected in his home district but he wasn't likely to survive on a national stage. Blaine had been working with coaches and consultants and hoped eventually to overcome this crippling defect. He was sixty, he still had time to run for president.

"Sir, did you see the video?" Hart asked.

Peter Berg answered, "We all saw the video. You want me to put it in now so you can point out exactly where the *spirits* show up. I guess I missed that part."

Berg went over and got the videocassette from a woman in her late thirties, another of Blaine's assistants, who kept her head tilted upward as if she suffered from a chronic nosebleed. She constantly dabbed at that nose with a handkerchief. Known as the hardest-working congressional assistant on Capitol Hill and indispensable to the running of Blaine's office, she was in love with the congressman, who had eyes only for his political career.

Along with Berg, the woman, and the congressman, there was an older man, also on Blaine's staff, who would frequently crouch over and whisper to the congressman. Hart thought of him as the Whisperer. Completing the ambush gang were two men who said nothing during the meeting but watched everything carefully with expressions of disapproval. They sat along the wall. One of them looked military and Hart thought of him as the Colonel. The other wore a sweater vest and thick glasses. Hart named him the Scientist.

As Berg was setting up the videocassette, Blaine said, "Agent Hart, is it necessary for us to look at this again? I mean, are you going to show us something that we might have missed?"

"The camera was focused on John Brown Dog, so what happened to those fluorescent tubes wasn't caught on tape."

"Exactly," Blaine said.

"You know what I see," Berg said, playing the tape without sound. "I see an Indian dancing like a fool, I see lights flickering, I see lights go out, then I see a bunch of cowboys come rushing in to whale on Tonto."

The woman laughed, covering her mouth, and then sniffed and then blew her nose.

"Melanie?" the congressman said. "You had something?"

She wadded up the handkerchief and wiped at the outside corners of her nose. "I wanted to ask the agent, if Indians were the ones who put the black substance on the arch, how did they apply it? Spray it on? Paint it on? Drop it from an airplane?"

Blaine said, "Good point. Agent Hart?"

This was all in the report; these questions served only to beat up on Hart. "As I wrote in the report, John Brown Dog said that he conjured shape-shadow spirits that came up from the river and these shape shadows were responsible for, as he said, cracking the arch's ribs, that is, damaging structural members, and then for staining the arch black."

The Whisperer came over and whispered to Blaine. "Oh, yes," Blaine said. "According to your report, if we want to make the arch shine again, we just pour milk over it, is that correct?"

Berg and Melanie laughed, the Whisperer smiled, the Scientist and the Colonel remained grim-faced.

Hart said, "I put in the report what John Brown Dog told me."

"Got milk?" Berg said.

Melanie laughed again as she searched through her pockets for a fresh handkerchief, and spoke as she blew her nose. "And it has to be raw, unpasteurized milk."

"Of course," Berg said. "Everyone knows you can't remove stains unless you use unpasteurized milk, stains that have proven impervious to any number of acids and other chemicals, stains that have to be burned off with acetylene torches that damage the underlying steel. But just splash on some milk and the stains are gone, is that right, Hart?"

"It's worth a try."

Blaine spoke sharply. "It is most certainly *not* worth a try. We've had a thousand suggestions on how to remove the stains and if we go around pouring on green tea or urine or trying any of the other odd-ball ideas we've received—including raw milk—we will look like the Keystone Kops. Agent Hart, did you know that some of our engineers are suggesting that the arch has been so severely damaged that it might have to be taken down?"

"Yes, sir."

"We're saying it's not terrorism, but everyone suspects exactly that. One of this country's greatest memorials, ruined, and people are afraid that terrorists are in possession of some powerful new technology capable of destroying structures in ways we don't yet understand. What's next? people want to know. Is the Statue of Liberty safe? The Washington Monument? Are any of us really safe? My committee has been trying to counter these fears with cold, hard facts. And now a special agent of the FBI has been foolish enough to *contribute* to the hysteria with a report that, frankly, I find so intemperate that I question your ability to continue in the Bureau, a concern I will be sharing with the director, I assure you."

The prospect of losing the job he loved made Hart sick to his stomach. "Congressman, I think if you analyze the substance that's in these two fluorescent tubes I've brought and compare it to the stains on the arch—"

"No, I'm not going to authorize that."

"You're not?"

"No. And do you know why? I'll tell you why. We do not lend credence to speculations of the supernatural. I don't believe in the supernatural. And as an elected member of Congress I tell you that the Congress of the United States of America does not believe in the supernatural."

"Sir, I saw it with my own eyes—"

"Oh, for crying out loud, Hart." This was Berg. "The Indian pulled some sleight of hand on you. That's why they call them magic *tricks.*"

Blaine said, "To state the obvious, in all of recorded history, there has never been a conclusive instance of the supernatural and—"

"Jesus Christ rose from the dead."

Which shocked everyone into silence, even Hart, who was immediately embarrassed at having taken a cheap shot. Blaine was an evangelical Christian and Hart had just used the congressman's religious convictions against him. If Hart's father had been in the room, he would've been disappointed in his son.

Finally Peter Berg spoke. "I think what the congressman meant was, there's never been an instance of *secular*—"

"I don't need you to defend me, Peter." Blaine's normally pale complexion was coloring. "Let me tell you something about Indians, Mr. Hart. As a young man, I worked in a Legal Aid office in Oklahoma and I discovered that Indians are their own worst enemies. All too willing to live on government handouts. Dwelling on wrongs that were committed not against them but against their increasingly distant ancestors. Sanctimonious about their nature-based, non-Christian spirituality. And I'll tell you something else that most people aren't aware of, Indians were also their own worst enemy in the past, when they were being defeated and losing their lands. They had such hatred of each other, such intertribal warfare and rivalry, that they preferred joining up with whites against other Indians who were their traditional enemies rather than banding together *against* the whites. In all the wars and battles we had civilizing the West, do you realize how many Indians fought on behalf of the U.S. Army *against other Indians,* happy for a chance to kill other Indians, their traditional enemies? Do you realize how many Indian scouts Custer had with him going into Little Bighorn? I'm going to tell you something and I want you to listen carefully, because truth is in short supply in this town but what I'm about to tell you is the God's truth: the historical arc of the American Indian that began with the arrival of Europeans ended with the United States in control of all land from coast to coast. Our American way of life has many enemies. The war on terrorism is going to be with us for a long time. What role do Indians play in all of this? None. Their time has passed."

The Whisperer made his way to Blaine, delivered a murmured message, then returned to his seat.

Blaine said, "Why was Cortes, with a small band of men, able to defeat tens of thousands of Aztecs? The popular notion is that the Aztecs couldn't deal with the superior weapons carried by the Spanish and had never seen horses before and were terrified of mounted Spanish soldiers, thought they were gods. But that's not true, or not entirely true. The Spanish were so ridiculously outnumbered that the Aztecs could've defeated them with rocks, with their bare hands. So how did the Spanish do it?"

John Brown Dog had told Hart that the Europeans' most effective weapons were guile and dishonor. He said Indians had no experience dealing with an enemy who would dishonor himself to win a battle. During tribal fighting in the West, the invading party would often send ahead a small group to announce to the village that the enemy was coming, giving women and children a chance to get to a safe place, giving warriors an opportunity to arm themselves and dress for battle. European soldiers, John Brown Dog said, would be court-martialed for warning an enemy. European commanders, such as Custer, made it their trademark to attack at dawn when an Indian village would be asleep and the people, unarmed, could be killed all the more easily.

"Mr. Hart?"

"I don't know, sir, how did the Spanish do it?"

"With Indian allies! The Aztecs were such terrible people, were so hated by their neighbors, that these neighboring Indians gladly joined with the Spanish to get rid of the Aztecs. I'll tell you a grisly story, an example of why Indians flocked to Cortes. . . . He had many more Indian allies fighting with him than he had Spanish soldiers, he couldn't have conquered the Aztecs without those allies. Oh, I know the Indian view of these things, I've heard it a thousand times. The Americas were Eden, the Indians living in harmony with nature, and then here come the despoiling, polluting, evil Europeans."

John Brown Dog had said that the Aztec city of Tenochtitlan was, at the time of Cortes's arrival, the most populous and, arguably, the most beautiful in the world, a city crisscrossed with canals, a city of public spaces and public art, pristinely clean, a thousand of its citizens employed to sweep the streets—at a time when the cities of Europe were cesspits, vile with disease, rampant with crime. Before the Europeans arrived, John Brown Dog said, all types of societies were represented in the Americas, from hunter-gatherers to great urban civilizations. Trade crisscrossed the North and South American continents. Some tribes were so ideally situated in their environments that the people could provide food and shelter by working a few days a week, the rest of their time devoted to leisure and play and philosophy. John Brown Dog had said, "I know what you were taught by your upside-down and backward history, Charlie, but it's not true that the Americas were sparsely populated, with a few tribes here and there, hunting deer and buffalo, planting a few seeds of maize. Before the arrival of the Europeans, one fifth of the entire world's population lived in the Americas."

Blaine continued, "One of the Aztecs' neighboring tribes tried to make peace with the Aztecs by offering their chief's daughter as a bride to the Aztec chief. When that neighboring chief arrives among the Aztecs on the wedding day, expecting to see his daughter in her bridal finery and to greet the Aztec chief as his soon-to-be son-in-law, instead he discovers that his daughter has been skinned alive, and her skin is now being worn as a cape by the Aztec chief, who tells the grieving father, 'Oh, we found her more useful as a sacrifice than as a bride.' Is it any wonder that the Aztecs' neighbors joined with the Spanish? I think the Spanish must've been welcomed in the Americas as liberators offering freedom from oppression."

Hart asked, "What do you want me to do, sir?"

"We want your report deleted from existence."

"I beg your pardon."

"If it gets out that the FBI is asserting the arch was damaged by supernatural means, my committee will turn into a three-ring circus. You're here so we can persuade you to withdraw your report. If I *order* you to withdraw it . . ." Blaine chuckled and nodded. "I've been around Washington long enough to know how these things work—if you're a true believer, you might follow my order and officially withdraw the report, but then you'll leak it to the press. Then, not only will the supernatural be injected into our investigation, my committee will also be accused of a cover-up."

Hart thought, This is exactly what *is* happening—a cover-up.

"Agent Hart, *are* you a true believer?"

"I saw what I saw, sir, and I reported it. I believe it would've been a dereliction of duty to have seen what I saw and *not* report it."

"Okay, we're making progress. It's not that you're a true believer but that you were hornswoggled into thinking you saw something that, in fact, is impossible. You were tricked. As Peter said, the Indian is probably a master of sleight of hand."

"I don't think that's the case, sir, but—"

"You can become a valuable asset to my committee or an embarrassment to the FBI; the choice is yours. What I'm asking is that you join our side, that you in fact recognize what side you're on. I'm asking that you voluntarily withdraw your report and give me your word that all copies will be destroyed and that you will discuss it with no one, not even your family. Can you give me that pledge?"

"I think my duty was to write the report as accurately and honestly as I could. If you and the Bureau decide the report should never see the light of day, that's your decision."

Blaine was coloring again. "Now you're performing the Washington slip-and-slide, trying to force us to make the decision and take the responsibility."

"I don't see how it can be *my* responsibility, Congressman. I'm not at the level to make the decision to kill this report. But what I will do, if this is okayed by the Bureau, I'll turn over all copies and disks of the report, I'll delete everything related to the report from my computer, and I'll promise not to discuss the matter with anyone, certainly not leak it to the press."

"Atta boy."

"I still hope your people will analyze what's in these two fluorescent tubes."

"You're backsliding. I can't officially take delivery of your *tubes* or anything else connected to your report without making note of it in the committee record. The president's supporters would love to catch me covering something up. I want *you* to go around the room and collect all copies of the report and I want *you* to take those tubes with you."

"And do what with them, sir?"

"Throw them away. In an environmentally safe manner, of course."

Berg, Melanie, and the Whisperer all laughed.

"One other thing I want you to do, Agent Hart. Were you aware that your Indian, John Brown, has been released?"

"Released?"

Berg said, "A fleet of lawyers sailed in after you left. A habeas corpus here, a habeas corpus there, the Indian having not been charged with anything, the Indian making noises about bringing brutality charges against the police, *voilà*, he walks."

Melanie said, "Someone with big bucks was behind it."

Berg asked her if she was making a pun.

The woman looked at him blankly and then explained, "The law firm that was brought in to free the Indian is the biggest and most expensive in the West."

Blaine said, "I know you traveled the entire day to get here, Agent Hart, but now we're going to ask you to travel all night to get back out there. And I'm going to be even more of an ogre by asking you not to contact your family while you're here, not to talk with any of your friends, your colleagues at the Bureau. Let's keep this whole unfortunate matter as quiet as possible until we can squash it like a bug. You reported that the Indian made veiled threats regarding Mount Rushmore. We need you to take him into custody before he starts trouble there."

"On what grounds?"

"*National security.*" Blaine let those holy words sink in, then said, "If that's all, we can call this meeting to a close—a successful close, I'm hoping. Right, Agent Hart?" Blaine stood and offered his hand across the big desk.

"Yes, sir." Hart stood, too. While shaking the congressman's hand, he spoke hesitantly. "Sir, there's one more thing I haven't mentioned yet."

Blaine looked suspicious.

"In the report, I explained a little about ghost dancing, which did not in fact end after the Wounded Knee Massacre but has been continued, passed down, for more than a hundred years. The promise of ghost dancing is that the old world will be reestablished with, as John Brown Dog says, millions of buffalo, not whites, occupying the land. But according to the promise of ghost dancing, the removal of the whites from Indian lands will be accomplished peacefully. No wars, no killings. How can millions of whites be removed without violence, without anyone being killed? John Brown Dog gave me the answer while he was in the hospital, his version of how the promise of ghost dancing would be brought about, which I didn't include in my report because I thought it was too sensitive."

Blaine told Hart he had everyone's attention, let's hear it.

"I was hoping, sir, I could discuss this with you in private."

"And you know what I'm hoping, Agent Hart? I'm hoping this is not another supernatural tale. Go ahead, these people have my complete confidence."

"John Brown Dog said that at some point women aren't going to be able to get pregnant anymore and that eventually the whole human race, except for certain native peoples, will die out—no one killed, we just all die out naturally."

Peter Berg laughed. "I know half a dozen women, friends of mine and members of my family, who are pregnant."

Melanie agreed. "My sister's pregnant, I have an aunt who's pregnant, also my best friend from college." She looked wistfully at the congressman.

Hart tried to explain. "John Brown Dog didn't say there weren't any pregnant women, he said that at some point in the near future women will no longer *become* pregnant."

"Tell me you don't believe this nonsense," Blaine said.

"If it turns out to be true, and I knew about it and I didn't tell you, I would feel pretty stupid and disloyal."

"Duly noted. If the human race cannot reproduce itself, we'll remember you told us first." This got another laugh from his appreciative staff.

Hart collected the copies of his report, hefted the cardboard box containing the fluorescent tubes, and left Blaine's office feeling sick. He had convinced no one of anything. Maybe he had kept his job at the FBI, which was the only positive thing that had come out of the meeting and it was only a maybe.

They caught up with him in the hallway. The one he thought of as the Colonel said, "We'll relieve you of that box," and the Scientist took it carefully from Hart.

"Did the congressman change his mind about having this stuff analyzed?" Hart asked.

The Colonel didn't answer. He was about forty, thick-chested and short-haired.

"Who are you guys? You're not on Blaine's staff, are you?"

Neither of them answered. The Scientist, older than the Colonel, had a little potbelly and a distracted air, though his was the more interesting face, struggling for recognition behind thick glasses.

Hart said, "Maybe I should see some ID."

The expressionless Colonel stepped uncomfortably close. "Hart, do yourself a favor and go back to South Dakota and catch your Indian, then keep your mouth shut." He took the box from the Scientist and strode off down the hallway.

The Scientist started to follow but hesitated and asked Hart, "What did you see?"

"Pardon me?"

"The camera was pointed at the Indian, not at these lights, I understand that. But you looked up. *You* saw it."

"I described it in my report. You must've read—"

"Tell me. Please. What did you see?"

13

WHEN JOHN BROWN DOG began dancing, I was embarrassed. For myself more than for him. Those local cops were watching everything behind the two-way mirror and I was letting a crazy Indian dance.

He danced and nothing happened. His dancing was fascinating, that someone could exert or exude such power with so little movement, dancing from one foot to the other, not lifting either very high, the haunting sound of his chanting. But I was still embarrassed, for me and eventually for him, too, so finally I told him to stop.

He continued.

I told him again to stop.

He said he was going to conjure shape shadows, he told me to watch the lights. Across the ceiling of the interview room was a bank of fluorescent lights, all except two of them covered with translucent plastic. On the fixtures for these two particular fluorescent tubes, the plastic was missing. John Brown Dog told me to watch those bare tubes. I did. Nothing happened. I'd had enough of this. Stop, I said.

He kept urging me to watch the lights. He said he was going to conjure shape shadows into the fluorescent tubes and I could take the tubes back to Washington, run tests, match what was in the tubes with the black stains on the arch, and prove the connection.

Feeling more and more like a fool, realizing the local cops were laughing at everything we said, I told him I didn't see anything.

He said keep watching, he was going to rock my world.

I told him to stop. I wanted to go over and physically force him to stop dancing, but I was afraid of provoking the local cops who would come in to "help" me and then use the opportunity to beat up on an Indian.

John Brown Dog told me to reposition the camera and point it up at the lights. He wanted me to catch the event, the evidence, on tape. I wasn't going to do that.

Enough is enough. I started to go over to John Brown Dog, intending finally to force him to stop, but then the lights started to flicker. The camera hadn't been moved, it was still on John Brown Dog, but once again I looked up at the two bare lights.

You asked me what I saw. Here's what I saw:

The *other* lights were flickering. The two exposed tubes were burning steadily. From one end of each tube, black things began to—it's going to sound crazy, but they began to *swim* into the tubes. I called them *things* but actually they were distinct, recognizable shapes. The first one was a tiny black frog. Not an actual frog but the black shape of a frog, oozing into the fluorescent tube as a liquid, I guess, and then as soon as it was in the tube, in the light of the tube, it formed the shape of a frog and began swimming—swimming through the fluorescent light, through the light itself—to the other end of the tube. Right behind it came other shapes. I remember the frog being first because I was so astonished to see it but I don't remember the sequence of which shapes came second or third and so on.

There was a fish. The black shape of a fish. A couple inches long, I guess, and obviously small enough to fit in the tube. It swam through the light, its movements exactly like those of a fish swimming through water and then when it reached the other end of the tube, it did the same thing the frog had done. It flattened itself and became a solid, I don't know, a solid plug of black. The frog had filled an inch or so of the end of the tube, the fish added a similar length, and now that end of the tube is solid black, no light, just black.

There came a parade, an armada, of shape shadows following the same pattern, flowing into the tubes as liquid, forming distinct shapes, swimming to the other end, adding to the blackness.

There was a dolphin. Seals. Sea turtle. Orcas. And the weirdest, the most unsettling, was the shape of a person, making his way, swimming underwater through the light.

While all this was going on, those parts of the two fluorescent tubes that had not yet been filled or plugged with black, kept shining brightly while the other lights in the room kept flickering. The shape shadows made their ways through the lights quickly and filled the tubes with black. That's when all the other lights, the ones that'd been flickering, also went off.

From their position behind the two-way mirror, the local law enforcement team couldn't see what I had seen, and they stormed in with flashlights—and pepper spray and truncheons. They were on John Brown Dog before I could stop them. In fact, I'm not even sure I tried to stop them at first, I was still in shock from what I had seen.

But then John Brown Dog called. I tried to get the local cops off him. I said I could handle it. They ignored me. There are easy take-downs and there are hard ones. This was a hard one. They were man-handling him onto his stomach, pushing his face onto the floor, kneeling on him, bending his arms behind his back, the cops livid—cursing him, hitting him, screaming at him to stop resisting.

No, he wasn't resisting. That's what he kept repeating, kept telling me, "Charlie, do you see, I'm not resisting."

In there just now with Congressman Blaine and his people, someone said the Indian had tricked me with those shape shadows, that it was some sort of sleight of hand. But what happened in that interview room with those lights and shape shadows, there was no way John Brown Dog could've conjured it as some kind of trick. No way liquid black plasma can enter through an electrical connection, form shapes of swimming creatures, and then plug those tubes with a solid black that's as heavy as lead.

I never before believed in the supernatural, in the spirit world. I do now. Because I saw what I saw. I suppose a Christian would say it's like the followers of Jesus who saw Him perform miracles. Under those circumstances, it's easy to become a convert. You don't really have a choice. But I also understand that for those who don't see the miracles but only hear about them—or in this case, didn't see the shape shadows and only have my word on it—I can understand how difficult it is to believe. If someone had told me what I'm telling you, I wouldn't have believed that person. So I don't blame you for being a skeptic.

Except the look on the Scientist's face was not that of a skeptic.

14

RIDING BACK OUT TO DULLES, Charlie Hart wanted to see his
wife and daughter. He wanted a shower. A night's sleep. He wanted
peace of mind.

Nothing in his life had prepared him for this otherworldly weird-
ness. He had never been fascinated with science fiction or interested
in the occult. Charlie was a plain-vanilla American, blue-eyed and
brown-haired, a big, good-looking nice guy who got along with
everyone, whom everyone liked. A hard worker. Loyal. He played
football in college, never a star but a solid performer. Coaches liked
him. Instructors liked him. He met the girl of his dreams, she loved
him as much as he loved her, they got married, had a daughter, and
now his wife was a real estate broker making twice his salary, they
had a great house, wonderful friends—all of this good fortune coming Charlie's way as if by entitlement.

Until now. Even if he finds John Brown Dog, Charlie figures he'll
never be back on the FBI fast track.

Charlie wished now he had hedged more in his report—he
should have written that John Brown Dog "alleges" this or that, and
"according to" the Indian, and "as incredible as it sounds, the Indian
actually claims . . ." Should have distanced himself from John Brown
Dog's assertions so the report wouldn't have come across as Charlie's

endorsement of what the Indian was saying. Except, Charlie believed John Brown Dog.

He remembered a camping trip with his father, whom he adored and respected. Still does. That was another of Hart's entitlements: growing up in a functioning and happy family, his parents obviously in love with each other, no one abusing anyone else, physically or mentally. Whenever the conversation among friends came around to how awful it was growing up, how terrible families are, Hart never had anything to say.

The camping trip with his father, one of many: they were gathering wood for the evening fire when they saw lights. Might have been a helicopter or a meteor or flashlights from hunters. Hart told his dad, "I wish a UFO would land. I'd love to see one up close. I mean if they exist. Wouldn't you?"

His father took a long time answering. In fact, it wasn't until they had the fire going that Charlie's father said, "I don't want to see a spacecraft up close or far away or anywhere in-between. You know why? What do you do with that experience, seeing something inexplicable, unbelievable? Do you report it? No one'll believe you. So you become obsessed with it. *I saw something miraculous.* Maybe you devote the rest of your life to trying to see it again, trying to convince others of its existence. It eats at you. To what end? Better you never saw it in the first place."

Thinking of what his father had just said, surprised by the emotion with which his father had spoken, Charlie got the idea that his father was referring to personal experience, that he had at some point in his life seen something miraculous and had become obsessed with it. Charlie had been brought up not to be afraid of asking his parents questions. "Did you ever see something supernatural?"

His dad poked at the fire. "No."

But in the middle of the night, his father shook Charlie awake and was so uncharacteristically distraught that Hart thought: bear.

"I've never lied to you, Charlie. So let me take back what I said before. I did see something . . . unbelievable. Camping alone in the woods when I was a young man. On a night like this."

"You're scaring me."

"I don't mean to."

"What did you see?"

"It doesn't matter."

To Charlie, it did.

"What matters," his father said, "was that the experience very nearly derailed my life. The obsession I was telling you about earlier. I very nearly dropped out of university. And to what end? I was never going to be able to prove what I saw. And the only people who were interested in what I had to say were other obsessed crazies. Doomed people. So I did the smart thing. Maybe not the brave thing or the intellectually honest thing. But I put the experience out of my mind and went on with life. Today, I've pretty much convinced myself I didn't see what I saw. Do you understand?"

Charlie didn't understand back then, but today, he knew exactly what his father had been trying to tell him. Hart wouldn't be in trouble now if he had been able to convince himself he hadn't seen what he saw when John Brown Dog conjured the shape shadows.

But another lesson his father taught him was to do what was right. Don't debate it, don't weigh the consequences, just automatically and consistently do what's right.

Hart had a headache. He wanted to be home, he wanted to make love to his wife. He regretted acting too meek during the meeting with Congressman Blaine and his people. He thought, I should've told that weasel Peter Berg to fuck off.

Charlie's wife once said he was too good for his own good. She later claimed she'd meant it as a compliment. But she was giving Charlie a message, trying to make a point, that his refusal to engage in office politics or criticize colleagues or jockey for position could damage his career, get him left behind.

By the time they arrived at Dulles, the Bureau driver had to wake

Hart, who'd been dreaming of his father. In the airport, drinking surprisingly good coffee, Hart finally decided he was glad he'd written the report exactly as he had. He got onboard with peace of mind. Even if the truth was subsequently buried and John Brown Dog discredited—along with Hart—at least the truth had been written in one place, at one time, written in words right side up and straight. He could sleep now, the plane racing away from a rising sun, giving Charlie a few hours to catch up.

15

DURING A LAYOVER in Chicago, Hart had shaved, washed, and changed his shirt at a courtesy lounge. In Rapid City, South Dakota, at the designated spot in the terminal, he was met by Bill Reynolds, maybe the last morbidly fat FBI special agent on active duty.

"I know what you're thinking," Reynolds said. "You're thinking, this guy has got to be the only obese S.A. left in America."

When Hart didn't reply, Reynolds said, "Let me see your ID."

"You're holding my paper there in your hands."

Even though that was true, Reynolds holding Hart's paperwork and photograph, he still insisted on seeing Hart's credentials.

"This is a first," Hart said, handing over his identification. "Maybe I should ask for yours, too."

Reynolds produced his identification and more or less forced it on Hart.

Charlie asked, "Why this . . . formality?"

Reynolds took Hart's suitcase and went outside. When they were away from the terminal but before they got into Reynolds's car, he told Hart, "You're radioactive."

For a fleeting moment, Hart took the statement literally—maybe those fluorescent tubes had contaminated him—but then he realized that Reynolds meant what Hart's boss had indicated: he was bad news.

"You're hotter than a firecracker, son. You're on fire. You glow in the dark. You're contaminated and anyone close to you will probably get contaminated, too. Which is why this assignment, assisting you, is a real career killer for me. There's no way I can handle you that's going to be the right way to handle you. And I got this assignment, babysitting you, because the FBI hates fat agents. Fat and fifty. Fat and fifty and a smoker, too." Reynolds produced a pack, tapped one out, lit it up. "Can't smoke in the car—the next person who uses it will rat me out." He inhaled a lungful, held it for several seconds, then blew out with relief. "What in God's name did you do in D.C. to get you so deep in water so hot? Man, I'd love to see your next evaluation. Even worse than the one I got. I told someone back at the office, this Hart kid must've screwed the director's mistress, gave her the clap, she gave it to the director, he gave it to his wife. This kid could bring in a whole terrorist network, hogtied and willing to testify, and *still* never get a promotion."

"Is it really that bad?" Hart asked as he stood there trying to stay out of Reynolds's smoke stream.

"You're kidding me, right?" The older agent's round face was so red with broken veins that Hart figured Reynolds had a third addiction, alcohol, along with food and tobacco. "Career-wise, you are a dead man walking."

Hart looked down, surprised to see his shoes were scuffed. Before all this happened, he wouldn't have been on duty with unshined shoes.

Reynolds finished his cigarette and then sprayed his mouth with a breath freshener that painted a spearmint odor over the tobacco stench. Hart could smell both.

"Look at it this way, kid. Call you Charlie?"

"Sure."

He shook Hart's hand. "Bill."

"Okay, Bill."

"Look at it this way, Charlie. You're young, you're good-looking, you'll fall into some other line of work, got plenty of time. Be happy you're not *fifty* and fat and looking at the end of your career. Too young for retirement, too old for a new job."

"You're really going to get shit-canned just by being associated with me?"

Reynolds took out a handkerchief and wiped his sweaty face. "I was heading for the shit can anyway. Being assigned to the most contaminated agent in FBI history is just a way of ensuring I don't wiggle through another evaluation. See, last one I had, I lost thirty pounds in preparation—"

"This your car?"

"Yeah." Reynolds laughed, which made him cough. "You're in a hurry. This trip is going to end with you getting fired and you're in a hurry to get there. Ah, youth."

Inside the car it was well over a hundred degrees, and Reynolds was having difficulty breathing as he started the engine.

"You okay?"

Reynolds looked at him with stricken eyes. "Don't ask me if I'm okay every time you see my face go red . . . or I start coughing or can't get my breath. Otherwise all you're going to be doing is sitting there like a parrot saying, 'Are you okay? Are you okay?' "

"Okay."

Reynolds laughed, coughed, turned the AC on high.

"I assume we're headed for Wounded Knee," Hart said.

Reynolds gave him a queer look.

"I thought we'd start there, looking for John Brown Dog. Wounded Knee is where I found him originally. He was the spiritual leader of the sun dance. I found him hanging from a lodgepole, suspended from rawhide that had been pierced through his skin and muscles. Why are you looking at me like that?"

"Haven't you heard? Haven't you seen TV? The Indians are massing at Rushmore."

"Massing?"

"Yeah. As in gathering, collecting, bunching up."

"To what purpose?"

"Trying to dance."

Hart had an image of shape shadows crawling over the presidents' faces, staining them black. "Indians shouldn't be allowed to dance at Rushmore."

"I thought you were the Indian lover."

"Out here, is 'Indian lover' used the same way 'nigger lover' used to be used in the South?"

"Hey, don't talk to me like that. I'm not a racist and you don't know me, so stuff your judgments."

Hart apologized. "John Brown Dog said that the African-Americans, actually he called them Africans, he said they had a better lobby than the Indians, which is why saying 'nigger' will get someone fired, labeled a racist, or shunned in polite society, but the football team of the nation's capital can still be called Redskins. It's the worst epithet a white man can call an Indian. What's the worst name you can call a Chinese person . . . Chink? Can you imagine a football team named the San Francisco Chinks? The Philadelphia Wops? Couldn't get away with it. But Washington Redskins? No problem."

"You want I should tell you about the Indians at Rushmore?"

"Sorry."

"You don't remember the seventies, all the shit that was going down, Wounded Knee Two."

"I wrote a paper on it."

"Of course. Golden boy. Anyway, all that shit, the occupation of Alcatraz, and the Indians came to Mount Rushmore, too. There were rumors they intended to pour red paint over the presidents' faces. You know, because the Black Hills are sacred to the Indians, the Hills were deeded to them in perpetuity by treaty and . . . hey, here's a funny story. Years ago I was teaching evenings at a community college, trying to polish up my evaluation, and I was reviewing the treaty that gave the Black Hills to the Indians and I asked the class if someone could define 'perpetuity.' This Indian kid answers. Real laconically. 'Yeah,' he says. 'Perpetuity means eight years.' You know, 'cause that's how long the Indians held the Black Hills before we took it all back after gold was discovered. Smart-ass kid. But, you got to give him one thing, he was *accurate*. So I marked him A for class participation."

"How many Indians are at Rushmore now?"

"I don't know. A shitload. Dozens. Maybe a hundred."

"And they're dancing?"

"Trying to get in to dance. The superintendent, Leonards, is there, trying to keep the Indians out. Lawyers, activists, pointy-headed liberals, everyone's there or heading there. I heard President Carter was coming. Leonards says dancing is a demonstration and demonstrations aren't allowed at the memorial. The Indians say dancing is their way of praying."

"Letting the Indians dance at Rushmore would be a gigantic mistake."

"Yeah, that seems to be the sentiment from D.C., too."

"It does?" Charlie wondered if the substance in the fluorescent tubes had been analyzed after all, if he and John Brown Dog had been proven right.

"State cops and our own agents being brought in to reinforce the park rangers," Reynolds continued. "National Guard being mobilized. After the arch was damaged, we went on heightened security at Rushmore. Just like the other national monuments. What's your connection? Were you investigating arch damage?"

"I'm under orders not to discuss anything with anyone."

Reynolds grunted.

They drove through the Black Hills, a six-thousand-square-mile cathedral of folding hills and dark pines. Hart saw immediately why this place was considered mystical, why it was sacred to the Sioux and to the tribes before the Sioux, succeeding generations of Indians who lived here, hunted here, worshiped here for thousands of years.

"Wow!"

Reynolds slowed the car and asked Hart what was wrong.

"I just saw the heads, there through the trees."

"You've never been here before?"

"No. They're spooky."

"It's un-American, you never coming here before."

"Big white heads sticking out from a cliff."

Reynolds laughed, coughed.

They came to standstill traffic filling the two-lane road.

"Going to have to take the shoulder," Reynolds said, putting a light on the dash. "I love this," he said, giving the siren a few blasts to warn motorists he was coming on their right, on the shoulder.

Tourists had been trapped in traffic long enough that some of them had stepped out of their air-conditioned vehicles to stand around and talk with each other in the shirtless heat. Many were eating, as were those still in their cars and RVs. Most were holding soft drink containers, big plastic bottles and big insulated mugs.

Hart said, "I wonder how long the average American tourist ever goes without consuming something? Thirty minutes? Ten?"

"Hey, don't make fun of fat people."

"I wasn't." But in fact, the majority of tourists here were grossly overweight.

"No, I'm just shitting you, go ahead and make fun of us."

They came to an area where Park Service vehicles were on the shoulder, blocking the way. With the road still full of tourists' cars and RVs, Reynolds and Hart had to continue on foot. Hart kept on his suit coat but Reynolds pulled his off and carried it over one arm.

"You going to walk in like that?" Hart asked him. "With your sidearm exposed?"

"Yeah, you going to write me up?"

"I'm beginning to like you, Bill."

"Because fat people are jolly?"

"No, because you're so un-FBI."

Although they were at an elevation of over one mile, the heat was oppressive and walking uphill was taking a toll on Hart, who was in great shape, so he could imagine how Reynolds must be suffering. He started to ask Reynolds if he was okay but then remembered he'd been warned not to.

When they reached the outermost parking lot, Reynolds and Hart were stopped at a checkpoint and had to produce identification, which was examined carefully by armed park rangers.

Reynolds turned to Hart and spoke quietly. "If it wasn't for you and me looking so white-bread American, if our heritage was Middle Eastern or, God forbid, Indian, we wouldn't get in carrying sidearms regardless of what kind of ID we had."

Hart nodded. As irreverent as he was, Reynolds's take on these things was dead accurate.

A grim-faced and heavily armed park ranger escorted Hart and Reynolds through the crowds, toward an air-conditioned trailer at the edge of the lot nearest the memorial entrance.

"I remember going to national parks as a kid," Hart said to Reynolds. "Park rangers were unarmed back then, they were guides, naturalists. They acted like they were the happiest people in the world with the best jobs in the world."

"And now they're storm troopers," Reynolds added quietly. "Not their fault, though. The rangers changed with the times."

When they reached the white trailer, the ranger told them to stay put while he went in to get the superintendent.

The superintendent came out, he was wearing jeans and a white shirt, not a uniform; he was short and compact with his white hair in a military buzz cut. He was sixty years old and definitely in charge.

"Another team here from Washington to help us," he said. "I'm Superintendent Marty Leonards."

Hart and Reynolds introduced themselves and offered their identification, which Leonards waved off. "I've been expecting you. Especially *you*," he said with a friendly tap on Hart's lapel. "I think I got your Indian."

"John Brown Dog?"

"He won't say a word, but I think he's your man—all the Indians here were deferring to him."

"Don't you have John Brown Dog's photograph?"

"No. Bureaucratic foul-up. All the stuff you got when you were interviewing him? All the videotapes, photographs, everything except what you took back to Washington with you—all of it got lost or 'misplaced' after the lawyers sprung the Indian."

"And you think that was a bureaucratic foul-up?"

"Why? Are you suggesting a conspiracy? Because if you are, I think I'm going to like you, kid. Never met a conspiracy theory that didn't fascinate me. Twenty years U.S. Navy, twenty years Park Service, that's forty years of conspiracies, from the Bermuda Triangle to Sasquatch."

Hart wasn't sure how much the superintendent was pulling his leg.

"I got the memorial closed right now," Leonards said. "But I'm fixing to open it up, with or without Indians being let in. Because keeping the memorial closed means the terrorists have already won."

Hart waited for a smile, a wink, a nod, but once again the superintendent played it with a poker face, giving no indication if he was being droll.

"Did you guys hear," Leonards continued, "that one of your own told Blaine that the arch damage was caused by Indians conjuring up spirits? Which is why we have such a high profile here today. What an asshole."

"I'm that asshole," Hart said quietly.

Leonards laughed and put a hand on Hart's shoulder. "I know you are, son—I just wanted to see if you'd 'fess up to it."

Reynolds was confused. "You told Blaine *what?*"

Hart shook his head.

Leonards laughed again. "The FBI is very good at keeping secrets from itself. Let me go in and clear out half the people in that trailer, the half who are in there strictly for the air conditioning, then I'll bring you in and see if we got the right Indian."

After Leonards left, Reynolds again asked Charlie what he'd told Blaine. "You actually said that Indian spirits damaged the arch?"

Hart was apologetic but said he'd been ordered not to talk about it.

"The superintendent knows," Reynolds pointed out.

"Not from me, he doesn't."

Reynolds turned away, took out his wrinkled handkerchief, and wiped his red face repeatedly.

Hart scanned the crowd looking for a small young woman with fish-eye makeup. Seeing the white middle-aged tourists, he wondered—if people of European descent were strong enough, ruthless enough, determined and disciplined enough to conquer the world, how did they end up in their current condition, with huge bellies and fat white thighs that pressed together all the way down to their knees, wearing stretch shorts and candy-colored T-shirts pulled tightly across their upper-body fat? The children fat, too. Grandparents in undignified track outfits that did little to hide their bulk. Or in T-shirts printed with stupid slogans. Everyone joking around, taking pictures, making videos, engaging in horseplay. No one serious, no one dignified. And three out of four of them eating, drinking, chewing gum, sucking on Popsicles, as if afflicted with an oral fixation that required constant maintenance.

Indians waiting to be let in to the memorial were somber, dressed in dark clothing, no shorts or T-shirts, no slogans on their clothing. Most of the men had long hair tied back with wind-rags, many of the women wore beaded dresses. They were a serious people, ready for whatever the day brought. Indian warriors going into battle would shout, "Hoka hey!," "It's a good day to die!" The white tourists, with a thousand-year heritage of conquering and subjugating people of color, didn't look as if they could defend their ice cream cones.

Reynolds was right, Charlie thought—I'm an Indian lover.

After a dozen or so people left the trailer, Reynolds and Hart were called in.

Reynolds said thank God for air conditioning as Hart looked at the Indian seated in the center of the trailer with several park rangers around him.

"That him?" Superintendent Leonards asked hopefully.

Hart shook his head. "John Brown Dog is in his early thirties."

The Indian here was seventy or older, his dark face creased by deep wrinkles. He had a large head and was wide between the eyes.

The grandfather, Hart thought just as the Indian saw him and smiled.

"You know this one?" Leonards asked Charlie.

"No. But I might know *of* him."

"We haven't gotten a word out of him. For all I know, he's mute."

The old Indian rose, the rangers around him taking positions as if to block his escape or take him down if he tried something ominous, like dancing.

When Superintendent Leonards told his rangers to back off, the Indian came over to Hart. "I've been waiting for you."

"So you *can* talk," Leonards said, then asked the Indian if he knew Agent Hart.

The old man said exactly what Hart had said, "I know *of* him." The grandfather smiled. "This one I will speak with. He is the one we call Listens to Indians."

Hart's face reddened.

The Indian smiled again. "Brown Dog said your face hides nothing, that you are that rare European without guile, and that you keep your word."

"You're the grandfather."

"I am."

"Do you have another name?" Leonards asked.

The grandfather smiled at the superintendent, too. "I am Sitting Bull."

In his usual laconic manner, Leonards said, "I'm Buffalo Bill."

"We worked together," the grandfather said.

Both men laughed.

Hart asked the grandfather why he was here at Rushmore.

"We want to come into your memorial and pray our prayers. You have prevented us from doing this. If a Catholic stands there before the four great white heads and crosses himself, your rangers don't throw the Catholic to the ground and cuff him. If a Presbyterian stands there at the viewing area and says a silent prayer while giving the Presbyterian high sign—Charlie, do Presbyterians have a high sign?"

"Not that I'm aware of."

"Then, if the Presbyterian bows his head and says a silent prayer, park rangers don't rush over and Mace him. Why then are Indians prohibited from praying?"

"Because," Leonards answered, "your prayers take the form of dancing, which is a demonstration, which is not allowed at the memorial. A Christian prayer, like you were mentioning, doesn't draw attention to itself. Your prayer, because it involves dancing, significantly interferes with the ability of others to enjoy the experience of the memorial. You know this. You're being disingenuous to equate your dancing with someone's silent prayer."

"Disingenuous? I might have to consult a dictionary."

Leonards wagged his finger at the grandfather. "You are a sly one."

The grandfather nodded. " 'Sly' is a word I know."

"I'll tell you what I'm prepared to do," Leonards said. "If we can come to an agreement on how many of your people intend to dance and exactly how long the dancing is to continue and if you also agree to no speeches, no handing out of literature, no signs or other demonstrations—then I'm prepared to open the memorial and see if we can't work this out."

"You have a generous heart," the grandfather said slyly. "Tourists out there are using their cell phones to call important people, news crews are arriving, thousands heading this way to find out why the Indians are being discriminated against, being barred from Rushmore. You do not want a confrontation, tear gas sprayed and shots fired and tourists wounded on your watch. To avoid all that, you have found a generous heart that would allow us to dance here in front of the big white heads carved on our mountain. We will agree to your terms. We will choose our dancers. They will dance for a set amount of time."

Superintendent Leonards turned to Hart and asked, "What do you think?"

"Yes, Charlie," the grandfather said, "what do you think of Indians dancing in front of the four great white heads?"

"Absolutely, unequivocally . . . *not,*" Hart said, turning to tell Leonards, "No Indian should be allowed to dance anywhere near here."

The rangers who were listening looked at the old Indian and waited for him to challenge Hart, to show his anger, but instead the grandfather smiled and put a hand on Hart's shoulder. "Charlie, I think we should give you another name in addition to Listens to Indians. You are the rarest of Europeans. *Believes* What Indians Say."

Leonards turned to Hart. "You better explain."

"Any Indian trying to dance anywhere near here should be forcibly stopped, cuffed, and taken away if necessary."

Leonards said, "Oh, Christ, you and—" He stopped himself and pulled Hart close so no one else could hear. "You and your goddamn Indian spirits again. Instead of sending you here to make everything worse, they should've put you under psychiatric observation. Listen to me, if you start talking about Indian spirits—"

"I haven't said a word about Indian spirits."

"If this gets out, I'm going to have a mob on my hands. Every nut within a thousand miles is going to want to see the Indians conjure spirits." Leonards stepped away from Hart and told his rangers, "Okay, listen up, people. I want everyone out of this trailer except Hart, me, and . . . this Indian. No one discusses anything with anyone. Is that clear? The three of us are going to stay here and settle this matter."

The grandfather said, "A suggestion. Instead of staying here in this trailer, the cold air killing my sinuses and provoking my arthritis, may I suggest we walk to the four great white heads and settle the matter there. The gates are locked, no one's in there, we will have privacy there. And since the fate of the four white heads is being decided, it is appropriate that we negotiate under their watchful eye."

"What do you mean, their fate is being decided?"

"We will negotiate. Please, from one old man to another. My air was not meant to be conditioned. And also, when my people see me walking with you, they will know I am not in this trailer being beaten for resisting arrest. The sight of me will calm them."

"All right. Just the three of us. You okay with that, Hart?"

Charlie looked at the grandfather and asked him, "Will you agree to no dancing?"

The old man was amused. "You Europeans are so afraid of dancing Indians."

"Dance until you drop," Leonards said. "I don't care."

But Hart was insistent. "Give me your word. No dancing while we're out there."

"You are troublesome. But I give you my word. While we're out there under the four great white heads, I will not dance them down."

16

"WHAT DO YOU MEAN, 'dance them down'?"

Instead of answering Leonards, the grandfather looked at Charlie.

But Leonards would not be put off. "If you're threatening to damage the memorial, we got a whole different ballgame here. Whether you're joking, whether your threats are hollow, doesn't make a difference, I'll have you arrested. And we won't be going to the memorial, we won't be negotiating any dancing, either. Now what did you mean, 'dance them down'?"

The grandfather apologized. "I promised Charlie I wouldn't dance and I promise you, Superintendent Leonards, that I will not speak of dancing. Let's go see the heads. Please."

Getting through the crowds required an escort, half a dozen park rangers with sidearms. Indians had bunched up near the entrance to the memorial to prevent anyone from getting in and several of them signaled the grandfather, getting close enough to ask if he was okay. The old man replied he was fine, let us pass.

Gate guards holding M-16s let the three men into the memorial, which was eerily quiet.

After passing the toilets and vending machines, they entered the avenue of flags, a double row of stone columns, each bristling with flagstaffs jutting out at forty-five-degree angles. The view was clear to the four great heads, at a distance and on a height.

They were simultaneously magnificent and unreal. Their massive size and position on the very brow of the cliff made the sculptures compelling, yet they were also dwarfed: heads on mountains. And ridiculous. *Heads on mountains.* A thoughtful person might walk to the edge of the viewing area and either be awed or double over in crazed laughter. Maybe both.

The grandfather and the superintendent walked ahead of Charlie Hart, who thought the men had a lot in common in spite of being on opposite sides. Both were feisty and ironic, both with a great deal of personal dignity that suggested neither would suffer fools or back down. They were short, though the grandfather was much thicker through the chest and arms. Both were gray-haired. Both dressed conservatively, the grandfather wearing jeans and a dark red western shirt. He was bow-legged. Both wore cowboy boots. You could almost imagine them as two old fishing buddies.

Except now the buddies were arguing. When Hart caught up, Superintendent Leonards was saying, "I won't listen to this, not another word of it."

The grandfather explained to Hart, "I was just telling the superintendent that this memorial is, spiritually, the ugliest place in America. These flags, these columns, those awful white heads. This is the kind of memorial the Nazis would've made if they'd won the war, carving Hitler's head—"

"I'm serious," Leonards interrupted. "We're here to discuss the conditions under which I will let your people in to conduct a dance, we're not here to listen to your blasphemy about Mount Rushmore."

"Blasphemy? I am familiar with this word. Let me define it for you. Your government granted the Black Hills to the Indians for all time and by official treaty, the Fort Laramie Treaty, approved by your Congress, signed by your President Grant, giving the treaty the same force of law as your Constitution itself. But your hero, Custer, leads an expedition into our Black Hills and it is confirmed, *gold*. Here's an interesting footnote for you, Charlie, who listens to Indians, who *believes* what Indians say. Black Hills gold made the Hearst fortune, which William Randolph Hearst inherited, allowing him all manner of extravagances, such as a castle by the sea and a vast newspaper empire. Hearst's newspapers created the Spanish-American War, which made a hero out of Teddy Roosevelt who became president and got his head on a mountain in the Black Hills that supplied the gold to make it all possible."

The grandfather turned to Leonards. "I'm sorry. I was defining blasphemy so that you might use the word more accurately. Your government broke its word, violated the treaty, dishonored its own Constitution and, after eight years, stole our sacred land, and *then* a racist European sculptor defaces one of our stolen mountains with these grotesque white heads of men who hated Indians—and your government makes all of this into a national monument: *that* is blasphemy."

Leonards had crossed his arms. "I'm not going to discuss this."

"But I am content because my children's children will once again possess Paha Sapa." Before Leonards could respond to this assertion, the grandfather pointed at the presidents and told Hart, "Look at their expressions, Charlie, and decide for yourself what is grotesque, what is not. Washington there has the look of someone who has just sucked a lemon laced with morphine. Jefferson! The most bizarre of the four, the way he's looking up as if sniffing at something, perhaps recalling how the African, Sally, smelled when he crept into her bedroom and pulled back—"

Leonards told him to shut up. "To avoid a crack in the rock, the sculptors had to raise Jefferson's face, that's why he appears to be looking up."

"Appears to be sniffing a woman."

"You're a real bastard, you know that."

The grandfather laughed. "And Teddy, tucked back there like a butch lover who has eyes for Lincoln, the only one of the four with enough dignity to look embarrassed by this grotesque blasphemy."

They continued walking, taking stairs down to the large viewing area, the grandfather speaking now to Hart and Leonards both. "I truly believe that someday this defaced mountain will become a national shame. And when that day comes, when the scales fall from the eyes of the Europeans, you will see how this holy place has been—"

Leonards interrupted to tell the old man he was crazy. "America will defend this memorial to the death. With tanks and troops, with jets and rockets, with whatever it takes. This place is precious to America. Mount Rushmore *is* America."

"You know what I think, Charlie? I think the Europeans should have their bellies full by now. You conquered us and took everything we ever had. You left us a broken people, the poorest people in this nation, the sickest people, the people most likely to be victims of violence, twice as likely as the supposedly violent Africans. But this is not enough for the ravenous Europeans, you stay hungry to hurt us more. I think you are disappointed there weren't more of us to kill. I think you are wistful that the era of unabashed Indian killing didn't last longer. You are a people who long to walk on the bones of your enemies. Or at least show them off to tourists. You dig up the bones of our ancestors and put them on display in your museums. You piss on us. That's what these four awful heads are doing, carved there on our sacred mountain—they are pissing down on any Indian who dares to look up."

With strained patience, Leonards asked the grandfather, "Do you want to discuss the conditions under which your people will be allowed in here to dance, or do you want to continue giving speeches about the poor downtrodden Indian?"

"I want to continue giving speeches about the poor downtrodden Indian. Charlie, look at those heads and tell me what is missing, what is the one feature on a person's head that is nowhere shown on those four great white heads? Eyes, yes. Noses, yes. Hair—"

"No ears."

The grandfather threw his head back and whooped. "No ears!

The racist sculptor, Borglum, got one thing right! No ears, because the Europeans will not listen."

Leonards said, "I'm prepared to allow a dozen of your people to dance here on Grandview Terrace for no more than thirty minutes, with all the other restrictions that I mentioned before—no signs, no literature, and no speeches like the ones you're now giving."

Ignoring him, the grandfather said, "Washington compared Indians to wolves, both being beasts of prey, differing only in shape. Jefferson said the government had only two choices when it came to Indians, drive them away or exterminate them. Roosevelt said that in nine out of ten cases the only good Indian was a dead Indian and he wouldn't like to inquire too closely into the case of the tenth. Lincoln approved the hanging of thirty-eight Indians at one time, establishing a national record, the largest public execution ever. And *these* are the presidents you carve on our sacred mountain."

Leonards tried appealing to Hart. "They got their own memorial right near here and it'll end up bigger than this one and it's being carved into their own sacred mountain just like this one is. And it's being done by Indians so—"

The grandfather interrupted. "Crazy Horse is being sculpted by a European."

"Hired, paid for, and sponsored by Indians."

The old man's dark face was troubled. "I knew Henry Standing Bear, relative of Crazy Horse, and the man who launched the Crazy Horse memorial, a good man but misguided. The Europeans are putting up what they call an Indian memorial at Little Bighorn, too. Also misguided. If Indians were to make a memorial it might be a twist of buffalo grass, an offering of tobacco. After the sun dance is completed we let the lodgepole stand until it returns to nature by weathering and rotting. That is our idea of a memorial. We would never make a memorial that required blowing up a mountain. We would not carve a giant Indian on a giant horse. Especially not to represent Crazy Horse, who in his lifetime never allowed a photograph taken or a sketch of him made, adamant about not having a representation of himself created, and now we carve him in stone to last forever. Shame on us. Indians are not blameless, I know that. We were not able to band together and resist the European invasion; shame on us for that also. I think when scales fall from *Indian* eyes, they will take down that terrible sculpture of Crazy Horse and he can rest again. Charlie, do you know why Crazy Horse was sculpted to be pointing as he is?"

"No."

"He is pointing to answer the eternal question of every European tourist—which way to the toilets?"

When Charlie laughed, Leonards told him to shut up.

The grandfather continued, "The Indian memorial at Little Bighorn was designed by European sculptors who had never even visited the battlefield, Crazy Horse sculpted by Korczak Ziolkowski and Rushmore by Gutzon Borglum. These are ugly names for ugly creations."

"Now who's being bigoted?" Leonards asked.

"Bigoted? Gutzon Borglum, celebrated here at Rushmore as a hero, was a member of the KKK."

"Oh, here we go. Borglum happened to be a member of an organization that has since become discredited, properly so, but at the time—"

"Your words are upside down and backwards. Borglum was not just a member, he was on the Ku Klux Klan national executive board, called the Imperial Kloncilium. Charlie, I am speaking straight words, you can look them up. Borglum's speeches and letters would embarrass the superintendent here even though he is charged with protecting Borglum's evil creation. Borglum wrote of the Nordic races subduing savages such as Indians. He wrote of race mixing as 'mongrelization.' And this is the bigot who made these awful white heads in service of what he called, in a speech he gave right here, the 'heart and soul of my race.' Rushmore was conceived in racism, created in bigotry, and dedicated with white hatred for the dark races, and I say to you, Superintendent Leonards . . . take down these heads from my mountain!" Although the grandfather's voice rose like a politician finishing a stump speech, his expression remained sly.

Charlie wondered if Leonards got the Reagan–Berlin Wall reference. It was hard to tell: the superintendent was off on a tirade of his own. "All right, that's it, buster. I gave you plenty of warnings, I've tried to be reasonable, I've offered compromises . . . and now I tell *you* this: get out of my memorial, take your people away from here, and don't come back until you can treat this place with the honor, dignity, and respect it deserves."

"But I *am* treating it with *exactly* the honor, dignity, and respect it deserves. Here, let me show you." The grandfather unzipped.

"Why, you son-of-a-bitch!"

The old men set to grappling with each other.

Charlie was about to step in and separate them when all three heard a familiar sound: gunfire.

17

THEY RUSHED BACK toward the entrance. Charlie Hart, the youngest, the fittest, and the only one armed, took the lead. After another round of gunfire, shotguns, the three men took cover behind a stone wall until they could determine where the shooting was coming from. Just outside the memorial's entrance, people were shouting.

"This is exactly what I wanted to avoid," Superintendent Leonards said.

The anguish in his voice convinced Charlie and the grandfather of his sincerity.

Crouching, they worked their way toward the entrance, reaching the glass doors in time to see an extraordinary scene play out.

There in the parking lot a young Indian man walked toward a dozen or so armed officers shouting for him to stop. The Indian, long black hair tied in back, wearing jeans and long-sleeved shirt, carried nothing in his hands, which he held out, palms up. He walked purposefully, eyes clear. This was not a man on drugs; he seemed, in fact, beatific. It was the armed officers who were acting crazy, whacked on adrenaline and anxiety, pointing weapons at the Indian, then lowering them, then raising them again, screaming a blur of contradictory orders—Go back, Stop, Get down, Raise your hands, Drop to the ground, Put your hands on your head, Turn around.

He kept coming. The cops and rangers swirled around him in a loose circle, so that if one had opened fire and missed, or if the bullet had gone through the Indian, an officer on the other side would've been shot, which was how most of the army casualties at Wounded Knee happened.

Hart, past the entrance now, recognized the danger of the setup but could do nothing to change it. If he shouted, the cops and rangers, screaming at the Indian, wouldn't have heard him. And if he rushed out there, coming into the parking lot from the blind side, the officers might turn and open fire on him.

The Indian was taunting them, reaching for them. As agitated as the officers were, Hart was surprised they hadn't already shot the Indian or jumped him or done something other than shout. Astonishingly, the young Indian man pushed aside a pistol being aimed at him and reached toward the ranger holding it, touching him on the head. With that, the Indian turned and began to walk away, slipping the grasp of several cops, one of whom tried to use pepper spray but managed only to stain the Indian's shirt sleeve. It seemed then that the officers were about to do what Hart would've advised them to do in the first place, holster their weapons and wrestle the unarmed man to the ground, but a dozen young Indian men shouting war cries came rushing across the parking lot. The officers backed away, allowing six of their number to step forward and fire. To Hart's relief, he saw they were shooting beanbags—fabric bags the size of teabags, filled with lead shot, and fired from twelve-gauge shotguns. They'll knock a man down at close range and are billed as nonlethal.

You could see the dark bags flying across the parking lot; most missed, a couple hit the Indians in their legs to little effect—the cops were too far away.

But now Hart saw that the Indian who had just counted coup was, in fact, on the pavement, holding his leg, which was bleeding profusely. A wound like that couldn't have been caused by the beanbags. Even in cases where they've been implicated in the deaths of suspects, beanbags create *internal* bleeding. Someone had shot this Indian for real.

Everyone got quiet. The Indians could charge en masse, prompting the officers to open fire with lethal weapons. Or both sides could back down. If it came to shooting, future generations might call this the Rushmore Massacre.

As the wounded Indian rolled over, holding his leg, the grandfather and the superintendent walked out together.

As in a stage play, everyone's eye went to these new characters. Who were they? Protagonists, antagonists? Had they come out in the middle of the action to shoot or be shot? Or make speeches? What chorus would they sing?

"You have counted coup!" the grandfather shouted at the Indians. "You have walked among your enemy and touched them. This tests the strength of your medicine, which is strong today. Now, gather up your wounded brother."

Meanwhile, the superintendent was among the officers, speaking to them, calming them, praising their restraint, and assuring them all would be honored for their action today. "No one's been killed," the superintendent told them. "That's the important thing. You could've opened fire at any time but you didn't. You used the beanbags . . . up until the last. And I want that man to separate himself, go to the trailer. Follow the procedure. You know, boys, your restraint reminds me of a different kind of Indian, those who were followers of Gandhi. They stopped British trucks by lying down in front of them. But you know, men, people forget that *two* things were required for that nonviolence to work . . . a willingness on the part of Gandhi's followers to lie down in front of those trucks and an *unwillingness* on the part of the British drivers to run them over. We hear a lot about the bravery of the Gandhi people but not much about the humanity of the British drivers. Today, you officers displayed that humanity."

"Fucking Indians," one of the deputies muttered.

"Come waltzing over here just daring us to pop one in their ass," another cop agreed.

The others chimed in with their complaints; no one was in the mood to be inspired by stories of restraint and humanity.

The Indians across the parking lot weren't happy either. Some had started chanting. Several shouted at the grandfather, telling him the time for talk had ended—they had rifles in the trunks of their cars.

The intensity of the moment was broken when an ambulance arrived. The Indians allowed the medics through. A gurney was wheeled out, an IV set up.

Tourists popped up from behind cars and RVs, raising their cameras.

After the ambulance left with the wounded Indian, news crews began arriving.

For his protection, the grandfather had been moved to the center of the Indian group while Superintendent Leonards went among the state and local cops, trying to get everyone to back off and stand down.

Two reporters, camera crews in tow, approached Hart and wanted to know if he'd seen what had happened: had someone tried to blow up Mount Rushmore?

Hart pointed out Superintendent Leonards. "He's in charge of the cowboys." And then the grandfather. "And he's in charge of the Indians."

Leonards refused to talk to the press until he could establish order, but the grandfather welcomed all reporters who came his way. He told them he had a statement to make. He asked whether the news crews would be sending their reports directly back to the studios and was told that satellite hookups hadn't been established yet, his statement would be taped. "I'll wait for you to make your satellite hookups, then I'll give you my statement, because if you put it on tape, your tapes will be confiscated."

While the grandfather waited, turning his back on the four great presidents behind him, he looked off into the distance with such a placid expression that you might have thought, *Here is a man with all the time in the world.*

Leonards came over with two armed rangers and said he was not going to permit anyone to make a statement.

Tourists began shouting him down. An unarmed Indian was shot for doing nothing but whooping! The Indians were peaceful! They just wanted to be let in to the memorial!

In face of this white tourist uprising, Leonards sent his armed escort away. He stayed but said nothing more about preventing the old Indian from making a statement.

Reporters were already shouting questions at the grandfather. What is your name? Are you the Indian leader? Do you intend to damage the memorial? Why are you here? Did your group have anything to do with damaging the St. Louis Memorial Arch?

The grandfather held up one hand and spoke slowly. "I will answer your questions after I make my statement. Before they shoot me."

Now that he had everyone's attention, the grandfather began speaking.

"What I am about to tell you will make no sense to you now, will not be believed by you now, but when it does occur it will be the biggest single news story on earth.

"Indians have many grievances and I will be happy to discuss them later. We want the Congressional Medals of Honor awarded for action at the Wounded Knee Massacre to be posthumously rescinded, we want Leonard Peltier freed, we want the Washington Redskins to change their name. But we will discuss all that later. First I will make my statement.

"I have been asked by ghost dancers and by our allies to present a demand to the United States government. If this demand is met, our allies will reverse a phenomenon soon to be—"

"What phenomenon?"

"Please," he told the reporters. "Let me finish my statement. Here's what will happen—no woman anywhere on earth will ever again become pregnant."

Reporters and tourists asked one another what the grandfather had just said. They heard his words but did not understand them.

"The human race will die out in its time. After a hundred or so years, no more people on this planet. The promise of ghost dancing will have been brought about without war, without violence, without anyone being killed."

Hart waited for the grandfather to describe the part that John Brown Dog had explained to him about certain Indian tribes and other native peoples being taken to a safe place where they would continue having babies, their small numbers eventually returned to their native lands after everyone else was gone.

But the grandfather didn't go into that. Instead, he outlined how this promise of ghost dancing could be avoided. "Our allies have required this of us, this offering of one last chance to make things right. We would have preferred to see the promise of ghost dancing brought about without discussion, without negotiation. But our allies talked with us and convinced us of their wisdom. Also, they are not without power.

"In exchange for our allies not preventing women from becoming pregnant again, Indians will receive, for their exclusive use and occupation, all parks and forests and other protected lands that are owned, controlled, and maintained by the United States government and all individual state governments."

Now people knew the old man was crazy. A few laughed at him.

One reporter shouted, "You want Yellowstone and Yosemite back? You want Mount Rushmore back?"

"It is good you ask if we want them *back*. And the answer is yes, the Black Hills, including this terrible memorial, will be returned to the Indians. As will Yellowstone and Yosemite. The Great Smoky Mountains National Park. The Everglades. The Grand Canyon. Shenandoah. The Adirondacks. Robert Moses State Park on Long Island. National and state forests. All of them, everything."

Superintendent Leonards, who had worked himself close to the grandfather, told him, "I thought you were a serious man, but I see now you are not."

"Don't you think it's a good trade? We're getting a lot of land, but you stole most of it from us in the first place and, in return, you are achieving the continuation of the human race as it now is, in all its numbers and chaos."

"You won't be given one acre of one park anywhere in this country."

"You mean your government would rather see the human race die out than to give land back to the Indians?"

"It's not going to come to that but if it does, yes, that's exactly what I mean. Not one acre."

The grandfather addressed the reporters. "I respect Superintendent Leonards and I fear he speaks the truth. But as I said, I am required by our allies to make this offer even though I think, as the superintendent says, it will never be accepted."

He was interrupted by air horns. Big gray diesel buses were pulling into the parking lots, buses with bars over their windows and escorted by armored military vehicles.

"Looks like your statement is finished," Leonards said.

"Film all of this," the grandfather urged the news crews. "Make a record of what they do to us. Don't surrender your tapes."

But the reporters, like Leonards, no longer took the grandfather seriously or considered this a legitimate news story. Tourists were changing their minds, too. It's one thing to root for the Indians to be permitted some kind of powwow in the park but now this old Indian is talking about giving them Mount Rushmore? He's crazy. Someone shouted, "If you don't like America, go back where you came from!"

Which amused the grandfather. "You forget yourself, sir. I *am* where I came from."

"Get a plane ticket and go to Iraq, see how they treat you there."

"*You* get a plane ticket and *you* go home . . . to Ireland or Holland or Germany or wherever *your family* came from," the grandfather told him. "My family came from here. I *am* home. You blue-eyed devils are illegal aliens."

Which elicited their boos, curses, and contempt.

"You don't even know your own history," he tried telling them. "In 1832, Superintendent of Indian Affairs William Clark sent to the secretary of war an order of extermination against Indians being led by the one you call Black Hawk."

But no one except the Indians was listening. With a sense that the show was over, tourists began wandering away.

Charlie Hart was trying to figure where to position himself in the coming action. He saw cops and troopers and rangers receiving earphones from heavily uniformed men who'd just unloaded out of the buses. Earphones? Hart wondered if they were rigged with radio receivers so that all law enforcement personnel could get orders from a central command.

At a signal, a flying wedge of men who'd organized themselves behind the buses made its way to the crowds. The men wore black body armor and massive black helmets with bulletproof visors, and carried five-foot plastic shields, batons, shocking devices, and handcuffs and plastic strips on their belts. They marched slowly, inexorably, accompanied by a heavy beat of baton against shield, of black steel-toed boots stomping in step.

It was brilliantly organized. Whenever the wedge encountered someone who was destined for the buses, he was pulled into the wedge and worked toward the back where a team was waiting to cuff, search, and then escort the person to the nearest waiting bus. If the person resisted, he or she was shocked or pepper sprayed or both, was struck on the shins with batons and dragged by shoulders or arms or hair to the search-and-cuff team.

Hart identified himself as an FBI agent and tried to show his credentials but the wedge was a living machine programmed to consume Indians and knock everyone else out of the way.

The grandfather shouted, "Where is Charlie Hart! Where is Listens to Indians!"

"Here!"

But their voices and all other sounds were suddenly drowned out by a terrible noise from an opened Heaven. You had to cover your ears or risk damage to your eardrums. The noise was so loud it shook the sac in which the heart is suspended and made people sick to their stomachs.

18

BILL REYNOLDS FOUND CHARLIE bent over retching. The parking lots reeked of vomit, the stench so bad that even those, like Reynolds, who had been wearing protective earphones were now becoming ill from the smell. Indians had thrown up before being loaded on the diesel buses and tourists were still vomiting, weeping, groaning, doubled over.

Reynolds handed Hart a cool, wet washcloth. When Reynolds said something, Hart tapped his ear and replied, too loudly, "I can't hear!"

Reynolds mouthed, *It'll be okay in a minute.*

Hart felt it would never be okay.

Walking among the sick—even those not vomiting were moaning and looking for help—Reynolds and Hart made their way toward the air-conditioned trailer where they'd first met the grandfather. After Reynolds fished out Hart's ID and showed it to one of the guards, they were let in.

Hart collapsed in a chair and Reynolds brought him an ice-cold Pepsi, which Hart drank all the way down, the best drink he'd ever had in his life. He belched.

"You're not going to throw up again, are you?" Reynolds asked, taking a step back.

"No." Then Hart realized he could hear. "What the hell was that noise?"

"Helicopters carried it in at treetop level. You didn't see the black helicopters?"

Hart shook his head. "What was it?"

"A new technology."

Hart shook his head again, this time in disbelief.

Removing the earphones from around his fat neck, Reynolds said, "You should've got yourself a pair of these."

Hart didn't know whether to laugh or punch Reynolds in the nose.

"I can't believe we used that 'new technology' on tourists. Can you imagine the lawsuits? They weren't doing anything except waiting to be let in and go see Mount Rushmore."

"I think we'll say they were sympathetic to the Indians, to the rioters."

"No one was rioting. The grandfather was making a statement to the press."

"I don't think that's what we'll say."

"Did the Bureau order the buses?"

Reynolds shrugged.

"This is going to be another Ruby Ridge, another Waco."

"Except no one got killed here."

"Yeah. Shot but not killed. Rounded up and taken away. Made sick. But not killed, not yet. Bill. Why the hardball tactics—do you know something I don't?"

"We got our marching orders. While you were with the superintendent and that old Indian."

"What marching orders?"

"I guess something you said to the Blaine Committee lit a fire because suddenly we're Code Red, hot as a poker."

"Bill, specifics."

"We got orders from Washington. Lock down this memorial. No one allowed in. Specifically, no Indians permitted within ten miles of this place. We're to round them up using whatever force necessary. No Indians at Rushmore. Dancing or not, no Indians. So whatever you said to the Blaine Committee, it made an impression."

Hart thought it wasn't what he said, it was what he'd brought—those two fluorescent tubes. The analysis must've been completed, must've matched the black stain on the Gateway Arch, finally convincing Blaine and the committee that Hart was telling the truth.

"Charlie? What do you make of that old Indian saying the human race is going to die out?"

"I guess we'll find out."

"Do you have kids?"

"A daughter."

"I got one each. Hey, and wanting all parks returned to the Indians, did you catch that?"

"Yeah."

"Looney tunes."

"I wonder if there's a line I can use to call my wife."

Reynolds brought him a phone. "Tell her you love her."

"I always do."

But Charlie couldn't get an outside line. Even after he explained who he was, he was told he had no authorization to call out.

Reynolds asked him if he was hungry.

"No."

"They got some great cheeses."

"No."

"Sliced ham."

"Bill."

"You should see the food they brought in for us, no expense spared. It's not the usual piece of orange cheese between two slices of Wonder Bread, they got pâtés, roast beef, a dozen different mustards, gourmet coffees—"

Bile rose in Charlie's throat.

"You okay?"

Charlie said no, he wasn't okay.

"I'll go fix us a couple plates, then I'll get you rigged up."

"Rigged up?"

"Body armor, earphones, gas mask, they've brought in everything you need."

"Need for what?" The Indians had already been corralled. Charlie wondered who the enemy was.

After Reynolds ate—Charlie was still too sick to contemplate food—he helped rig Hart with enough equipment to go into battle. Body armor. Two-way radio. Rations and water and medical gear and ammo. A Remington Model 870P, seven-shot twelve-gauge pump-action shotgun loaded with three-inch magnum shells, double-aught buck. You could blow off barn doors with that weapon, you could cut a man in half. Hart also got a gas mask and protective earphones.

Reynolds told Hart he had to be issued one last item and led him to several huge cardboard boxes filled with black and dark blue nylon jackets. One box was full of jackets with POLICE on the back in bright fluorescent orange lettering. In another box, the jackets were printed with BATF. Another, with BIA. Reynolds fished around in the FBI box until he found one to fit Hart.

"What's in this other box?"

Reynolds took out one of the jackets and turned it: DEA.

"DEA?"

"Charlie, you ever see their budget? Bring in the DEA, get them to spread around some of their green. And guess what? Every operation they're made a part of, someone ends up finding drugs."

"No SPECIAL OPS jackets, huh?"

Reynolds frowned. "Don't joke about that, Charlie." He lowered his voice as people did in the Middle Ages when speaking of God. "They're not wearing jackets that say so, but they're among us."

After leaving the trailer, Reynolds took Charlie to the operations commander for an assignment, when a young man in a POLICE jacket came after them with a message. Special Agent Charles Hart was to report to the holding area where the Indians rounded up at Rushmore were being kept and was to locate and identify the Indian he had interviewed near Wounded Knee, one John Brown Dog. Upon identifying this Indian, SA Hart was to facilitate John Brown Dog being taken into custody by the Bureau of Indian Affairs. This assignment, identifying John Brown Dog and taking him into custody, was to supersede any other orders or assignments. All appropriate authorities would render whatever assistance necessary to ensure the successful completion of this assignment.

After Hart finished reading the fax, POLICE asked him if he needed an escort to the holding area.

"No, just give me directions." He returned everything except his FBI jacket to Reynolds, who asked, "You sure you don't want to hold on to any of this gear?"

"What for? I'm going to be off this mountain, where it's safe."

"Safe?"

"Yeah, away from those heads."

A DEA jacket surrendered his Crown Victoria, and Hart headed on down the mountain. He had to turn on his headlights, dusk being forced into night in this steep forest, dark pines.

The sodas he'd been drinking compelled him to pull off the road. When he doused his headlights, the blackness seemed complete. But after Hart got out of the car, he noticed a high half moon that illuminated parts of the forest, wherever moonlight could make its way through the trees and reach ground.

He took a few paces and peed. Hart again remembered camping trips with his father, how dark the nights were, scary but exhilarating. They talked about everything. His father told him Indian legend stories and . . .

Charlie stopped peeing when he heard something, a rhythmic beating or hammering. It was difficult to determine where it was coming from, the sound so soft or so far away, Hart couldn't tell which.

Walking a hundred yards along the shoulder, Hart thought he was getting closer to the sound but he also recognized the foolishness of leaving the car, which had a radio. He returned and drove along the shoulder with his window open, stopping occasionally to turn off the engine and listen.

Nothing.

Are woodpeckers nocturnal? That's what it had sounded like, a woodpecker working on a hollow tree.

Hart drove another hundred yards, stopped, got out.

Nothing.

Reaching for the car door, Hart heard it again. More like a drum than a woodpecker.

This dark mountain forest was cold now and Hart zipped up the FBI jacket. The sound was close. Hart checked his semiautomatic pistol and found a flashlight in the car. He considered reporting in— but to whom, and what would his message be, that he thought he heard a drum or a woodpecker, he wasn't sure which? By the time backup got here, whatever was making the noise would be gone.

Charlie walked into the woods, an armed FBI agent. He was not frightened but felt goosey, as if he might jump or yelp if a branch fell behind him or an owl flew near his head. Enough moonlight was making it through the canopy that Hart could see his way with the flashlight off.

The drumming had stopped but he could hear something else now, a voice, a single low voice, talking.

He drew his weapon. Following the voice, Hart moved as his father had said Indians moved while hunting, placing their toes first and choosing exactly where to position each step.

There.

Hart stopped breathing.

There by a small stream, on a grassy spot no larger than a living room, a single Indian was dancing, had danced a circle of flattened grass, was chanting low and steadily.

Hart opened his mouth and breathed shallowly.

The big Indian wore only a breechcloth, a flap front and back, the two pieces of leather connected top and bottom with leather straps.

He was oiled, his dark skin shining in the moonlight. Barefoot, he wore bands of fur around his ankles. Feathers were fixed to leather straps around his large biceps. Across his forehead a war rag kept his long black hair in place.

He was magnificent—but under the circumstances, Hart knew that a dancing Indian was a threat to Mount Rushmore and had to be stopped.

Charlie looked around. He could see those four giant white heads through a gap in the trees. The heads looked even more peculiar than usual. The presidents were being kept illuminated so that more than a hundred government agents could stand watch over them with powerful weapons.

But the danger was here, this lone Indian dancing in the Paha Sapa.

Hart remembered what his father had told him, that before you put yourself in a dangerous or awkward situation, know what you intend to do. The Bureau had taught him the same lesson. Charlie was also remembering what Davy Crockett said: *First make sure you're right, then go ahead.*

He planned to take another few steps then shine the flashlight on the Indian and point his pistol and say, *FBI! Freeze! Put your hands on your head! I'm armed and I will open fire if you don't follow my orders.* And then . . . and then . . . if the Indian didn't stop dancing, or if he tried to get away, Hart would shoot him. Shoot to kill. No doubts, no compromises. No foot chase through the forest. No attempt to wound the Indian. Kill him if he doesn't stop dancing.

Hart hesitated.

A warm calm came over him as he foresaw what would happen in the next few moments, that he would challenge the Indian, the Indian wouldn't obey the order to stop dancing, and Charlie would kill the Indian to save the presidents on Mount Rushmore. Charlie was as sure of this sequence as he was of gravity. He checked the pistol's safety.

When Hart turned on the flashlight, the Indian turned to face him.

19

JOHN BROWN DOG. Charlie had known it all along even if he hadn't admitted it to himself. John Brown Dog stopped dancing, the flashlight making him squint. He wanted to know who was there.

"Charlie Hart."

John Brown Dog's expression lifted. "Listens to Indians."

"I have to take you in."

"Put that light off my face, Charlie."

Hart kept both the flashlight and the pistol aimed at John Brown Dog. "I'm armed. I will shoot you if you don't comply."

" 'Comply'?" John Brown Dog cupped a hand above his eyes. "Are you really Listens to Indians? Or someone imitating his voice? Shine the light on your face; show me it's you, Charlie."

"It's me." Realizing he didn't have cuffs with him, Hart was trying to figure out how to take the big Indian into custody.

"You must be a hero to your government, Charlie—being proven right about the arch."

"Sometimes being right is the worst possible place to be."

The Indian grunted his agreement. "What was that terrible noise carried by those helicopters?"

"A new technology."

John Brown Dog smiled.

"Did it make you sick?" Hart asked.

"No, I was far enough away. But I don't want to hear it again."

"Me either. I met the grandfather."

"Good! He began negotiations?"

"He said all state and national parks and forests had to be returned to the Indians if we wanted to stop the human race from dying out."

"Charlie, it is good you said *returned* to the Indians. What do you think your government's answer is going to be?"

"I think the government is going to put a world of hurt on Indians."

"Nothing new."

"Who are these allies I'm hearing about? The grandfather said the Indians are following your allies' advice. Are they from another country?"

"The whore is one of them."

"But who are they?"

John Brown Dog hesitated but finally said, "I just found out about them recently."

"They're terrorists, aren't they?"

"If I told you, Charlie, it would blow your fucking technology-biased mind."

"The people who will question you after I bring you in . . . it's not going to be like the talks we had before."

"I know, Charlie. I enjoyed our talks."

"You won't enjoy the next round. Let's go."

The big Indian stayed where he was.

"Will you walk back to the car with me and promise not to run off? I don't want to shoot you. But I will."

"Charlie, it's too late."

Hart got that feeling of someone watching him, someone nearby. He shined the flashlight all around.

"Put it off," John Brown Dog told him, more of a warning than a demand.

Hart did.

The Indian said, "I brought them from the Badlands."

"*Who?*"

"Can't you sense what's around us?"

Hart could, the hair on his arms and at the back of his neck stood on end, his mouth was dry, his heart a tom-tom.

He wondered what he'd do if he ordered John Brown Dog to accompany him to the car and the Indian refused. John was too big to drag or carry. And if it came to a wrestling match or fistfight . . . Hart didn't want it to come to that. Not knowing how he should proceed and wanting to ease the tension, Hart asked, "What's that around your neck?"

John Brown Dog was embarrassed, then amused. "Damn whore. I keep taking off the Miraculous Medal, she keeps putting it back on."

"Maybe it has magical properties."

"Hey, Charlie, I know you're pulling my leg but, considering who the whore is, you might be right."

"Who is she?"

"I told you, one of our allies."

"And I've asked you, *who are they?*"

"I'll give you a hint."

"I don't want a hint, I want an answer."

"They've taken up residence in the Badlands, in the worst of the Badlands, where no creature can cross, nothing lives. After you left for Washington and I was sprung from jail, I went to the Badlands and conjured an army to bring here, Charlie. I assembled an army of our allies, who are not without power."

"John—"

"I kicked up Badlands dust, stomping along the clastic dikes, which are naturally formed walls; Europeans used to wonder who built those Badlands walls, going nowhere. Brother warriors beat the drums as I danced the Badlands battlements."

"John."

John Brown Dog continued talking, his voice sounding more and more like a chant. "Out of the Badlands they came, our allies, like smoke gathering in the low parts, then black streams flowing the wrong way, Charlie, flowing *up* the furrows, against gravity, what do shadows know of gravity, gathering themselves into shapes, twisting their way up the battlement on which I danced and chanted and conjured."

"Okay, that's enough."

"Shape shadows, liquid black, standing snakes. Included among them were bad spirits gone good, but they were not the majority, Charlie. Some of them were briefly shaped like women, who changed to fish that swam in the night air, thick with heat, thick with dust. Some were like buffalo running among us, stampeding over the edge into the Badlands, sweeping the gorges. Some were wolves, slinking like sins made at night."

John Brown Dog began dancing.

"No!" Hart shouted. "By God, I'll kill you!"

"Kill me you might," the Indian chanted as he danced, "but not by God."

"Stop!"

"I brought the army here through a doorway—they're all around us."

In his peripheral vision, Hart saw someone and turned in time to see the tall figure duck behind a tree. "I don't know how many Indians are here with you but if I'm attacked, you're the first one I'm shooting."

John Brown Dog stopped. "Europeans who came out here, they used to believe Indians could make themselves temporarily invisible. How else to explain it? You're a European sodbuster at the edge of a field and suddenly an Indian is standing next to you. Didn't see him, heard nothing, no cover he could've used to sneak up on you. Impossible unless the Indian could make himself invisible."

Hart turned to see a tall thin black figure so close he could touch him if he dared, a foot taller than Hart, two feet taller, three feet, growing, the impossibly long arms also growing until they touched the ground whereupon black fingers walked the forest floor to encircle Hart.

He leapt back bumping into someone big and smelling of wood smoke.

Charlie whipped around. John Brown Dog. Charlie put his pistol to the Indian's head. "Call them off."

"Better turn off that light, Charlie, it's drawing them to you."

When Hart flashed the light back to where the tall thin figure had been, it was gone. Then John Brown Dog was gone. He saw other figures moving among the trees, moving *in* the trees, heading for the stream. Hart came very near to opening fire, but how do you shoot a shadow, where do you aim?

Still, he had to warn those guarding Mount Rushmore.

A bear came for him at a lumbering but determined gait, huge, nearly the size of a horse, half a ton of grizzly but black, all black, flat black. The bear's eyes were holes and its massive head swung back and forth with each step.

Hart raised his arms and shouted, *"Hey!"*

The bear came faster but veered off and ran headlong into a large tree, splashing the trunk with black, wrapping its bear shape around the tree, blackening the bark ten feet up from the ground.

Then the black began oozing down the tree, pooling at the base of the trunk, running off into a thickening rivulet that became a snake slithering toward Hart who high-stepped but couldn't avoid it, the black snake flowing over his shoes and into the stream where Hart's flashlight showed black fish the size of marlin fish skittering against the current while, over the water, a black cloud of insects roiled. On both shorelines black wolves loped.

Hart felt the ground shake. All around him were black buffalo running among the trees.

Hundreds, maybe thousands, of shape shadows heading upstream, toward Mount Rushmore.

Hart raised his pistol and emptied it into the air, hoping those guarding Mount Rushmore got his message: *They're coming.*

20

PULLING A CLIP from his belt, Charlie Hart was about to reload when someone grabbed his elbow. Thinking it was John Brown Dog, Hart turned to say something, but then—all at the same time—he smelled curry and cheap cologne and saw her startling face looking up at him, a small, mad face marked here and there with blue dots and blue stars, her eyes made up with thick black lines, the ends of the lines crossing to make her eyes look like fish, like two fish staring at each other across the bridge of her nose just as John Brown Dog had described. The whore's eyes were crossed.

Except this couldn't be her. This woman was older than Hart, was in her forties.

It's the whore's mother, Hart thought.

She said something in a singsong voice Hart didn't understand and held tightly to his elbow, so tightly it began to hurt. She wore a buckskin dress and was barefoot.

Remembering himself, that he was an FBI agent, by God, Hart told this woman, half his size, that she would have to come with him. She began ululating and pointing, Hart trying to pull loose so he could subdue her, how difficult could it be manhandling a woman half his size? When he lifted his arm, she held to his elbow until her feet came off the ground. It was like being gripped by a snapping turtle.

I'm going to have to hit her, he thought.

Apparently sensing this, the woman leapt for Hart's face, grabbing his jacket, her mouth open wide, teeth showing.

At the last available moment Charlie maneuvered her to the side so that she'd miss his face. He also kept propelling her in the general direction of her momentum and threw her over his shoulder.

Unfazed, she hit the ground rolling and ran right back at him.

He was prepared to knock her down with the heavy flashlight, but she ducked and bit his forearm, bit through nylon jacket and dress shirt, through skin and into flesh.

Which hurt with a sharp electrical pain, Charlie now more interested in getting his arm out of her mouth than in capturing her.

Someone grabbed her from behind and, with one powerful heave, lifted her off the ground, away from Hart, tossing her to the base of a nearby tree, the woman grabbing the trunk and scurrying up like a monkey in a dress, climbing all the way to the topmost limbs.

Hart was holding his right forearm where he'd been bitten, telling John Brown Dog, "I hope she's had her shots."

"Let it bleed free, Charlie."

"Who the hell is she?"

"I thought you'd know. From everything I'd told you."

"Elena?"

"Yes, the whore."

They both looked up at her, growling down at them.

"But you told me she was young," Hart said. "You were even afraid of her being underage."

"Yeah, I know. Damnedest thing, ain't it?"

"I don't understand what's happening, but you're both going to have to come with me."

John Brown Dog looked at him but didn't laugh, Hart grateful for that.

"Let's stay for the show," John Brown Dog said.

"Show?"

John Brown Dog took Charlie gently by the shoulders and turned him to face Rushmore.

21

SHAPE SHADOWS HAD LEFT the stream and flowed uphill through the trees and to the base of the monument.

Federal and state agents saw the fingered black mass and threw on even more lights. Helicopters were ordered airborne. Fighter jets so high overhead they couldn't be heard were told to drop low and be prepared to open fire. Night vision goggles were adjusted, laser sights trained, their red dots dancing on the faces of American heroes.

Everyone waited for the order to fire.

But those responsible for issuing that order were unsure. The field commanders had set up on Grandview Terrace with communications centers and support personnel in the buildings behind them. The commanders had been trained for a variety of contingencies and could've repelled a small army—but how do you stop what looks like liquid tar, a foot deep, from being sucked up a mountain at a steady pace?

Nearly half a million tons of granite were removed from the mountain to make the presidents, dynamited and chipped out with air hammers, and all of it fell on the side of Mount Rushmore, where it remains to this day. As originally designed, the presidents were to be sculpted to the waist and, in fact, Washington's figure shows lapels. Money ran out. When the sculptor, Gutzon Borglum, died, his son, Lincoln, took over, ultimately leaving the figures unfinished. It is this unfinished nature that imbues Rushmore with its power. Washington has fully emerged and Jefferson nearly so, but Roosevelt and Lincoln look as if they are caught in the process of being born from the cliff. Standing far below, a viewer looking up has the sense of catching the mountain giving birth to these giant heads, the debris of those births still visible on the mountain's lap.

It was this debris, hundreds of thousands of tons of granite, that was now being covered by a thick tarlike liquid. And then the shape shadows stopped.

A man wearing a BIA jacket (but who in fact did not work for the Bureau of Indian Affairs) asked the FBI field commander how many cameras were recording the event.

"We have two official film teams, set up there . . . and there." He pointed over the railing of the terrace. "They're shooting film. We also have half a dozen teams shooting video, using different kinds of tapes and cameras to catch everything regardless of available light."

"I want—"

FBI interrupted: "And I've seen the local cops with their own cameras, some official and some personal."

"I want a team assembled immediately to confiscate all tape and film, all cameras. Everything. Official, unofficial, local, personal. I don't want anything getting out of here, not even a disposable camera, not even a hand-drawn sketch."

FBI replied in the affirmative, then, looking again at the stained debris field, said, "I wonder what that black crap is?"

"Have one of the helicopters drop a team down and get samples before the damn stuff dissolves or evaporates."

"We're lucky it got only halfway up the mountain."

No sooner was this said than the black mass came alive again and began seeping upward, flowing toward the peak of the debris field, heading for Teddy Roosevelt.

"Should we open fire on it?"

"Damned if I know. Have one of the gunships strafe it."

The order was issued. The other helicopters flew to a safe distance and held there as an Apache gunship strafed the debris field with an M230 chain gun, the 30mm rounds kicking up rock dust and ricocheting so wildly off the hard granite that all sorts of commanders, even those without radio equipment, began shouting, "Cease fire! Cease fire!"

The gunfire only caused the liquid black tar to accelerate toward the gap between Roosevelt and Lincoln, eventually oozing onto the tops of the presidents' heads.

DEA came running up. "You know what we need? We need some high-pressure water lines capable of carrying superheated water, or maybe pressurized steam, spray that shit back down the mountain."

The other commanders stared at him to see if he was joking. Even with all the power of the federal government and complete access to the DEA budget, it would take twenty-four hours to assemble steam lines and high-pressure hoses and heaters and industrial pumps on the mountain and put them in working order.

Meanwhile, shape shadows were approximately two minutes away from pouring down onto the faces of the presidents—huge faces sixty feet from chin to hair, their mouths eighteen feet across.

And indeed, two minutes later, the "black shit," as the field commanders now called it, rolled off the tops of the presidents' heads and onto their faces. Washington was first to be stained, the black covering his wide forehead, his disdainful eyes, his twenty-foot nose, and his fussy, thin mouth. Then Jefferson, made blacker than any slave he had owned or raped statutorily. Roosevelt was blinded when his eyeglasses turned black; then the black covered his mustache as if he'd been eating licorice. And finally, the Great Emancipator, who emancipated no Indians, was made completely black, even his mole, sixteen inches across.

"Holy Mother of God," said FBI.

From somewhere off to the command center's right, a lone gunman began firing at the presidents, striking Lincoln in the head and hitting the mountainside several dozen feet below Roosevelt's chin.

The commanders thought this might be the assault they had been prepared to repel, that at this point they sorely wished for . . . but it was quickly ascertained that a local cop with a high-powered rifle and night scope was so disgusted by the disfigurement of his presidents that he was trying to shoot the black shit off. When his big rifle was taken away, he cried like a baby.

FBI asked pseudo-BIA, "You might confiscate all the film and video that's being taken right now, but how the hell you going to stop news helicopters from putting *that*"—and here he gestured toward, but could not bear to look at, the blackened presidents—"on the news tomorrow morning?"

"Ever hear of a no-fly zone?"

"You going to shoot down a CNN helicopter?"

"You better fucking believe it."

DEA said, "Hey, look, that black shit's moving again."

They grabbed their binoculars.

The solid blackness that had settled on the presidents' faces was swirling as if the presidents were covered with churning black plasma.

Although the Rushmore granite is stable, a geological survey found one hundred and forty-one cracks in the rock that makes up the presidents' heads. These are routinely filled with silicone to prevent water from seeping in, freezing, then expanding and widening the cracks. To monitor the cracks and any movement in the granite, sixty-three sensors have been embedded in the mountain, some as deep as fifteen feet. Five miles of cable link the sensors to various monitors, which have shown that movement on the mountain is limited to barely five hundredths of an inch per year.

The shape shadows darkening the presidents' faces were in search of these one hundred and forty-one monitored cracks and for older fissures that were created millions of years ago when the granite was formed, then cooled. These cracks later filled with molten magma to create pegmatite dikes, several of them visible as the white streaks on the foreheads of Washington and Lincoln before those foreheads went black.

"What's that shit doing?" asked SECRET SERVICE.

Finding ways in. The pegmatite dikes were harder to displace, but all of this stuffing—silicone and granite dust and solidified magma—was soon replaced by shape shadows. Within a few seconds all the black was gone.

"It's going away," FBI said.

"Is it over?" NSA asked.

Almost. Once embedded in the presidents' heads, the shape shadows began expanding. Everyone on Grandview Terrace heard it, a deep-rock popping noise, a granite-groaning noise, as if the presidents were grinding their teeth so hard that molars were breaking, jaws fracturing. And then it seemed you could hear every bone in their faces crack.

Even after the impossibilities they had just witnessed, those on Grandview Terrace were astonished to see Washington lose his nose, twenty feet of granite, hundreds of tons, sliding off, hitting his chin, end over end down his lapel, landing at the top of the debris field.

Followed quickly by Jefferson losing his jaw. It just dropped off, hitting Washington's shoulder and tumbling faster and farther than Washington's nose had traveled.

FBI got on the radio. "Everyone stationed anywhere near the debris field is to vacate *immediately.*"

Roosevelt's face came off in the strangest way. A variety of deep canals formed up and down his head and then all his features seemed to dissolve, the granite turning to gravel, which poured down the mountainside kicking up massive clouds of rock dust.

Jefferson's jawless face came off in massive chunks, one of which carried away his right cheekbone and his entire nose; then he lost his forehead, and finally Jefferson was no more, was only a rough surface of jagged rock where once his face had turned skyward.

Washington's entire head came loose as if guillotined and rolled down the mountain with such force that it seemed the Father of His

Country might reach Grandview Terrace and crush the agents of his government. But what was left of Washington's head stopped short of the terrace and cleaved in half like a cut grapefruit.

Lincoln held on to the last and gave the spooky night its spookiest moment. A crack had formed across his mouth, and when this fissure slowly opened, it seemed as if Lincoln were about to speak. Government agents braced to hear his mountainous voice—with the voodoo-native-jive magic they'd already seen, why wouldn't they believe that a president made of granite could speak? The crack opened wider and wider, men below the mountain running to get even farther away, terrified of what Lincoln might say.

His nose fell off, his heavy brow collapsed, and only then did the crack across Lincoln's mouth open wide enough that he lost his jaw. What remained of Lincoln's face turned to gravel, as Roosevelt's had, and poured down the mountain in a cloud of dust.

Part III

To the Sea, Turning Black

22

IT BECAME KNOWN as the calamity. In some ways, the defacing of
those four granite presidents was more frightening to many Americans than the events of 9/11. No lives were lost at Mount Rushmore,
but the unexplained nature of what happened there, *how* it could
have happened, infected Americans with a strain of hysteria. After
9/11, the perpetrators' identities, their methods and means and moti-
vation, all became clear within a relatively short time, but nothing
was clear or understood about the destruction of Mount Rushmore
and the damage to the St. Louis Memorial Arch, except that the two
events were obviously linked by the mysterious black substance.
Who did it? How did they do it? Who hates us now? Why do so
many people hate us? Most U.S. citizens thought America should be
beloved worldwide; in fact before 9/11 and then the calamity, many
citizens had assumed that America *was* beloved worldwide.

To tourists and law enforcement officers who'd been at Rushmore
before the calamity, Indians were, of course, the first and most obvious suspects. They had been trying to demonstrate and the grandfather had made explicit statements. But his interview was never
shown on television, because all the stations and news crews surrendered their tapes in the holy and terrifying name of *national security.*

The public in general considered Indians too spiritually attuned with Mother Earth to go around knocking down mountains. And many people thought Indians were incapable of organizing anything more intricate than a powwow, much less a successful attack on a heavily defended memorial. The consensus, then, was that Indians were nothing more than the unwitting patsies of some sinister group, well organized, powerful, and capable of masterminding the calamity.

Truth be told, what unsettled Americans most of all was the black substance, which apparently followed no laws of nature. If a hundred armed government agents, backed up with jets and Apache helicopters, couldn't stop that tar from destroying our beloved presidents, what would prevent it from flowing into our towns and cities, our school and businesses, our basements and attics?

Church attendance went up. Nuts crawled out from under Internet rocks to spin a mind-numbing web of theories. UFO sightings proliferated. People hoarded food and water. Gun purchases soared.

The federal government raised the threat level to red and mobilized its domestic forces. But to what use do you put a National Guard unit when your enemy is a shadow?

After the destruction of Rushmore, the Black Hills were searched by air and ground but no Indian army was found. All the Indians who had been taken into custody at Mount Rushmore were accounted for except the grandfather; they simply could not find him. John Brown Dog and Elena had escaped, too; they slipped away while Charlie Hart watched the presidents' heads roll down that mountain. Hart had been debriefed repeatedly and was assigned to help in the massive search for the three most wanted individuals in America.

When no other guilty parties were identified, rumors spread about what had happened between the Indians and law enforcement officers at Rushmore. Pirated copies of the interview with the grandfather were offered on the Internet. And people began thinking: maybe

Indians *are* the terrorists. Not foreigners this time, but our very own Indians.

Out west, attacks on Indians became commonplace. Their schools and museums were vandalized. Indian police set up roadblocks at reservation boundaries to ensure that outsiders weren't bringing in weapons or explosives. In South Dakota, two men drove their Chevy pickup to within range of the Crazy Horse monument and shot at it with high-power rifles until they ran out of ammo and beer. In Congress, bills were introduced calling for the retaliatory destruction of the Crazy Horse monument, for all aid to Indians to cease immediately, and for the arrest and imprisonment of any Indian found acting suspicious near any national monument or memorial.

At airports, men and women mistaken for American Indians readily identified themselves as Arab-Americans. People who once proudly declared themselves to be one-eighth or one-sixteenth Indian now renounced that heritage. The travel writer William Least Heat-Moon went back to using his real name, Bill Trogdon, and the Washington Redskins became the Federals.

Charlie Hart got a call from the President of the United States.

"Charlie, you're our go-to man on this deal. Find those three Indians and bring them in."

"The woman isn't an Indian, sir."

"Find 'em. The full resources of the federal government are at your disposal. I want to tell you something, Charlie. Powerful forces are trying to convince me to round up all Indians everywhere and put their feet to the fire, so to speak, and to close all parks and monuments and memorials and basically turn this country into a police state. So far I've been able to hold these dark forces at bay. But I don't know for how much longer. I need your help."

"I'll do everything I can, Mr. President."

"Atta boy."

Charlie was in Keystone, South Dakota, studying maps and plotting his next move. He had finally been allowed to put a call through to his wife and daughter, assuring them he was okay and would be with them soon. His wife wanted to talk about Mount Rushmore, but Charlie told her that he couldn't discuss it. She asked if he was okay, had he been injured. He said he was fine.

Which wasn't true. Something was wrong with Charlie's right forearm, around the area where he'd been bitten by the wild woman in the woods, the one John Brown Dog said was Elena. Charlie went to see a doctor, who gave him a tetanus booster and told him that while many human bites can turn nasty because of the bacteria normally present in the mouth, Charlie was lucky—his wound was clear, no infection. But the area around the bite mark had begun to discolor. He went back to the doctor, who took tests and reassured Charlie there was no infection. The discoloration must be latent bruising.

A few hours after talking with the president, Charlie received a call from Congressman Blaine.

"I've made it official. You are formally assigned to my committee. The director himself has okayed it."

"Yes, sir." He didn't tell Blaine about his conversation with the president. Charlie had no illusions that he was the go-to man for either Blaine or the president. Every third person in the federal government was working on this.

The congressman called him son. "You are going to become a hero and you are going to have any job you want at the Bureau or anywhere else in the federal government. But I have to know where you stand."

" 'Stand'?"

"We didn't have a happy first meeting, but now I'm behind you one hundred percent and I need to know if you're on my team."

"I'll check with the Bureau in the morning and if I've been assigned to your committee, I guess that's where I stand."

"You know America will fight this to the death. We won't give up an acre of land, not an inch of land."

"A hundred and fifty years ago, Indians fought to the death, too, Congressman, and were just as determined not to give up—"

"Son, you start talking like that and I'll start worrying about where your loyalties lie."

"I will do whatever is necessary to defend my country."

"Atta boy. And my committee will give you any support you need to find that John Brown Indian and the old Indian and the woman they're running with. Do you have any idea where they might be or where they're heading?"

"I think Little Bighorn, sir."

The congressman was silent a moment, then said, "There's no significant memorial there."

"No, sir. Just a small obelisk marking the burial spot of the soldiers and then the Indian memorial, which was added recently."

"I would've thought their next target would be another major monument—the Statue of Liberty or one of the monuments here in Washington."

"I think John Brown Dog and the woman were intending all along to make certain stops. St. Louis. Wounded Knee. Rushmore. And now Little Bighorn."

"What's their plan for the Little Bighorn?"

"I don't know."

"Do you think you can hold on to them this time?"

"Yes, sir."

"She bit you, did she?"

"You heard about that, huh?"

"Have you been looked at? She didn't give you rabies or anything like that, did she?"

"No, sir." *But my arm is turning black*, Charlie thought.

"I've talked with the director about your plan for Little Bighorn."

Then Blaine had known all along?

"Going in with a small group," the congressman continued. "No other agencies represented so those wily Indians don't get tipped off. Clever thinking."

"Yes, sir."

"I tell you this in strictest confidence, Charlie. The president wants to close all monuments, memorials, parks, and all other potential targets. He wants to shut this country down and create a police state. He also wants to authorize the largest roundup of American citizens, specifically Indians, since Japanese-Americans were interned in the Second World War. You don't want that to happen, do you, Charlie?"

"Of course not," Charlie answered warily, the president having told him just the opposite, that it was he, the president, who was trying to hold these dark forces at bay.

"None of us wants that. So you see what's at stake. You must bring those three individuals into custody. The woman, the old man, and Brown."

"John Brown Dog."

"Yes. We're counting on you, Charlie. The whole country is."

"Yes, sir."

After hanging up, Charlie went into the bathroom and looked at the discoloration on his forearm. The area felt normal. There was no pain when he pinched the skin. But, either he was becoming a hypochondriac, and paranoid at the same time, or the blackness was spreading.

23

"SEE THIS?" BILL REYNOLDS dropped a copy of *USA Today* on the restaurant table. The banner headline read, "The Arch Shines Again!"

"What do you make of it?" Reynolds sat down and looked at a menu.

"I don't know, Bill, I haven't read it yet."

"You ate already, you didn't wait for me?"

"All I'm having is coffee and toast."

"You thin guys, you really kill me."

"Let me read the article."

Scientists working with Congressman Blaine's committee had devised a liquid solution that removed the tarry substance that had attached itself to the arch. A test portion of the arch had already been cleaned with spectacular results, more photos inside. But engineers, speaking on condition of anonymity, suggested that the arch might not survive the next windstorm and should be taken down before it blew over.

"Charlie!"

"What?"

"Don't read the newspaper at breakfast. You're shutting me out. We never talk anymore. When's the last time you brought me flowers?"

"Hey, I requested you for this assignment, didn't I?"

"Let's see. Am I happy you requested me? The last time we were together, I saw the destruction of one of the greatest sculptures ever created, an American icon turned to gravel, so I can hardly wait to see what this assignment brings. Traveling with you is like running through a thunderstorm carrying a lightning rod."

"You're welcome."

"Speaking of storms." The fat agent pointed out the restaurant window to massive thunderheads developing in the west. "That's the direction we have to go."

Half an hour later they were headed for the Little Bighorn Battle-field National Monument in southeast Montana, a day's drive from Mount Rushmore. Reynolds was behind the wheel, with little room to spare. "When you talked with the president, what did he sound like?"

"Presidential."

"Fuck you, Charlie."

They drove in silence toward thunder.

"You ever been in a Dakota-Montana storm?" Reynolds asked.

"They bad?"

"You get a preview of hell."

"Appropriate."

"Hey, Charlie, before that black shit took down the presidents, did you believe in anything supernatural?"

"No, not before meeting John Brown Dog, I didn't."

"I still don't think it's anything supernatural. I think that black shit is some kind of plastic polymer space-age plasma stuff, some kind of newly invented substance and we're going to find the Indians in possession of a tanker truck full of it somewhere."

"If you'd seen the shapes those shadows took, you wouldn't be thinking that."

"This calamity is going to turn out to be the worst possible thing that could've happened to the Indians."

"Maybe the calamity was inevitable."

"Bullshit."

Hart shrugged. "John Brown Dog said every great sin has to be atoned for. The European movement into the Americas was the biggest theft of land and the largest sustained genocide in history. Never accounted for, barely even acknowledged by us."

"'Us'? I didn't do anything to anyone. And I don't feel any personal guilt for anything any previous people did to the Indians, whether or not I was related to those previous people. If I didn't do it, I'm not guilty of it."

"It's not about personal guilt."

"What's it about, then?"

"The moral arc of the universe."

"Charlie! Such a comedian!"

"Yeah."

"You want to give the Indians all our parks?"

"It'll never happen."

"You can bet your ass on that. I'm hungry, can we stop for a cheeseburger?"

Over lunch they discussed the operation scheduled to start tomorrow morning. Hart and Reynolds would meet this evening with six special agents, who would go undercover at the Little Bighorn Battlefield and be prepared to assist in the apprehension of John Brown Dog, the grandfather, and the whore. One, two, or all three. Whoever was there. It was only Hart's hunch that any of them would be visiting the battlefield this week.

After lunch, Reynolds again driving, wave after wave of motorcyclists passed them, men with scraggly beards and wearing black leather, alone or with tattooed women riding behind.

"Rolling thunder," Reynolds said.

"They going to a rally somewhere?"

"Coming from Sturgis," Reynolds speculated.

"Not heading for Bighorn, I hope."

"Don't worry, they're going to hit that storm we're heading for and have to hole up at some beer joint."

They reached Billings at day's end. Reynolds waited with Hart in

Hart's motel room. The six special agents arrived over an hour's time to avoid drawing attention. The two female special agents would pair off with two of the men and go in as tourist couples; the other two male agents would also be undercover as tourists, two fishing buddies stopping off for a look at the battlefield where Custer made his last stand.

Hart went over the rules of engagement. The six special agents would stay focused on Hart and Reynolds. Assuming the targets were at the battlefield, Hart would signal identification of John Brown Dog, the old Indian, and the woman known as Elena or God's whore. One of the undercover couples was assigned to take the grandfather into custody. The other undercover couple would go after Elena.

"Don't underestimate her because of her size," Hart told them. "She's very strong, very slippery, and she can climb like a monkey. Get her on the ground, get cuffs on her wrists and ankles, and get her in your vehicle. Our information on her age is a little dicey but if she's in full makeup there won't be any mistaking Elena. Also, she bites, so be careful." Charlie rubbed his arm where he'd been bitten. No pain. It was turning black but there was no pain. "You have photographs of the old man, the grandfather, that were taken at Rushmore."

The two remaining male agents would help Hart and Reynolds take John Brown Dog.

"Will four of us be enough?" Reynolds asked. "He's one big . . . individual."

Hart nodded. "He's good at slipping away, which he did while Rushmore was being destroyed, but he's never resisted me or tried to use force against me. I don't know what's going to happen tomorrow, however, so we have to be prepared for anything. Not only is he a big guy, he has powerful medicine."

The other agents didn't know what Hart meant by this, but no one asked.

"Our goal with all three is to get them down, get them cuffed, get them out of there. No deadly force. This is critical to the operation. Use pepper spray or your stunners or Tasers only if it seems your target is about to escape. But no firearms, even if they *are* escaping. No shooting under any circumstances. We don't want to wound tourists and we certainly don't want to kill any of the targets. The Blaine Committee, the FBI, and just about everyone else in the federal government wants to interview them. If they escape, we might be able to recapture them. But if they're dead, this operation will have been a total failure. Is that clear?"

Everyone indicated it was. These were good agents, Hart thought—professionals, not cowboys.

"I was even thinking of requesting that you go in without your sidearms." He could see the disapproval in their faces but sensed they would comply if he asked them to. "I don't think that's necessary, however. I'm confident you're all going to follow the rules of engagement. Questions?"

One of the agents had written a short report on the Little Bighorn monument. After passing around copies, he gave the highlights.

"The battle took place June twenty-fifth and twenty-sixth, 1876. The Indians won, but—"

Reynolds laughed. "Yeah, that was Custer's conclusion, too, the Indians won."

"What I was going to say, this was a classic case of winning the battle but losing the war. News of Little Bighorn reached the east on July 4, 1876, our country's centennial. The United States was in the middle of this huge celebration and then there's this terrible news of a Civil War hero being killed, his entire command wiped out. The country decided to resolve the Indian question for good. Which basically we did, except for skirmishes. Indians are never again a threat."

"Until Rushmore," Reynolds said.

"Yes," the agent agreed, then continued. "The Little Bighorn battle is popularly known as Custer's Last Stand and until 1991 the site was officially called the Custer Battlefield National Monument. It's located within the Crow Indian Reservation. A narrow road, Battlefield Road, follows a ridgetop through the battlefield. For the guided tour, you can drive to the southern end of the road, near where the battle started, and then make your way back north to where it ended, at Last Stand Hill, which is near the visitor center. No trees, no cover, just dry grasslands and a series of hilltops and deep ravines, which they call coulees out here. If we catch up with our targets anywhere on the battlefield, there's nowhere for them to escape.

"Back toward the main entrance, however, there are various structures that the Indians might try to take over: a superintendent's house, toilet facilities, the visitor center. Around these are the parking lots. There's a national cemetery where soldiers from various wars are interred. At the start of Battlefield Road, there's a small stone monument marking a mass grave of soldiers killed in the battle. Across from it is the more recent Indian memorial. Throughout the battlefield, small white markers show where various soldiers were thought to have fallen. These aren't actual graves. The bodies were moved to the mass grave. I think officers' bodies were taken to various places and reinterred. Custer is at West Point."

"I guess we don't have to worry about the Indians trying to dig up his bones," Reynolds said.

The agent who'd been giving the report replied that he had wondered about exactly that. "Do we think the Indians might try to use that black stuff to defile gravestones or what? Or do we think they want to destroy the monuments, which like I said are pretty small?" He asked Hart directly, "Why do you think the Indians are going to be at Little Bighorn?"

"I've been studying their route. It's a hunch. I don't have any better idea where to look for them. All of the above."

The agent asked, "Where should we try to take them? There's likely to be crowds around the parking lots and visitors' center. We might have more room to work and less chance of interference if we wait until the targets are actually on the battlefield, if that's where they're heading. Like I said, there's nowhere for them to hide once they get on the battlefield, no building to take over or compromise."

Hart said he was inclined to take them as soon as he saw them. "They're elusive, even the grandfather, who's probably in his seventies. Somehow he got out of the holding center after Rushmore was destroyed. I say again that I have no direct evidence that any of the three will be at Little Bighorn. I'm just making a calculated guess. We'll go to the memorial every day for a week, give them a chance to turn up, and then play it by ear."

One of the female agents said, "Ever since Rushmore, there's been trouble at the battlefield. Tourists and locals getting into arguments with Indians, even with Indian guides working for the Park Service. Motorcyclists have been showing up in substantial numbers, harassing Indians and giving the rangers a hard time, too. Programs marking the anniversary of the battle will run until the end of the month, so attendance is up and the park superintendent is making noises about closing the memorial if the trouble continues. We might find ourselves trying to take three Indians into custody in the middle of a riot."

Hart said he didn't know what was going to happen. "But the eight of us are working independently of any other agency. I've been assured by Washington that there will be no federal or local personnel at the memorial who know about this operation, no one from any other agency, just the eight of us. If there's trouble between tourists and Indians, let the rangers handle it. We have to focus on taking our targets into custody and getting them out of there."

As the six agents were preparing to leave, again following a staggered schedule, the other woman told Hart, "It's an honor going on this assignment with you. After what happened at Mount Rushmore, I feel like this is going to be the most significant thing I ever do in my life."

An hour later, after the last of the six agents were gone, Reynolds teased Hart. "And it's an honor for me to go anywhere with you!"

Hart told him to get stuffed.

Reynolds flipped on the television, catching a news report that said the cleaning of the Gateway Arch had been progressing ahead of schedule when a windstorm toppled the structure just hours ago. No one was injured, but the arch was a complete loss.

Hart said, "That should crank up the general anxiety."

"You want to order in a couple pizzas?"

Hart told him to leave.

Reynolds opened the door. "It's weird that storm hasn't hit yet. But you can smell it coming."

24

IN SPITE OF CHARLIE'S anxiety about the upcoming operation, the heavy rain that night did not wake him. When he opened his door the next morning he saw that the parking lot was flooded at its lower end. He felt lethargic and headachy. While drying after his shower, he looked at where Elena had bitten him. The actual teeth marks had cleared up. There was still no pain. But he could swear that the discolored area was bigger. He found a pen and drew a red ink outline around the discoloration so he could monitor its size.

Reynolds was chirpy at breakfast, Hart asking him, "Did you have a smoke this morning?"

"Why, can you smell it on me?"

"No, I was just asking."

"Have you ever smoked?"

"No."

"Ever abused alcohol, not counting college? Let me answer for you: No. Ever cheated on your wife? No. Ever fudged on your taxes or expense reports? No. I'm glad we didn't share a room last night, your halo would've kept me awake. Tell me you got a flaw, Charlie; give me a reason for living."

"I can be moralistic and preachy."

"Really? That's so hard to believe."

Hart laughed. "My wife says that sometimes I'm too earnest."

"Gosh, where did she ever get that idea?"

"I come by it honestly, from my father. He's the most honorable man I know. The kind of guy who drives back to the store when he discovers he got too much change even though the store is a part of a billion-dollar chain and the clerks don't care about the change and don't have a way of entering it into their accounts. The old man leaves the money there on the counter and says, 'It's yours, not mine.' Riding back home, I point out to him that the store didn't want the money back, he could've kept it. He said he returned it for *his* benefit, not the store's."

"You people who had happy childhoods, who admire your parents and want to be just like them, you're from a different planet."

It was sixty-five miles to the Little Bighorn battlefield. Charlie drove. He told Reynolds he was going to offer John Brown Dog a chance to surrender before trying to subdue him. "Stay close but don't jump in unless he resists, unless there's a struggle or he tries to run."

After arriving at the battlefield's main entrance and paying to get in, they drove around a few minutes looking for a parking space. The other six agents should already be there. It was their job to watch for Hart and follow his lead, so he wasn't concerned about spotting them or making sure they were in place. What did concern him were the dozen or so riot-geared state cops armed with rifles and shotguns.

Reynolds said he'd check it out and, after showing ID to several of the officers, was finally directed to their field commander. Returning to Hart, Reynolds said, "Not to worry, Charlie, they're not after our Indians; they don't know anything about that. They're here because of the fights they've had between tourists and Indians, motorcyclists and Indians. Apparently the superintendent wanted to shut this place down but Washington ordered him to keep it open."

Hart began making his way through the crowd gathered outside the visitor center. A ranger was using a bullhorn, telling people that they'd be allowed to visit the memorial and drive through the battlefield as soon as order could be established, no more altercations, no more speeches or name calling. He sounded like a high school teacher talking to rowdy students on a field trip.

Coming back to pick up Reynolds for another sweep through the crowd, Hart noticed several of the armed riot officers staring at him. Something about their intensity made him uneasy; they had dead eyes beneath the oversized helmets and did not look like the usual run of state cop.

The second time in the crowd, he saw John Brown Dog.

"I got him," Hart told Reynolds.

"Where?"

"Up against the visitor center there, right against the building. Stay close but don't say or do anything until—"

"Yeah, I know. Go on. I got your back."

Hart was able to walk right up to John Brown Dog, close enough to touch him, before he was spotted. Charlie was proud of this, thinking he must have powerful medicine, too.

When John Brown Dog turned and saw Charlie next to him, he registered flashes of surprise and anger but quickly resumed his implacable Indian face and said, "I'm sad to see you, Charlie."

"You have to come with me this time."

John Brown Dog stared into the distance as he spoke. "Of all of Christ's disciples, which one was the most vital to His mission?"

"I don't know what you mean."

"Any of the disciples could've spread the word and built the church, but Judas was absolutely critical because Christ had to be betrayed—to complete his destiny."

"Turn around and put your hands behind your back. Let's do this quietly."

"Kiss me," the Indian said.

"What?"

"That's how Judas did it, Charlie. Betrayed Christ with a kiss. You know, to identify him to the soldiers."

"What are you talking about?"

He stopped looking off into the distance and pointed at his chest. "These."

John Brown Dog had on a blue shirt, and now Charlie Hart could see that the shirt was marked by a constellation of laser dots, dancing bright red on this overcast day.

25

WHEN THE SHOOTING BEGAN, tourists and park personnel closest to the visitor center tried to get in but the doors were barred by grim-faced men with guns and no sympathy. People scattered, trying to reach their vehicles; some tourists hit the ground, others ran into the cemetery to hide behind the gravestones of soldiers. The toilet buildings filled quickly. Forty-eight people ran past the two memorials and into the open spaces of the battlefield itself.

Operations Commander Harlan Wickett ordered repeated fly-overs by helicopters with thermal imaging gear. The data sent back to Wickett's computers in the visitor center showed forty-seven people standing on Battlefield Road and one individual hiding deep in Medicine Tail Coulee, lying down.

The people cowering in their vehicles, in the toilets, behind gravestones, were rounded up and processed, fingerprinted, photographed. John Brown Dog wasn't among them. Wickett thought he must have been with the crowd that ran into the battlefield and was the one apart, hiding in the gully. Capturing him would be a matter of deploying a tight circle of men around the Indian's location and then sending in a few lads to flush him out like bird dogs putting a quail to flight.

In fact, why not use real dogs? "Any K9 teams available?" Wickett asked the field commanders.

DEA put up his hand like a schoolboy. "We got four teams."

Wickett grinned. He was a tall thin man, slightly bent as the result of an injury unrelated to the military, a car crash, a DWI that crippled the other driver, a judge, and almost cost Wickett his career. Although gruff, Wickett had a winning smile, which he now deployed. "You think your dogs can flush out an Indian?"

DEA consulted with one of his men, then sheepishly admitted, "The dogs have been trained to locate drugs. These particular dogs have never been used to go after suspects per se."

"Per se?"

"One's a beagle."

"A beagle?" Wickett grinned again, this time in frustration.

A local deputy said, "We got two dogs that'll flush an Indian out of a hole, you betcha, Cap'n."

"Breed?"

"Both of 'em German shepherds. Big males."

"Good. Get them up here pronto."

"You got it."

Wickett summoned the field commanders to gather around a model of the battlefield and asked BATF if he was familiar with the Little Bighorn battle.

"Only what's on that old Budweiser painting."

Careful to maintain interagency goodwill, Wickett didn't come right out and call the guy an idiot. He indicated Medicine Tail Ford on the Little Bighorn River. "This is where our man is going to try to cross the river, then make his way down to here." Wickett pointed to a highway, Route 90. "His confederates will probably be waiting, try to pick him up and spirit him away. I got people deploying to the highway right this minute. Or maybe he's heading for the railroad. We're getting that covered, too. Doesn't matter in the end, because he's not going to reach the river. How do I know this? He's hiding here." Wickett touched the spot in Medicine Tail Coulee where thermal imaging had placed the single individual. "He's waiting for dark or for this storm to hit or both; then he's going to hightail it. Which direction? Not back to the road, which he knows we'll have covered. Not along the bluffs, which will expose him. He's going to follow the coulee down to the river.

"Darkness is not going to be a problem for us because the thermal imaging works at night, but if a storm grounds our helicopters we're going to lose the ability to track him. Which means we have to deploy now. On the off chance that our Indian is hiding among the forty-seven standing out on Battlefield Road, I want each of those people checked. Anyone who's Indian, even slightly resembles an Indian, bring them here."

FBI said, "We still don't have a photograph of him."

"I don't care. Any big male Indian, I consider guilty until proven otherwise."

"Hart could've identified him," FBI said.

"Well, your Agent Hart got himself shot, didn't he? Listen, people. Any big buck we find, we bring in. Now let's go out and process those forty-seven people on the road. Last report I got, they were walking back this way. Then let's throw a human net around this location." Wickett again pointed to the spot where John Brown Dog was supposedly hiding. "Come up here and mark it on your maps. We're going to deploy a hundred yards back from where he's located, whatever the terrain allows. I want people along the road, along the bluffs, and in two lines between the road and the bluffs. Space your men close enough that no one can get between them. If this operation goes past dark or if the storm hits, I want your men close enough to hold hands. If we have sufficient personnel, we'll create a second perimeter ten or twenty yards outside the first. How many tranquilizer guns do we have available?"

FBI said a dozen. Men from other agencies had never heard of using tranquilizer guns on suspects.

"Deploy them equally spaced around the first perimeter and make sure they're in the hands of personnel who got the training." Wickett paused. "No firearms. I know this is a tough one for you guys to accept, but I want each of your men checked. No firearms. No rifles, no shotguns, no sidearms, no little backup revolvers tucked in ankle holsters, nothing except pepper spray, stun guns, Tasers, cuffs. The entire point of this operation is to bring the buck in alive."

Local sheriff's deputies were talking among themselves.

"What is it?" Wickett asked.

"We don't like going in there unarmed."

"The Indian has never been known to carry a firearm."

"With all respect, sir," one of the deputies said, "you don't know Indians like we do. Could be he stashed a rifle in that coulee, planning to dash in there all along. And if he jumps out of a hole with a M-16 or such, I don't want to be standing there with nothing but my dick in my hand."

The other deputies murmured their agreement.

"You men have the option of being dismissed from this operation; you can keep your firearms and go guard the tourists."

"We want to come along, it's just—"

"Listen to me, all of you. I'm bringing this Indian back to Washington, D.C., *alive*. I don't care if you kick him, shock him, gas him, bite him, or tickle him until he wets his breeches, whatever it takes to put the bastard in cuffs and get him to me, but I am not going to have him shot with anything more powerful than a tranquilizer dart. I'm also thinking of your own safety. We're going to be deployed all around him out there, facing each other. At night. Someone lets off a nervous shot, half of you open fire and end up killing the other half. I won't have it. No firearms on this operation. I'll bust any man who disobeys that order." Wickett realized that he couldn't make good on the threat to bust them in rank, these men weren't under his military command. "People. Listen. When you capture this Indian, you're all going to be heroes. But only if you bring him in alive. So let's do it."

The storm hit full force a few minutes later, but Wickett caught a break when the last helicopter got a great thermal image of the Indian, who had worked his way a little farther south and west down

Medicine Tail Coulee, heading for the river as Wickett had predicted. But now the Indian had holed up again.

The forty-seven tourists on Battlefield Road were processed, no Indians among them, and put on buses to shelter them from the rain. A hundred men from various federal agencies along with state cops and local cops, all of whom had taken the no-firearms pledge, were stationed around the Indian's last known location.

Two big black and tan German shepherds were brought in. Wickett ordered them held; he wanted to speak to the handlers.

"You run these dogs find-and-bark or find-and-bite?"

"It's more find-and-scare-the-shit-out-of-him," one of the handlers said.

Wickett brushed back his short gray hair with both hands; he didn't have time for this happy horseshit. "Will they attack when they reach him?"

"Shouldn't," the handler said.

"Not unless he runs," the other added.

"And if he does run?"

"He won't get far, not with two shepherds clamped on his red ass."

The dogs were whining in anticipation, straining against heavy leather collars, oblivious to the driving rain.

"Hold on to them," Wickett ordered the handlers. "I want to tighten up our circle."

"Oh, hell, Cap'n, let 'em go, they ain't going to eat him," one handler said.

The other one added, "That Indian's going to get dog bit, is all, not killed."

Wickett radioed three field commanders, one stationed with men along the bluffs, one to the east of Medicine Tail Coulee, one to the west. Wickett had personal command of the men along Battlefield Road, just north of the coulee. He told his commanders that the dogs were about to be let loose and when the shepherds had the Indian located and held at bay, Wickett would give the command to rush in and secure the target. "Don't use the tranquilizer unless it's absolutely necessary. With the dogs on him, you probably won't have to use spray or stun guns either."

He asked the handlers if they had to be down there to call the dogs off or could anyone do that.

"It's better we do it, but basically any white man can pull them off an Indian."

"And from up here we'll know when they have him?"

The handlers both smiled largely, one of them saying, "Oh yeah, Cap'n, we'll know."

The leather muzzles were removed and the big dogs let loose, at a dead run now, into the coulee. Wickett, standing in that rain with the two handlers, waited for a sound from the dogs, signaling they had caught the Indian in his hole. But the shepherds were silent.

"What's going on?" he asked the dog men.

They weren't worried, they were grinning . . . Any moment now, just wait, listen for it, listen.

One dog yelped in the distance; the other began yipping, sounding timid and frightened.

"If that goddamn Indian . . ." one of the handlers started to say.

Then both dogs came out of the coulee yelping, running toward them, running past them, running for the Ford van carrying their cages. They cowered at the van's back door, whining to be let in.

"What's he done to them?" one handler cried.

Both dogs were black.

The handlers and Wickett hurried to the dogs.

"Son-of-a-bitch sprayed them with something," one handler said, stroking the dogs' fur. They were all black as if painted black from toenails to tail tip. The handler checked his hands. Whatever had been sprayed on the dogs wasn't coming off.

"Same shit they used on Rushmore," Wickett said.

"We got to get it off the dogs before it kills them."

Back on the radio to his field commanders, Wickett warned them that the Indian might have a supply of the black substance that brought down Rushmore. Two of the commanders radioed back for permission to arm.

Wickett had to shout into the radio to be heard. "Permission denied, move—"

Gunfire to the south. Wondering if the locals had been right, if the Indian had stashed a gun and was now shooting agents, Wickett called the field commander along the southern perimeter. "Where's the gunfire coming from?"

No answer, another round of small-caliber shots. *Someone's using a pistol.*

"Goddamn it, who's shooting?"

The commander radioed back. "Indians!"

Wickett pulled his hood over his face and tucked the radio more tightly to his ear. Had the southern commander said Indians, plural? Wickett shouted into the radio, demanding to know what was happening.

"Indians!" came the call again.

"Who's shooting, what's your situation?"

Silence. Then, from the radio and from the coulee in front of him, Wickett heard men shouting, crying out in surprise and pain and terror, men screaming like women. It had been a mistake to send them in unarmed.

The field commander on the southern perimeter was on the radio again. "Hundreds of Indians. We opened fire."

"*You* opened fire? With what?"

"Some of our men brought in their weapons . . . disobeyed your orders . . . pistols and . . . opened fire when we were attacked . . . They're still coming . . . hundreds of Indians . . . Oh John! . . . among us now . . . going among us now . . . *touching* us."

"Report your situation!"

The radio crackled and went dead. Wickett tossed it to one of his subordinates. "I'm taking four men with me." He pointed to them, one-two-three-four. "We're walking over to the southern perimeter.

You, go to that van and break out five riot guns, twenty rounds each, let's hit it."

Armed now with shotguns, extra rounds weighing down their wet pockets, Wickett and his four men walked east on Battlefield Road, stepped off the pavement, and headed south. Wickett gave orders not to fire unless he did.

There couldn't be hundreds of Indians out here. The infrared cameras showed one, only one. Where could hundreds have been hiding? In tunnels? Dug at night when the park was closed? Just like the goddamn sneaky Vietcong.

Sloshing through the mud and wet grass, Wickett's group found four black men half dressed, desperately pulling at their boots and trying to get the rest of their soaked clothing off.

Wickett asked if any of them had been wounded.

They didn't answer.

"Where's your unit?"

The four men still didn't respond, stripping down to their skivvies and checking themselves as if searching for wounds.

Wickett knelt and quietly asked one of the men, "What happened, son?"

"They came up the gulley, behind us, they came right up to our perimeter. They touched us."

"Turned us black," another of the four said, his eyes large and white in his black face.

"What do you mean, turned you black?"

"They touched us and where they touched us we began turning black and . . . look, sir." The man was very nearly weeping. "We're all . . . *black.*"

Wickett touched the man's bare arm and felt nothing unusual, just wet skin, African black, but the man's features were Caucasian, narrow nose and thin lips and eyes bright blue. Wickett stepped to another of the men and put his hand on the man's bare back. Again, the skin felt perfectly normal, no indication it had been sprayed with black paint or stained with a tarlike substance. This man also appeared uninjured, a black man not wearing a shirt—but he, too, had Caucasian features.

Wickett wasn't sure how to ask the question. "All four of you are . . . white?"

The men responded vigorously. *Yes, yes,* we're white, we *were* white. They looked at him with beseeching eyes.

"You got to do something."

"Get it off of us."

"Are we going to stay like this, stay *black?*"

Wickett ordered one of his group to accompany the four men back to the visitor center where a medical facility had been set up. "Get dressed, get going."

But the four kept looking at their legs and arms and torsos and feet, amazed that everywhere they looked they were black.

With his remaining three armed men, Wickett continued across the muddy prairie, heading for the bluffs above the Little Bighorn River. They came to another dazed group, some of the individuals in various stages of undress, stripped to the waist, one with no pants on, one completely naked—every one of them black.

"Are any of you men wounded?"

"I had a forty-five with me," one of them said. "I know you ordered no firearms, but I had it with me anyway and when they came on up out of the gullies, out of the grass, out of the ground—"

"Tunnels!" Wicket exclaimed. "I knew it."

"Not tunnels, sir. They just kind of *oozed* up out of the ground."

Another man wanted Wickett to know that there were hundreds of them, hundreds of Indians, some of them mounted.

"Horseback?"

"Yes."

The man who'd been armed with the .45 continued, saying he had opened fire on the Indians. "I put holes in some but that didn't stop them, they kept coming. Walked right among us, between us, touching us. And now look, look what those bastards did to us. . . . Will it come off?"

"That officer will take you back to the medics."

One man sat off by himself and Wickett helped him to his feet and said, "I'm sorry you're black but I guarantee you, son, we'll do everything in our power to get you white again."

"Fuck you," the African said quietly.

Wickett started to apologize but then turned and walked out to the bluffs with his remaining two men. Rain had stopped. Their boots made loud sucking noises, pulling at the new mud. There was ozone in the air. The night had chilled in the aftermath of the rain. With the moon out, they didn't need flashlights or infrared to see what was crossing the river, coming toward their side. Indians on horseback, thirty or forty. They were black. Not black-skinned and not dressed in black: they were black the way crepe paper is black, they were cutout figures riding silhouette horses. Once across, the mounted Indians began climbing Medicine Tail Coulee in total silence.

Wickett's two men took backward steps, distancing themselves from the impossibility they'd just seen, and then they turned for the hard road, for the safety of vehicles parked there. Wickett didn't bother trying to call them back; he was rattled, too. *It's got to be some kind of mass hysteria*, he thought. *I am not seeing what I am seeing, it can't be.*

Other men had abandoned the perimeter that had been cast around where the big Indian was supposed to be hiding. Some of these men had been blackened, others were white but dazed, all walked as if dreaming.

By the time Wickett returned to Battlefield Road, nearly his entire command was there. The fight had gone out of them. Some wept openly. Wickett couldn't send them back to the coulee, not with thirty or forty of the enemy waiting, black-shaped Indians on silhouette ponies. Even if he armed them with rockets, Wickett doubted his men had the wherewithal to soldier on.

A white DEA man who had been turned black came to Wickett and asked about the solution that had cleaned the St. Louis Arch. "Do you think it can be used on us?"

Wickett said he didn't know.

"I don't want to stay black."

"I know you don't."

A local deputy asked, "This is the Indians' plan, isn't it? Make us all into niggers."

Looking around to see who might have been offended by the word, Wickett tried to figure out which of the black faces were authentic and which were brand-new.

He wanted to get his men on their feet, up out of the mud, instill some sense of duty, tell them of their obligations, speak of honor. But these men had been cored. And Wickett himself was so disoriented by what he'd seen that he was unable to assume command.

Then . . . they were frightened by something terrible all over again, by a woman ululating loudly from down in the coulee, like a banshee in a hole—and now here she came in the renewed rain, a small woman in a buckskin dress, barefoot, holding her arms up, wailing that terrible tongue noise.

Behind her walked John Brown Dog, naked to the waist, wearing buckskin britches and moccasins. White splotches painted like hail covered his face and torso. He carried his medicine, a small medal on a chain in his right hand, a wide strip of leather in his left.

Wickett knew who these two were, the big Indian and the whore he was traveling with, two of the three wanted for interrogation, two of the three whose capture would heal his career forever. Wickett tried to rally his troops. "Courage, boys, we've got 'em now!"

But the agents and deputies and cops shrank back as Elena and John Brown Dog approached.

Wickett was going to attempt a capture by himself but thought better of it when horsemen came up from the coulee. He stepped to the far side of a truck, not wanting to be turned black.

As Elena and John Brown Dog walked among the defeated men, she stopped ululating and began shouting, grunting, calling out the courage chant that announces a true warrior, "Hun-hun-HE! Hun-hun-HE!" Passing near enough to touch the enemy cowering in the mud, the whore exalted John Brown Dog, telling the white men made black, "This is Loon Heart! *Mahn-go-taysee!* This is Strong Heart! *Soan-ge-taha!*"

They believed her.

26

BEFORE THE BATTLE, when Charlie Hart first approached John Brown Dog near the visitor center, when the Indian accused him of betraying him and Charlie saw those red laser dots dancing on John Brown Dog's blue shirt, Hart's first instinct was not to use his own body to shield the Indian, but that was how the incident was reported because that was what in fact happened.

Charlie had wheeled around and stepped to his left to see who was aiming laser sights at John Brown Dog, putting himself between the Indian and the state cops (who were actually federal agents), two of whom got off shots. One hit the side of the visitor center, the second struck Hart in the neck.

Charlie woke up hours later in the visitor center, with Bill Reynolds sleeping in a chair next to the cot. There was a heavy bandage on the side of Charlie's neck, and when he sat up his skull felt as if it had been cracked open.

Charlie's groan roused Reynolds. "Hey, buddy, you okay?"

Charlie gingerly pulled off the bandage and touched the wound, which was not bleeding. Mumbling to himself, he wondered how the hell he could still be alive, if he'd been shot in the neck like this.

"A tranquilizer gun," Reynolds explained. "They were aiming for the Indian, of course. Meant to dope him, rope him, take him to

Washington. But then you jumped in front of him and took one in the neck for your friend."

"I didn't mean to."

"That's not how it looked."

"What the hell were they doing here? I was promised—"

"Charlie, come on."

" 'Come on,' *what?*"

"The President of the United States might've given you a personal telephone call, but you ain't even a sideshow in this particular production."

"I know that."

"No, you don't."

"Did he get away?"

"He ran out onto the battlefield with a bunch of tourists. Our people brought the tourists back, then went after the Indian."

"And?"

"And I officially don't know anything." Reynolds bent low to the cot, Charlie could smell him, flop sweat and stale cigarettes. "But unofficially, I know it's not going well out there for our side. From what I can gather, listening to the radio communications, the Indians are using that black shit on the agents."

"Indians? Who else besides John Brown Dog?"

"I don't know. One report said hundreds."

"Shape shadows."

"Do you think that black shit's going to kill those agents?"

"I don't know."

"Speaking of black, when we took your shirt off we saw your arm. Practically your whole forearm is black."

Charlie looked for himself. The blackness had spread beyond the red outline he'd drawn that morning. "It's where she bit me. It's getting bigger and bigger."

"Does it hurt?"

"No. What's happening out there?"

Reynolds said he thought the battle was ongoing.

"Help me outside."

Reynolds told Charlie it was a bad idea for him to go out there. "It's raining and everyone hates you for letting the Indian get away in the first place."

"If he hasn't escaped yet, maybe we can catch him, you and me."

"See, you don't think you're a sideshow, you think you're the main event."

"We can do this."

"Charlie, you're wobbly and I'm fat, what're the chances?"

If he had to, Hart would go it alone. But his head was in a muddle, he was unsteady on his feet, and he was grateful when Reynolds came along and took his arm and walked him out of the visitor center into the rainy night.

They reached the battlefield entrance just as John Brown Dog and the little whore were walking out.

Hart told Reynolds, "Put a cuff on my left wrist, leave the other cuff wide."

"You going to cuff yourself to him?"

"Yeah."

"What a spectacularly bad idea."

But Reynolds did what he was told and slipped the key in Charlie's pocket. Charlie, refreshed by the cold rain, made his way to John Brown Dog.

The whore acted as if she was about to attack Charlie, but John Brown Dog held her back and told Charlie he was grateful that he had taken the dart for him.

"I didn't mean to," Charlie replied, reaching out to shake hands. While he gripped John Brown Dog's big hand, he cuffed himself to the Indian's right wrist.

"Sneaky white man!" John Brown Dog said, more amused than angry. Then he echoed what Reynolds had said earlier. "Cuffing us together is a really bad idea, don't you think?"

"This time you're coming with me."

"I still have magic to do here."

"No, you're done. You're coming with me, with us." Charlie looked around. Reynolds was standing there with his pistol out.

John Brown Dog waited patiently, holding Elena back with his free arm. "Your move."

Hart didn't have a next move. Where was the car he and Reynolds had been using? Hemmed in behind the buses. Where were all the federal agents Reynolds said had assembled here?

"Your move," John Brown Dog said again.

"Is that your car over there, the black Thunderbird?"

"That's it."

"You got the keys?"

"*She* does."

"Get them from her."

From behind Charlie, Reynolds asked nervously, "What're we doing?"

"We're moving these two away from here before someone gets killed."

Hart directed Elena and Reynolds to the backseat of the Thunderbird but realized he couldn't drive, not with John Brown Dog cuffed to his left wrist.

Still outside the car, Charlie told Reynolds he'd have to drive.

Reynolds stayed in the backseat. "We wait right here for backup, that's what we do."

John Brown Dog volunteered to drive. "I'll go wherever you say, Charlie."

Reynolds was astonished that Charlie agreed. When all four were settled in the car, its engine started and wipers on high, John Brown Dog asked, "Where shall I go, Charles?"

Reynolds said, "They're coming out of the visitor center, they're armed, Charlie."

Half a dozen agents, this time carrying M-16s, not tranquilizer guns.

Watching out the back window as the agents from the visitor center broke into a trot, Charlie told John Brown Dog, "Get us out of here."

From the backseat, Reynolds said, "Wait for the agents."

Charlie turned, Reynolds had his 9mm pointed at Elena's head. She didn't seem frightened but her fish eyes were completely crossed.

"Holster that," Hart told Reynolds, who shook his head and said again to wait for the agents.

"Charlie, remember about being on the right side? Those agents are on *our* side."

"Yeah, Charlie," John Brown Dog said, "whose side are you on, anyway? Should I go or should I stay?"

"Those agents don't intend to take you prisoner."

Seeing that the agents had stopped to set up a firing line, Reynolds cursed. "They're going to kill us all."

"When we're safely away from here," John Brown Dog told Charlie, "and it doesn't look like we're in any immediate danger of being shot on sight, then you and I will talk about whether I'm going with you or taking this woman to see her mother like I promised her."

"Okay, *go*."

But as John Brown Dog dropped the car into gear, Reynolds said, "Wait a goddamn minute," and opened the back door.

He got out and tapped on Charlie's window with the muzzle of his pistol.

"I'll stay here and tell them you've been taken hostage."

"What?"

He leaned closer. "Charlie, *her face is coming off.*"

Hart turned. Elena had both hands over her face. Through the back window he could see the armed agents taking aim. "*Go,*" he told John Brown Dog just as they opened fire.

27

TWO HOURS LATER the Thunderbird was still flying along two-lane roads. Whatever rounds hit the car back at Little Bighorn were not disabling, at least not yet. Charlie had removed the cuffs and John Brown Dog had dressed in clothes he took out of his garbage bag.

"She's coming apart, Charlie."

"What does that mean?"

John Brown Dog looked over the seat at Elena, asleep sitting up, and then back at Charlie Hart, who was now driving. "It means she was put together to help us and now she's coming apart."

"You promised me once you wouldn't talk in riddles."

"I keep that promise as best I can."

"She looks old."

"I know."

"Does she have that advanced aging disease, what's it called?"

"Charlie, you keep trying to come up with scientific explanations for what you see happening."

"Because no one will tell me *what's really happening.*"

"We keep telling you but you don't want to hear it."

They kept to small roads, heading for Wyoming. John Brown Dog said he wanted to show Elena what she was helping return to the Indians, Yellowstone and Teton and all the rest. Then they'd go to Las

Vegas, which Elena wanted to see before she came completely apart. Then to the California coast to find her mother.

Charlie Hart knew this magical mystery tour wouldn't be completed. The feds would stop them first, or he'd talk John Brown Dog into surrendering, or Elena would die in the backseat, or all three of them would get shot to death at the next roadblock.

Driving through the night, Charlie said, "You told me what you did to the St. Louis Arch. I saw what you did to Rushmore. But I don't know what you did to the Custer Battlefield."

"It's not called the Custer Battlefield anymore, Charlie—it's the Little Bighorn Battlefield. And what we intended to do we didn't get done. You intervened. Once again, a hero to your people."

"They think I'm a traitor."

"But it's you who stopped us. Listens to Indians has powerful medicine. You better pull over again."

Charlie did, John Brown Dog got out, opened the back door, and took Elena in his arms. He carried her up and down the roadside, in the rain. After a few minutes he returned her to the backseat, both of them soaking.

"It's the only thing that helps," he told Charlie. "Keeping her wet."

With the overhead light on, Charlie saw her face. "She doesn't look too bad now. Just old."

An hour later, the Indian asked if Charlie wanted a break from the driving.

"You can take over when we reach Wyoming. What did I prevent you from doing at the Little Bighorn?"

"After we left the troops scattered and demoralized, I was going to conjure another army of shape shadows to raise all the buried *wasichu* from all the graves, not only the soldiers killed with Custer but all those buried at Greasy Grass in the years after the battle, more than five thousand in total, raise up their bones and turn them black and leave those black bones scattered over the prairie."

"But you didn't get it done?"

"No, Charlie, you captured me."

"Be glad you didn't disinter five thousand soldiers and scatter their bones. If the government and the American people—"

"Europeans, Charlie. *We* are the American people."

"If they don't despise you enough for what you did to the Memorial Arch and Mount Rushmore, digging up our dead soldiers would've done the trick, would've put all your people in internment camps."

"You mean, reservations?"

"Why did you want to dig up those soldiers?"

"So that my people can walk on the bones of our enemies. It is a prophecy, Charlie."

"And making the bones black? Turning the arch black? Making the presidents black before you destroyed them?"

"Look at me." The Indian reached over and turned on the inside light. "What color is my face? They call us redskins, but what color is my face?"

When Charlie looked, he remembered seeing John Brown Dog's face for the first time, and how surprised he'd been that the Indian's skin was so dark.

"When you get a chance, Charlie, study old photographs of Indians taken in the West before there was intermarriage with whites and Spaniards and Mexicans. Our eyes are set wide apart, our cheekbones are high, and our skin is . . . You tell me, Charlie, what color is our skin?"

"Black."

"The white federal agents on that battlefield thought we had turned them into Africans, but we turned them the color of Indians." John Brown Dog switched the light off. "But in the end, African or Indian, it doesn't make much difference, Europeans become what they hate the most."

"If men who've been made black are washed in raw milk like the arch, will they become white again?"

John Brown Dog laughed.

"What's funny?"

"Charlie, I saw your forearm."

"You don't think I should worry about my arm turning black?"

"If our allies stop human reproduction and doom most of the human race to extinction in a hundred years—I think *that's* what should concern you, not the possibility you might end up looking like me."

A few miles later, Charlie touched the puncture wound on his neck.

"Are you okay?" John Brown Dog asked.

"My neck hurts like hell and I have a headache that feels like my skull is being cracked apart."

"Yeah, that horse tranquilizer is a bitch."

28

JUST PAST THREE A.M. they stopped at the side of the road in Wyoming, no traffic, a big sky scattered with stars, animal calls in the distance. Elena slept in the backseat, John Brown Dog in the front. Charlie Hart went outside and paced.

His father had told him always to do what was right, not to debate whether or not he can get away with doing wrong, not to try to balance the risk against the potential advantage, just do what is right. But his father, who grew up in the 1950s, hadn't warned Charlie of situations in which right was wrong.

The Bureau would almost certainly rule that Charlie did wrong by going with the big Indian and the little whore; he should've held them at the battlefield, made sure they were taken into custody even at the risk of getting them shot. But Charlie's own sense of right and wrong told him it would've been wrong to let John Brown Dog and Elena be killed at the Little Bighorn Battlefield, which would've been their fate considering the general hysteria there.

The Thunderbird's front passenger window came down and a blanket was tossed out. "Your pacing on the gravel is keeping me awake," John Brown Dog said.

Charlie spread the blanket a little distance from the road. He saw lights in the distance, in the direction from which they'd come. Hart waited for the car but its lights went out and the road stayed dark behind them. He stretched out on the blanket and tried to sleep.

He knew what was happening: *They're following us.* "They," meaning the FBI or other agents of the federal government. *Following at a distance to find out where we're going.* Charlie wondered what Bill Reynolds had told them. Did the government now consider him a hostage . . . or a turncoat? He wished he could call his wife and assure her that no matter what she heard about him, he had done nothing wrong, or at least he'd done what he considered right even if it was wrong.

Although the ground was hard, dawn came too soon, too brightly, awakening Charlie with the wish for another hour's sleep. He was folding the blanket when John Brown Dog got out of the car.

They walked off a distance and peed, returning to the Thunderbird to see Elena sitting up front putting makeup on.

"You look a lot better this morning," Charlie said. "How're you feeling?"

"Fuck you and give me some privacy."

"She apparently considers it mandatory," John Brown Dog said, after they had walked off a ways. "That eye makeup."

Elena honked the horn when she was ready to go. John Brown Dog got behind the wheel.

"I think they're following us," Charlie said after he was seated and belted on the passenger side.

"Yeah, I've seen them back there."

"We have to talk about the surrender. I mean, let's be realistic. At some point, they're going to stop us and take you into custody. Why don't we do it on our terms?"

John Brown Dog turned to Elena. "We can get to the ocean a lot faster if we don't have to drop down and go through Las Vegas."

She put on an exaggerated pout, her big dark eyes crossing to make the fish stare at each other. "Vegas!" she chirped. "I want to see the lights! I want to see water that dances! I got tricks to turn."

Charlie shook his head. "We won't make it to Vegas. We won't make it another hundred miles."

John Brown Dog pulled onto the narrow road and hit the accelerator hard.

"You know, Charlie Hart," Elena said from the backseat. "You could come back here and get a nice blow job while John Brown Dog drives, how's about that . . . on the house!"

"No, thank you," he said quietly.

The Indian laughed. "That's the politest refusal of oral sex I've ever heard in my life."

Which made Charlie laugh, too . . . and then Elena joined in with her own high-pitched laughter, though after a moment she asked, "What are we laughing about?"

Hours later they stopped in a little town for gas, for lunch at a small diner with a long white counter and round stools topped with bright red vinyl. The stools twisted all the way around and Elena kept turning complete revolutions, saying "Whee!" She wasn't expressing joy and delight as much as she was reciting a word she'd been taught.

The counterman, beer-bellied and three days past his last shave, was not amused. He wiped his hands on a formerly clean apron and looked only at Charlie Hart. "Yeah?"

"I hope it's not too early for lunch."

Impatient, the counterman asked, "What do you want?"

"I'll have an egg salad sandwich, cup of coffee."

John Brown Dog looked at the counterman, who still wouldn't look at him. "I'll have a cheeseburger, order of fries, cup of coffee."

Elena turned around and around on the stool, occasionally grabbing for John Brown Dog to keep from being spun off.

"Tell that crazy old lady to stop fucking around," the counterman told Charlie as if he were the only one of the three with any authority.

John Brown Dog reached over and gradually slowed Elena's revolutions.

"What'll she have to eat?" Charlie asked John Brown Dog.

"She'll order something but I doubt she'll eat anything."

"Cheese and tomato on rye!" Elena shouted, then went spinning. This time, she lost her balance and ended up on the floor, laughing.

The counterman leaned over and, with coffee breath that made Charlie wince, said, "Tell the Indian and his little cunt to leave before I kick all three of you out."

Charlie started to say something but John Brown Dog touched his arm and said forget it. Then he helped Elena stand and suggested Charlie get the sandwiches to go. "She'll drink sweet ice tea."

In ten minutes the counterman was back with three sandwiches on paper plates, two coffees in paper cups.

"And an ice tea, sweet," Charlie said.

The counterman got the tea. "You want it sweet, add your own. Sugar's over there."

"You got a paper bag I can put this stuff in?"

The counterman produced one. He picked up the top bun from the cheeseburger and spat on the patty, then picked up the top bread from the cheese-and-tomato sandwich and spat on it, too. He didn't touch Charlie's egg salad. After replacing the bun and bread, he said, "That'll be twelve bucks."

"I ought to make you eat those sandwiches."

"You been watching the news lately, pal? You heard of the calamity? You see who they're saying's responsible?"

Charlie was going to flip out his FBI identification and try to scare some decency into the guy but thought better of it and headed for the door, leaving the lunch order on the counter.

"You still owe for this food, twelve bucks."

Boy Scout or not, Charlie told him to go to hell.

When he got to the car, John Brown Dog asked about the food. Charlie shook his head.

The Indian didn't question him further.

In another town, they got lunch from a drive-up Wendy's and then drove west toward Yellowstone, followed by dark cars and spotter planes. They studied maps to skirt the park.

"I wish I could've shown it to Elena," John Brown Dog said.

"If you did get the parks back, which you never will, but if you did, what the hell would you do with them? We're already preserving them, they're already *parks.*"

"Do with them? I don't know. Maybe tribes will live there, hunt there. Or, and here's a radical idea for you to get your European mind around, maybe we'll close off Yellowstone and let no people enter and not *use* Yellowstone at all. Keep it that way, unused, for, say, five hundred years, see how the place rebounds from all the roads and hotels and concessions. Just because something exists, it doesn't have to be used. Maybe all over this country, not just the parks, we'll let the trees grow and live and die and rot without ever being *used.* Let the buffalo live and breed and die and rot back into the earth. Let the oil stay in the ground. Let the gold and lead stay in the ground. I don't know, Charlie. Maybe we won't *use* anything."

"Noble of you. And you can pull it off, too, if there's only going to be a few small tribes of Indians. We put this country to better use than your people did, we're supporting a population that's, what, thirty times the size of the Indian population back before Europeans arrived. And when a country has a population in the hundreds of millions, people have to be accommodated. You have to have hospitals, schools—"

"Prisons."

"Yes, prisons."

"I don't know, Charlie. Indians were here for a thousand years and we didn't build prisons. Or hospitals or schools or orphanages. People took care of each other. Children learned from parents and grandparents. Criminals were ostracized, not imprisoned."

"But like I said, that's because there were so few of you."

"Millions of us, Charlie."

"Relatively few . . . for such a big country."

"Maybe that's what's needed, to keep populations small. Oh, I forgot. You need big populations to sell things to, don't you, Charlie? Like all that fucking Iowa corn we drove through. Agriculture supports an overpopulation that supplies customers for capitalism that supplies the chemicals for agriculture."

"Commie," Charlie muttered, half joking.

"No, Charlie—*reader.*"

They drove on in silence, around Yellowstone, heading for Las Vegas and using the interstates now because what was the point of keeping a low profile when their every move was being plotted by airplanes and satellites, a posse keeping out of sight but following them nonetheless.

In Idaho, one motel owner saw the big Indian in the front seat and refused Charlie a room. At the next motel, he parked away from the manager's office and got the last vacancy.

"Two beds," John Brown Dog said when they entered the room. "You got a choice, Charlie. Sleep with an Indian or sleep with a whore."

"How about this—I get one bed, you two can share the other. You're traveling partners."

"I can't sleep with her, she makes too much noise."

"I'll sleep on the floor, it won't be as bad as last night out on the ground."

John Brown Dog smiled. "If we sleep in the same bed, Charlie, I promise not to bugger you."

"Thank you, but I'll sleep on the floor all the same."

Charlie and John Brown Dog went out for pizza and toiletries; when they got back, Elena was asleep. They watched television while eating. News reports from around the country concentrated on the calamity, showing people stocking up on groceries, buying generators, arming themselves. The federal government had lifted the ban on televising pictures of Mount Rushmore and the faceless mountain was being shown on all the stations. Agents who'd been at Little Bighorn were also shown and interviewed. Their facial features hadn't changed but their skin color remained dark. Commentators and government officials spoke carefully when discussing this matter: they couldn't exactly come out and say that being turned black was horrible, a terrible tragedy, the worst thing that could happen to a white person. The feds were concentrating on what they were now calling "dark matter," pledging to analyze it, map its properties, find antidotes, devise weapons to combat it.

Delighted with the television coverage, John Brown Dog couldn't get over the fact that everyone was thinking of shape shadows as an actual substance, something invented in a laboratory, a chemical manufactured at a clandestine factory. "Your government, Charlie, is a hoot! Instead of treating this as chemical warfare, they should be deploying spirits against us. Conjure up your Christian angels and see if they can't whip our shape shadows. The archangel Michael is a warrior, isn't he? Get his bad ass down here and see what he can do for your side. Send out battalions of people who do nothing but pray. Put your magic against ours." He laughed. "I forgot! You don't believe in magic, do you, Charlie?"

"Your talk of Indians being spiritually superior is getting old."

"No, Charlie, not old! Not yet! Let me talk a few hundred years about superiority, give me a chance to catch up with you guys."

"I'm going to sleep. The faster I get you two off my hands, the happier I'm going to be."

"You mind if I keep the television on? Seeing all the terrified Europeans is a tonic."

"Turn the sound down."

"Charlie, pictures are enough for me!"

That night, Hart dreamed of drums, of shape shadows settling over him, of water running.

He awoke to see light under the bathroom door, both beds empty. Charlie got up and listened at the door. "Everything okay?"

John Brown Dog said, "I'm giving her a bath. Come here."

"Why?"

"Charlie, come here."

Stepping into the small bathroom, Charlie saw Elena on her back in a tub half full of water. She was shockingly thin, her limbs spidery, her breasts small and sagging. She looked eighty years old. Her eyes were closed. "Is she okay?"

"No," John Brown Dog said quietly as he knelt at the tub. "Look at her feet, Charlie."

The whore's small feet were twisted oddly, as if her left foot was on her right ankle, her right foot on her left ankle.

"Birth defects?" Charlie whispered.

Elena opened her fish eyes but said nothing.

Charlie spoke quietly, "I don't understand who she is, what she is."

"She's an ally," John Brown Dog said as he stood and wiped his hands on a towel. "I think I'll let her soak awhile. Water's the only thing that keeps her going. When I first put her in the tub, her right ear started to peel off."

"Peel off?"

"Yeah, I—" The Indian stopped talking when he looked up and saw Charlie's face.

"What?"

John Brown Dog stepped out of the way so Charlie could see himself in the mirror over the sink. But Charlie Hart didn't believe what he saw. That is, he couldn't accept it as real, that the familiar face staring back at him was black.

29

NOBODY COULD SLEEP after that. The men showered and took Elena's suitcase to the car, then set off for Utah. In the backseat, Elena was quietly sick. Charlie Hart and John Brown Dog alternated between long stretches of brooding silence and bitter argument as the Thunderbird raced through the night, one headlight cocked at a crazy angle.

Charlie accused John Brown Dog of thinking it was amusing that Charlie had turned black all over . . . in fact, maybe while Charlie slept, John Brown Dog conjured shape shadows and completed the conversion that had begun with the whore's bite.

John Brown Dog refused to answer these accusations, and asked Charlie if this was the worst thing that could ever happen to him, becoming dark-skinned.

"That's not the point."

"I think that's exactly the point. You took a long shower before we left, were you trying to wash it off?"

Charlie *had* tried to wash off his new skin color but resented being made to feel guilty about it. "This is not a joke."

"Oh, no, Charlie, you look like an Indian, and that's not comedy, that's tragedy."

Hart almost took a swing at him.

They drove the eastern edge of the Great Salt Lake and then through the booming exurbs of Salt Lake City, the two men silent until one or the other made a sharp comment, an accusation of bad faith.

Whenever they passed signs for a route to a national forest, national monument, national park, John Brown Dog would say, "That'll be ours someday."

Charlie told him he was full of shit. "If you think *anything* is going to be turned over to you, you're crazy."

"The Mormons have a lot to answer for."

Charlie made a soft sound of contempt.

John Brown Dog ignored it and said, "Over a twenty-year period, a hundred thousand Mormons trespassed across Indian lands to reach Salt Lake Valley. This they did in open defiance of the law. When a Mormon's cow got shot by an Indian, the Mormon was offered payment by the chief they called Conquering Bear, but the stupid Mormon wanted his exact cow back, which was impossible, it had been butchered and eaten by hungry Indians who had been denied their—"

"You know what? I'm tired of hearing this litany of wrongs against the Indians."

"You know what, Charlie? I'm tired of singing it. After the Mormon cow incident escalated into soldiers killing Indians and Indians killing soldiers, General William Harney took six hundred soldiers to a Brulé camp on Blue Water Creek and killed a hundred Indians— men, women, and children. Harney was a butcher but he was only following orders, to exterminate Indians. His men cut off the genitals of Indian women and stretched them as hatbands. To honor Harney's atrocities, Europeans call a mountain after him, Harney Peak in our Black Hills."

"You should've fought harder."

"You're a son-of-a-bitch. I've heard that joke many times, Charlie. We did fight hard and we never stopped fighting. Our fighting eventually took the form of the ghost dance, which we've been dancing for more than a hundred years. And guess what, Charlie . . . it's working."

"We'll see."

"Yes, we will."

"Boys!" Elena said from the backseat.

When John Brown Dog stopped for gas, Charlie bought a quart of milk and took it in the men's room. He rolled up his sleeves and poured milk over his arms, rubbing the milk in and wiping hard with paper towels. He didn't become any whiter. Raw unpasteurized milk had removed the stains from the St. Louis arch, but Charlie didn't know where to get raw milk or whether it would work on skin as well as it did on stainless steel.

He looked in the mirror. The darkness of his skin did not appear to be a dye or stain or makeup; it looked completely natural. His formerly light brown hair was as black and straight as John Brown Dog's. What would his wife think? And if she approved of his new look, his new race, what would Charlie think of that? *I shouldn't be so troubled about this,* he lectured himself, *it's not life-threatening.*

A big white guy came into the men's room and stared angrily. And said, "You people."

What did he mean? Charlie didn't ask, but the man told him anyway. "How come a hundred white guys can use this room and it looks like it did when I cleaned it this morning, but one of you people come in and it's a pigsty?"

Charlie looked around at all the milk he'd spilled. "I'll clean it up."

"You people never—"

" 'You people' *who?*"

The man stared at Charlie's dark skin and Caucasian features. "Whatever you are. African-American." The words came out *African-American* but the tone and intent were clearly *nigger.* "Mexican." *Beaner.* "Puerto Rican." *Spic.* "Indian." *Redskin.* "Arab." *Raghead.* "Whatever you are, you're all the same, no consideration for others. Act like pigs. Drive off without paying. Shoplift. I been in this business twenty years and it's always you people causing the trouble, making the mess. And if you don't like how I'm talking to you, get a lawyer."

Although the white man's words were aggressive, he backed away from the door to let the colored man pass.

When Charlie got to the Thunderbird, John Brown Dog was sitting on the trunk, but Elena wasn't in the car.

"Where is she?" Charlie asked. "In the bathroom?"

John Brown Dog shook his head. "I took her to a little cemetery. She's talking with an older woman she met there."

"Her mother?"

"No, her mother's in a castle on the California coast."

"Of course, how could I have forgotten that?"

"Don't start."

"I don't understand how she could've known to meet someone here."

John Brown Dog said he didn't understand either. "The old woman looked like she was waiting for us, looked like she was all dressed up for church. Wearing a wide-brimmed hat with flowers all over it, plastic flowers."

"Crazy."

"Come on, let's go pick her up."

On the way, Charlie told John Brown Dog about the incident in the bathroom.

"You were using milk, trying to get white again?"

"Don't start."

Then he told John Brown Dog about the guy spitting on the sandwiches.

"I figured it was something like that," the Indian said.

Elena was sitting on the curb outside the cemetery, no one else around. She wore the hat John Brown Dog had described, wide brimmed, with plastic flowers, and she looked forlorn but not as damaged as before. As John Brown Dog pulled over, Charlie tsked. "Man, she's *ancient.*"

"I'm hungry," she said when she got in the car.

"You never eat," John Brown Dog said.

The whore insisted she was ravenous.

A few minutes later, Charlie pointed. "Let's stop over there, at that little diner."

"We better find a national chain restaurant, they're more concerned about bad publicity and lawsuits. Your food doesn't get spat on in front of you. They do it more discreetly, back in the kitchen."

Even with a national franchise's reputation to maintain, the hostess kept them waiting for a table and seated two parties who came in after them. When Charlie called her on it, she said she was waiting for just the right table, it was difficult to seat a party of three. "Pretend we're four," he said. She made a *you people* face and put them at a table in the back, near the restrooms.

"Everyone's staring at us," Charlie said.

"Trying to figure out if we're the terrorists."

"Well, you are, aren't you? You and the whore are the terrorists, you've earned these stares."

"But not you, huh, Charlie?"

"What do I look like? Tell me. Do I look like a white guy whose skin has been turned dark, or do I look like I'm not white at all, never was?"

"This really has gutted you, hasn't it?"

"How would you like it if you were turned white?"

"People of color have I-woke-up-white dreams all the time, Charlie. And to answer your question, you're looking more and more like an Indian. Your eyes have started to slant."

Charlie felt his eyes, John Brown Dog laughing softly.

"I think Elena is why everyone's staring," Charlie said after they'd ordered. "Wearing that buckskin dress, going barefoot, her crazy makeup. And now that crazy hat, as if she needed something else to make her look conspicuous and provocative."

"Elena," John Brown Dog said, "you are conspicuous and provocative."

Staring blankly, she didn't respond.

When they were halfway through their meal, a woman from another table made her way toward them. Plump, white, in her seventies, wearing a blue dress, she looked like a grandmother. Charlie smiled when she came to the table; he was thinking she was about to say something supportive, apologize for all the staring, but then he saw the madness in her eyes and put up his arm just as she grabbed a fork and tried to stab him.

He managed to deflect several of her jabs; she was sputtering about Rushmore, about Indians who should be grateful for all they've been given by America, and America being the greatest country on earth, how our only problem is that we're too good to people, *you people,* and you take advantage of us and if you don't like it why don't you go live in some other country, see how you're treated there—and then as Charlie tried to scoot out of the booth, she stabbed him hard in the chest.

Not that hard, she was an old lady. It didn't hurt nearly as much as getting the tranquilizer dart in the neck. But the fork momentarily stuck there. Charlie could see its stainless-steel handle rise rhythmically with his breathing.

The grandmother, amazed at what she'd done, backed away speechless.

"I'm not an Indian," Charlie said, pulling the fork out. There was remarkably little blood. "I'm not an Indian." For some strange reason, he handed the fork back to her and, stranger still, she accepted it.

Other patrons booed and cursed the three of them. John Brown Dog escorted Elena toward the door, Charlie headed for the cashier. People began throwing things. The cashier waved Charlie off, telling him to forget the check, just get the hell out of there.

John Brown Dog was behind the wheel when Charlie arrived at a run. Pulling out of the parking lot, John Brown Dog said, " 'I'm not an Indian,' " quoting Charlie. "You should make a sign and hang it around your neck. *I'm not an Indian.* Not an African or Puerto Rican either. Not a mulatto or a half-breed. *I'm all white. I just look dark.* It would have to be a pretty big sign."

"I just got stabbed in the chest for being an Indian, you should cut me some slack."

"Charlie, you got stuck by an old lady."

"Go to hell." Then he laughed. "An old lady *with a fork.*"

John Brown Dog laughed, too. "She really stabbed you, didn't she?"

Charlie touched the wound, which was shallow and nearly painless.

They drove into Nevada with the temperature topping a hundred, the car's air conditioning working poorly and then working not at all, blowing hot air until Charlie turned off the fan.

"This heat is not good for Elena," John Brown Dog said.

She was sitting up in the back, her eyes half open and glazed. She could've been ninety years old.

"We have to get her to water," John Brown Dog said. "This heat is killing her."

Charlie tried the air conditioning again, filling the car with the sick-sweet odor of antifreeze. "Stop at a motel," he said. "We'll put her in the swimming pool."

"I think she needs cool water. In this heat, a swimming pool will be like a hot tub."

"Let's surrender."

"Surrender?"

"Pull over and let them catch up, indicate we want to surrender."

"That's a bad idea, Charlie."

"They'll get her all the medical help she needs."

"She doesn't need medical help, she needs water."

"Pull over."

"Charlie, you gave me your word."

"I'm *asking* you to pull over and give up."

"You know what's going to happen if we stop and try to give up? You're going to run up to them and say, *Hey, it's me, Charlie Hart, I'm an FBI agent.* But they're not going to see a white FBI agent, they're going to see an Indian and tell you to drop to your knees and you're going to insist you're the FBI and they're going to take that as evidence of resisting arrest and, boom, you're going to get shot."

Charlie looked down at his black hands. "They might not think I'm an Indian; they might think I'm African-American."

"That'll help your case?"

"Will I stay dark like this forever?"

"Not forever, Charlie. If they dig you up in a couple hundred years and put your skeleton on display in some museum, like they do with Indians, your *bones* will be white."

They approached Las Vegas from the northeast, through scrub desert blowing with trash. Charlie looked outside. "Have you ever seen anything so ugly in your life?"

"No."

Plastic bags, thousands of them, had scattered everywhere, catching on fences and desert plants. There were tires and parts of tires just off the roadway. Someone had lost a shoe. A torn blanket half covered an auto battery. In the distance was the bright neon of the big casinos on the strip.

Elena coughed softly and in the front seat Charlie and John Brown Dog could smell her fetid breath.

"Gotta find a motel," John Brown Dog said. "Put her in a tub of water and ice."

"Something out of the way."

"I don't know Las Vegas."

"Turn there."

They stopped at a motel on a high-volume street flanked by convenience stores and porno shops, tawdry little wedding chapels and down-at-the-heels casinos. Construction sites blasted noise from behind hastily erected chain-link fencing. At gas stations, the cashiers stayed behind bulletproof glass. Every fourth business was a motel, each skankier than the last. Sidewalks were crowded with people who looked lost—geographically, mentally, spiritually, and financially at a loss.

"I'd rather spend another night sleeping outside," Charlie said as they sat baking in the motel's parking lot.

"We have to get her in water."

"I know." He opened his door.

John Brown Dog stopped him. "When you were white, Charlie, you were useful for getting a motel room. But now I'll go in myself, because I think you got a chip on your shoulder about your skin color."

After flashing a lot of cash and dealing with a Pakistani nearly as dark-skinned as he was, John Brown Dog was given a room that faced west, the sun no less hot for setting. It was hotter in the room than it was on the asphalt parking lot. While John Brown Dog ran a bath, Charlie fiddled with the air conditioning.

"If this is all the cool air we're going to get," he called to John Brown Dog, "we might as well sleep in the car."

John Brown Dog came out of the bathroom. "I'll get some ice."

When he returned with approximately a gallon of melting cubes, he told Charlie, "This place is crazy. They make you pay for ice. The machine is at the edge of the parking lot, in the heat, and the first three quarters didn't work—"

"Give me some."

"I want to put it in her bath."

Charlie took off his shirt and stepped to the metal door, placing both hands on it. "You should feel this door."

But John Brown Dog was already in the bathroom.

Charlie, sweating and miserable, turned on the television. While flipping channels he looked down at the fork puncture wound but was more fascinated by how dark his chest had become. All the news was about the calamity.

John Brown Dog came out and turned the television off.

"What's wrong?"

"She's in a bad way. The cold water comes out of the tap luke-warm. The ice is melted already. I have to check on something, will you keep an eye on her?"

"Check on what?"

"Something I saw when I was getting the ice."

"Tell me."

"I'll be back in fifteen minutes."

"You're going to leave us, aren't you?"

"No, Charlie, I'm not going to leave you. I'll be back in fifteen minutes."

"What should I do about her?"

"Bathe her. I mean, just keep pouring water over her head. That's where she seems to be deteriorating. From the head."

"I don't feel comfortable—"

John Brown Dog was out the door.

Charlie wasn't about to give the whore a bath, but he heard splashing and worried that Elena might be drowning.

She had slipped and was struggling to right herself. Charlie grasped her elbow and helped her up. Her body looked ravaged and he was embarrassed to see it. He drained some of the water and then turned on the cold tap. It came out warm, as John Brown Dog had said. Charlie used the ice bucket to pour water over her head.

This close to Elena, he could smell her vividly. Not curry and cologne, now she stank of bad milk and old tuna cans. She slipped again; he pulled her upright again. Her skin felt greasy, as if baby oil had been put in the water. "Who are you?" he asked aloud to himself, and was surprised when she answered.

"God's whore."

"What does that mean?" He was frustrated by not getting answers, by people talking in riddles and codes. Did they think their evasiveness was clever?

She drifted off. Charlie kept pouring water over her head. He noticed a V-shaped gash on the top of her right ear, then realized it wasn't a gash, that her ear was coming loose from her head. Black hair floated in S's and U's across the water's surface; Charlie saw where it had come out in patches, leaving parts of her skull bare.

He didn't think he could keep doing this, keep bathing her, keep touching her.

At one point he worried she had died and he put his hand to her neck to feel for a pulse.

With her fish eyes still closed, Elena grasped his wrist and pulled his hand down to cover her breast.

It felt like an empty sack and he immediately took back his hand.

When she opened those fish eyes, they slowly crossed and uncrossed. "You're black," she said matter-of-factly.

He nodded. "We should take you to a hospital."

"Charlie Hart."

"Yes?"

"Take me to the ocean."

30

HEARING THE DOOR to the room open and slam shut, Charlie came out of the bathroom with pistol in hand.

John Brown Dog's eyes asked, *What's wrong?*

Charlie said, "The way you came crashing in here, I thought you were being chased."

"I had to hurry so they wouldn't see which room we're in."

"Who?"

"How's Elena?"

"She's dying. I offered to take her to a hospital—"

"But she wants to go to the ocean."

"Yes. Right now. No more side trips."

"Okay. I moved the car."

"Where?"

"I parked it a couple blocks away. Put your shirt on, Charlie, let's go."

"Who did you mean, you didn't want them to see what room we're in?"

"I saw Vikings."

"You saw—"

"That man I killed in Kentucky, the big blond storm trooper I called a Viking. When I went out to get the ice I thought I saw him across the street."

"The man you killed is across the street?"

"Charlie, listen, okay? I saw a guy who looked like the Viking. Same size, same long blond hair, same black coat reaching the ground. When I went out just now, I snuck around a little and spotted four of them. They look like they could be brothers. It's very clear that they're looking for us."

"How do you mean?"

"They're walking in and out of motel parking lots, checking cars."

"Feds?"

"I don't think so. Your people are trailing us, hoping to find out where we're going, who we're going to meet up with. They don't have to search parking lots, they know exactly where we are."

"Then who are the Vikings?"

"I think they're Elena's people. Allies. I think, from things she's told me, I think they're part of an opposition group in the allies, a group that doesn't agree with what we're doing to bring about the promise of ghost dancing. That guy in Kentucky wanted to know where Elena's mother was, exactly where she was on the California coast. His group wants to get to her mother first. I'm not sure why. Kill her. Get information from her. I'm speculating." When John Brown Dog checked the front window, opening the curtain just an inch, he said, "Shit, they're out there in the parking lot."

Charlie came over and watched carefully until one of them came into view, the size of an NFL lineman, dressed in a long black coat, which was crazy in this heat, and he was looking in car windows, feeling hoods, checking tires.

Charlie asked John Brown Dog what the plan was now. John Brown Dog said he didn't know. "We might have to shoot our way out."

Charlie had another idea. "There's an exhaust fan in the bathroom. I noticed it was just sort of propped or wedged in the window, not built in."

"Let's do it."

While John Brown Dog worked on removing the exhaust fan, Charlie stood at the big bathtub, where Elena was still naked and half submerged.

"Let me do the fan," he told John Brown Dog. "You get her dressed."

"You know what, Charlie, instead of dressing her I think we should soak a sheet in water and wrap it around her, that way she can stay wet in the car."

Charlie began stripping the bed. When he got the sheet off he noticed it was so worn he could see the blackness of his arm through the material. He checked out the window. Two of the long-coat Vikings were at the far end of the parking lot, still checking cars. Just then, Elena began crying, and, the damnedest thing, both Vikings lifted their heads and looked in Charlie's direction. It couldn't be. They couldn't possibly have heard her crying from that distance, through the heavy metal door—but both of them went on alert like dogs responding to a distant whistle. They looked at each other and started walking toward the room.

"Keep her quiet," Charlie said when he brought the sheet into the bathroom and used both hands to submerge the threadbare material. The big exhaust fan was on the floor and John Brown Dog was sitting on the toilet lid, holding the wet and weeping Elena. Charlie asked what was wrong.

"She wants to put her makeup on."

"That's crazy, we don't have time. They somehow heard her crying and they're on their way."

"Get her makeup from the suitcase."

Rather than arguing the matter, it was easier, quicker, to do what John Brown Dog suggested. Charlie went into the other room and opened the suitcase, which was full of silver discs, clear jars of colored liquids, several jumbo boxes of prophylactics, and one small striped cloth case similar to the makeup bag Charlie's wife used.

When Charlie returned to the bathroom, John Brown Dog had

already wrapped Elena in the wet sheet. While John Brown Dog began making up her face, Charlie tried to open the window wider, but the sash was stuck three quarters of the way. "It's going to be a tight fit." He put his head out and looked both ways. The alley was filthy with trash but free of storm troopers. "I'm going to check the front again, see if they're here yet, if they were able to pinpoint our room." He paused briefly to look at Elena's face. John Brown Dog had used a heavy hand and the lines above and below Elena's eyes were thicker and blacker than ever before. He had made red X's on her forehead and diagonal blue lines on her cheeks, more like warpaint than makeup.

Looking out the window onto the parking lot, Charlie got the fright of his life, when he pulled the curtain aside ever so carefully—and saw a big face looking back at him. Right there on the other side of the glass. A big white face with devil blue eyes. It smiled. As malevolent a smile as Charlie had ever seen. The Viking, and however many were with him, began kicking the door, which was thick and all steel but Charlie could tell from the force of the blows that it wouldn't hold long.

He rushed into the bathroom, closing and locking the door.

John Brown Dog had propped Elena on the floor against the tub, sheet-wrapped like a mummy with only her sad little war-painted face showing, while he tried to get out the window. He put one arm and shoulder through first, then ducked and forced his head through—finally getting his upper body out and working himself upside down until his hands touched the alley and he could kick his feet free.

All the while, Charlie silently urged the Indian, *Hurry, hurry, any moment now the Nazis are going to be in here with us.*

John Brown Dog, outside now, stood at the window, the opening level with his head. "Hand her to me."

As Charlie picked up Elena, the Nazis broke into the motel room and hit the bathroom door hard. It was wooden, not nearly as stout as the front door, and it split immediately. But it held. Charlie carefully guided Elena's head and shoulders through the window opening.

From the other side of the bathroom door, they were kicking at where the wood had cracked, enlarging the opening until one of them got his heavy boot through. But the boot got caught. "Go, go," Charlie said, still inside the bathroom. "I'll catch up."

He considered firing into the door, killing whatever storm trooper had his boot caught, but what if they were federal agents?

Though he wasn't quite as broad as John Brown Dog, Charlie still had trouble fitting through the window. He was halfway in, halfway out, when, *shit,* he felt a powerful grip on his ankle. Charlie kicked and dove, pulling free, landing on his hands in the alley, cutting himself on broken glass but thrilled to be out.

One big Viking stuck his head out the window. Charlie aimed his pistol at the man's face, barely three feet away from him, but the big blond just smiled, daring Charlie to shoot.

Instead, he put the semiautomatic away and ran down the alley. No way would the Viking fit through that window; he and the others would have to go back to the parking lot and try to head off Charlie—and John Brown Dog, who was somewhere up ahead, carrying Elena.

When Charlie reached the end of the alley, he looked both ways and saw a crowded summer night, poor people on vacation, Vegas hot, sidewalks so packed that pedestrians were forced into the street. *I'm lost,* he thought. *I'll never find them in this crowd.* He had the strongest sense that John Brown Dog and Elena had abandoned him.

But there, down the block to his right, he saw John Brown Dog carrying her and occasionally turning to see if Charlie was coming. Charlie had a hard time catching up. Breathing was difficult, the tourists' white faces red, armpits sweating in big stink circles. All day they'd been in and out of this crippling heat, scurrying from one chilled casino to the next in search of luck and comps, betting money they couldn't afford to lose and desperate to make up some small portion of their losses by cashing in on every freebie offered, every low-cost buffet, all the comp drinks they could get sent their way. Some of them pulled along cranky kids. The sidewalk was littered with coupons and free newspapers and flyers that advertised escort services and strip joints. A few of the kids had grabbed these flyers and were astonishing each other with photographs of massively titted women and buffed half-dressed boys, SEXXX spelled with three or more X's.

When Charlie did catch up, he offered to carry Elena but John Brown Dog said they were almost to the car, just there.

Charlie looked, didn't see it, then realized how many people were staring at them, a big Indian carrying a sheet-wrapped little woman, Elena's eyes drawn in like fish, her cheeks painted for war, the thin motel sheet dripping water—*We must look like hell's own refugees,* Charlie thought. *We.*

They reached the black Thunderbird, it was unlocked.

"I'll keep her up front on my lap," John Brown Dog said.

Charlie held the door open. As John Brown Dog was turning sideways to get in the car without bumping Elena on the door frame, someone fired a shot from across the street.

A few people in the heat-addled crowd stopped walking and looked around, but most discounted the sound as a car's backfire or something to do with the construction. Charlie Hart knew gunfire when he heard it, however, and instinctively ducked, while John Brown Dog looked across the street, searching for where the shot originated. Then he saw, on top of that wedding chapel, a lone gunman crouching to shoot again.

"Charlie!" John Brown Dog struggled to hold Elena with one arm so he could point with the other.

Charlie drew his pistol, held it with both hands, took careful aim, shot three times. People all around ducked and ran. With a handgun, Charlie was unlikely to hit the target at this distance but the three shots made the assassin crouch down, giving John Brown Dog time to get into the front seat with Elena.

The street crowds were panicking now, those who had seen Charlie shoot had put up the alarm, black man with a gun, *Indian with a gun. Goddamn Indians. Now they're killing tourists right here in Las Vegas.*

A couple of white guys came at Charlie but he pointed the pistol at their faces and warned them, warned them with his eyes and grave expression, how very willing he was to kill them, and they backed off long enough for him to get behind the wheel.

People threw rocks at the car and shouted racial epithets.

The traffic was terrible, but there, good luck, a sign for Interstate 15—

"Charlie!"

He touched the brakes, *What's wrong?*

"Oh God Charlie."

"What's wrong?"

John Brown Dog lifted his hand, palm wet with blood shocking red.

31

THE CALAMITY HAD CONVINCED some Americans that hell was at hand—and now Charlie Hart was driving the road that led there, Interstate 15 from Las Vegas to the California border on any given Sunday, losers beating their ways home, hungover and sick and feeling gutshot, got to go to work in the morning, lost too much money, maxed out the Visa, should not have slept with that mortgage broker from Atlantic City, he was married, I was drunk, we didn't use a rubber, should not have gone with that hooker, my last cash and now God knows what diseases, warts, viruses, rot I have in my body, stayed too long at the tables, I was up at one point, should've quit then, lost *one thousand dollars* or fifty thousand, or five hundred, it was meant for the rent, the mortgage, the tuition, the baby's doctor or the baby's goddamn new pair of shoes that keep getting referenced at the craps tables . . . traffic running fifty miles an hour with less than ten feet between your front bumper and his back, then some asshole hits the brakes . . . every accident causing a new backup as far as you can see, and on this terrible highway you can see forever, you have to wonder about the men who built it, did they despair paving a ribbon across so much desert?

The lone gunman's first shot hadn't missed after all, it had hit Elena's head at an angle, glancing off with enough force to knock out a skull chip the size of your palm, she was bleeding all over the thin wet motel sheet, all over the Indian's lap.

Charlie Hart said, "We should be finding a hospital."

But John Brown Dog insisted that doctors could do Elena no good, she had to be taken to the ocean, to her mother.

"We won't get there until dawn."

"Drive."

"We'll be putting her *corpse* in the ocean."

"Charlie."

"Okay."

There was an accident just ahead. A car was on fire. On the shoulder, cars sat overheated, radiators steaming. People at the side of the road looked bereaved. There were no cops, no wreckers, no ambulances, no hope.

Charlie wanted to know if the apocalypse had begun.

John Brown Dog asked what he meant.

"You guys are—"

"Which guys, Charlie?"

"You Indians and your allies, you're bringing about this calamity, but there are things you haven't told me. Secrets you're keeping. Is this how it ends? This madness. Look at those two guys, fistfighting. That woman, her blouse is off. Is it like this all over the country?"

"No, Charlie, this is just the road back to Los Angeles after a weekend in Las Vegas, is all this is. Take the shoulder."

Hart was able to speed past dozens of cars, their drivers and passengers outraged he was breaking the rules like that, but then he came to an overheated RV blocking the way and needed to reenter the traffic stream except no one would let him in, *Payback time, asshole,* so he pulled out in front of a compact car, which hit the Thunderbird's left rear panel and caused a small pileup when the car behind the compact crashed into its rear bumper. Charlie Hart drove on.

"Sweet Jesus," John Brown Dog said, looking at Elena cuddled on his lap: her head had turned to reveal part of her brain swelling outward from the skull hole.

Charlie saw it, too, a glistening red bulge the size of a navel orange—he almost crashed into the car in front of him.

John Brown Dog found a plastic bottle half full of spring water and he gently poured the warm water over Elena's wound.

Charlie wanted to know if she was dead.

The whore answered for herself without opening those fish eyes. "Not yet, Charlie Hart." Her voice more breath than sound.

The swelling went slowly down. Charlie drove on.

They passed isolated casino-hotel complexes built all by themselves, surrounded by nothing but parking lots, luring travelers from California who couldn't wait for Vegas to lose their money. They saw Joshua trees in supplication by the thousands. And then it was dark and they saw nothing but car lights.

More casinos at the California border, traffic finally thinning out, the Thunderbird overheating, they could smell the radiator burning dry.

Charlie said, "Even if *she* makes it to the coast, this car won't."

"Drive until it stops."

"Then we're stranded in the middle of nowhere with a dying woman."

"Charlie, you're making my head hurt. What do you want to do?"

"We need a different vehicle."

"It's nighttime, we're driving through the Mojave Desert, what do you suggest?"

"Next truck stop, if we make it to the next truck stop, we'll get another car."

"How?"

"Commandeer one."

"You mean steal it?"

Charlie admitted that was what he meant.

"And you a special agent with the Federal Bureau of Investigation. It must be the Indian in you, Charlie, turning you toward grand theft auto."

"My skin's been discolored is all, I don't have any Indian in me."

"More's the pity."

They got to Baker with the Thunderbird's engine crackling. Charlie said if he turned it off, it would never start again. "The cylinders will seize, I'm surprised they haven't already."

John Brown Dog said he wasn't going to be able to help Charlie jack a car. "I can't put her down."

"Before I shut this off, I'm going to fill it with gas, just in case."

"Good idea."

"Can I get you anything? Something to eat? You want me to hold her while you use the can?"

John Brown Dog shook his head.

Charlie filled the Thunderbird with its engine running, then drove to a dark portion of the lot, switched off the ignition and left John Brown Dog and Elena in the car.

Halfway to the office to pay for the gas, Charlie was met by an attendant, a tall thin white kid who said, "I thought you were driving off without paying, I come to see if I could get your tags."

"I'm paying."

"Didn't you see the sign? 'Pay before driving away from pumps.'"

"I guess I didn't."

"Also you got a headlight that's screwed up."

"I know."

Back in the office, Charlie gave his credit card, which the attendant ran skeptically. And he was right, the card rejected.

"That's impossible," Charlie said. "There must be a mistake."

"Yeah, we get that a lot. You holding cash, I hope."

Charlie paid for the gas with cash, used the toilet, and then bought two gallons of spring water. "Where can I get water for my radiator?"

"There's a hose out there but I already turned it off for the night."

"Can you turn it back on?"

The attendant shook his head.

"Are you saying no?"

"I'm just . . . always with your special requests, ain't it? Can I run your Visa one more time, will I take rolls of coins for twenty dollars' gas, can I give you a jump start, can you use my phone."

"Listen, I have a sick woman in the car—"

"Yeah, I hear that a lot, too. Got a sick woman in the car, a pregnant woman, a hungry kid, a crippled-up grandma."

Charlie was about to pull his pistol when the kid sighed and said, "Drive around to the side there, I'll turn on the hose."

Returning to the Thunderbird, Charlie saw the attendant watching him.

"What's up?" John Brown Dog asked.

"I got this water for her." Charlie handed over the two jugs. "That kid's eyeballing me, I'm not going to be able to jack a car without him calling the cops. We get involved with the local police now, they notice the shape she's in, we'll never get out of here."

"See if this Thunderbird won't start and take us to the ocean."

Amazingly, the engine turned over on the first crank. Charlie drove it to the hose and filled the radiator. He looked around the engine to see if he could find where it had been damaged, what was leaking.

The attendant crept up and startled him. "You going to be on your way now, or you got another favor to ask?"

Charlie closed the hood and took a twenty from his pocket. "This is for you, for being a good Samaritan."

The kid gripped the money, his expression changing from disdain to embarrassment. He didn't apologize, but he did say, "I catch a lot of shit working here at night, especially Sunday night, people coming back from Vegas broke and in a bad mood."

Charlie waved him off.

The Thunderbird drove smoothly for twenty miles through the high desert and Elena seemed to be resting comfortably as John Brown Dog gently poured water over her head. But then the Thunderbird began overheating again, and the two gallons of water were soon enough gone. Elena moaned.

"It's swelling again," John Brown Dog said.

Charlie turned on the interior lights. A lump of brain tissue the size of a softball had ballooned out of Elena's skull. "I don't know what we should do."

"Make it to the ocean is what we should do, Charlie."

"I'm going to have to stop and fill the radiator again. If you want, I'll take care of her for a while. I don't mind. You can stretch your legs, use the bathroom."

They drove the night in silence, smelling the engine's heat, the whore's decay.

At one point, John Brown Dog said he wished he'd had kids.

"Maybe you still will."

"No parks, no pregnancies."

"Except for certain Indians, you said that yourself."

"Not me. I won't be one of them. I'm not going to survive this trip."

"What do you mean?"

"I mean, once we get Elena to the ocean and reunite her with her mother, you'll be taken in for debriefing and they'll probably give you a dose of reeducation, but they ain't going to let this particular redskin walk away, you know that, Charlie."

Charlie thought it was probably true, but promised to do what he could.

"Indians spoil their children, did you know that, Charlie?"

"No."

"We try to teach them to be tough, but as long as they're honorable they get away with murder. Never spanked. Never yelled at. The most parents do to you when you're an Indian kid, the worst they do to you, is be *disappointed* in something you've done or failed to do. Did you know, in Colonial days when settlers and Indians fought, it was common for children to be taken by whatever side won the battle. Indians took white kids and raised them as their own. Settlers took Indian kids and integrated them into white society. Back then, kids in white society got hard discipline and long hours of work. Many of the ones who'd been taken by Indians and were later returned to settlers would run away and find their way back to their Indian families. They loved the Indian life, what boy wouldn't? Hunting, fishing, riding horses. It was unheard-of for Indian kids who'd been taken by whites and then returned to the Indians to run away and rejoin white society. People don't know this. They think being kidnapped by Indians would be the worst fate in the world."

"How did the girls and women fare in Indian culture back in those perfect days?"

"Yeah . . . well . . ."

"Yeah, well . . . let me fill in the blanks. They did all the domestic work, struck camp, set up camp, did the planting, cooking, making clothes, in fact women did virtually everything that was considered beneath the manly arts of war and hunting and politics. In many tribes, they weren't simply second-class citizens, they were the slave class."

John Brown Dog shrugged.

"Everything you say about Indians is suspect because you absolutely refuse to acknowledge anything negative. Everything you say always ends up being whites versus Indians with Indians coming out on top, owning the moral high ground. It was interesting hearing you talk about how Indians spoil their children. Who knows, maybe that's the greatest way in the world to bring up a kid. Spoil them with love and they prosper. But then you have to point out how Indian child-rearing is so superior to white child-rearing that white kids in Colonial days ran back to their adopted Indian families. Indians win again. Always. In every story you tell."

"I think it's because we lost so bad, we have to tell stories that make us sound like winners. But I know it's tiresome."

"I'm not trying to—"

"No, you're right, Charlie. I'm too fucking strident for my own good. It comes from being a ghost dancer and dancing every day for sixteen years to correct the old injustices. It comes from being indoctrinated by the grandfather. But I can stop preaching to you, you've listened to enough of it."

"That's who I am. Listens to Indians."

"How much farther?"

"It's a long way to the ocean."

32

BARRELING THROUGH THE NIGHT, Charlie's mind overheated like the Thunderbird's V8. "I've never been a road warrior," he said, "fueled by caffeine or cocaine or whatever road warriors are fueled by, driving around the clock, driving thirty-six or forty-eight hours. My friends, in college, they used to tell me about their road trips, not stopping for anything but gas and toilet and drive-through food, hitting the zone, they used to say, when you're beyond exhaustion and achieve a state of mind that's—"

"Easy, partner."

" 'Easy'?" Charlie checked the rearview mirror. "What do you mean, 'easy'?"

"You're all hyper, man."

"I'm barreling."

"I'll take over driving at Barstow. See if we can find a gas station with the toilets outside so I don't have to go walking through a store to get to a sink."

"To get to a sink."

"Where I can clean up."

"Where John Brown Dog can clean up."

"Man, are you even going to make it to Barstow?"

"That's the question, isn't it?"

They were just outside Barstow, on the edge of the desert, when the reality began to take hold of Charlie Hart: they could make it to the ocean.

They stopped at a station where Charlie topped off the gas tank and refilled the radiator. He craved coffee. He unfolded a map on the hood of the Thunderbird. "We can make it to the ocean," he muttered over and over.

John Brown Dog put two large coffees on the edges of the map to hold it down.

"*Coffee.*" Charlie's voice reverential.

"*Man,* this hood is hot."

"Keep the coffee hot."

"Are you wigging out on me, Charlie?"

"Wonder where that comes from, *wigging out.*"

John Brown Dog studied the map. "The closest way to the ocean is here." He pointed to Long Beach. "But I don't know if it's the quickest way. What do you think traffic will be like, this time of night?"

"I don't know, what time is it?"

"You're the one with a watch, Charlie."

"Half past ten." He peeled back an opening to his large coffee and looked at the map as he drank carefully. "Damn." Charlie put a finger on San Simeon, on the coast halfway between Los Angeles and San Jose. "The Hearst Castle. William Randolph Hearst's San Simeon estate, a castle overlooking the ocean, wasn't that where she said her mother is?"

"Yes."

"Let's take her there," Charlie said excitedly. "Not just to the ocean but to her mother, let's finish what you started in Tennessee. *We can make it.*"

"San Simeon is a lot farther than just cutting west from here."

"She wants to see her mother, doesn't she?"

"Can we get in? No one lives there, do they—at the Hearst Castle?"

"I don't think so. It's open to the public."

"Not by the time we get there, it won't be open to the public."

"You think her mother works there, is being held there, what?"

"Don't know, Charlie." John Brown Dog gently opened the passenger door. "Elena? Can you hear me, hon? Is your mother at the Hearst Castle, at San Simeon?"

She murmured something that neither Charlie nor John Brown Dog understood.

"We can take you to the castle to see your mother," John Brown Dog told her, "but it'll delay getting to the ocean by several hours."

She said, "Mother."

"I'll drive," John Brown Dog told Charlie.

Charlie quietly said, "If we can't get into the Hearst Castle until tomorrow . . . she won't be alive tomorrow."

"I know."

Charlie put his coffee on the roof and carefully took Elena in his arms. She and the sheet were soaking. Even wrapped in several layers as she was, she felt bony to Charlie; he became queasy from the smell, soured milk and bad meat, and from the warmth of her wetness on his skin.

John Brown Dog didn't start the engine until Charlie was seated with Elena curled on his lap. "Can you reach the water jugs there on the floor? Pour a little bit at a time on her head, up and down her body."

"Do you think it's doing any good?"

"Yes. How's the wound?"

Charlie didn't want to look, but slowly turned her head. The opening in her skull seemed to have crusted over and the brain swelling had gone down, no longer ballooning out.

When John Brown Dog pulled away, Charlie's coffee spilled over the roof and down the back window.

They took Route 58 toward Bakersfield, the traffic heavy but moving. John Brown Dog never went more than five miles over the speed limit, Charlie wanting to urge him on, get in the passing lane, floor it, we'll take the risk of getting stopped for speeding—but he kept his mouth shut and was soon rocking Elena as he once had rocked his daughter.

Later, he told John Brown Dog, "Sometimes I feel something tingle, almost like a leak of electricity. We had an old lamp with a weak electrical short in it and if you touched it in a certain place, you'd feel a buzz or tingle. Not a shock, just the presence of electricity. That's what this is like. I feel it in my arms, on my legs."

"I know, I felt it, too."

"Is she wearing some kind of electrical device and all this water is causing it to short out?"

"Charlie, she's naked under that sheet."

"A pacemaker or—"

"Come on, Charlie."

"She's not . . . real, is she?"

"Real? What're you holding if she's not real?"

"I mean . . ."

"Yeah, I know what you mean."

Before leaving Bakersfield, they filled the car again and took on more water for the radiator, for Elena.

John Brown Dog asked Charlie how he was fixed for cash.

"I got about thirty left."

John Brown Dog gave him more. "It's from the stash the Viking turned over to Elena. I think you'd better buy some five-gallon containers. Four of them. I don't know if we can make many more stops. You know what I'm saying?"

"Mad dash for the ocean."

"You want me to hold her, you drive?"

"Okay." Charlie felt guilty for being so relieved to get Elena off his lap. It wasn't just her smell or the fact she was dying, it was her otherworldliness that made him feel creepy.

The idea of one last unbroken dash to the coast had been appealing in theory, in Bakersfield, but, hours later, both men were exhausted and itchy-eyed and felt like they couldn't drive or ride another hour. How far was it yet? They debated stopping, if not for the night, at least for a rest, a quick nap, a chance to stretch the kinks in their muscles. But what if Elena died an hour before they reunited her with her mother and it was that hour they took to rest? Better keep barreling. Switch drivers. The needle of the Thunderbird's temperature gauge was on the edge of the *H* but seemed to stay there, hot but getting no hotter.

Traveling west on Route 58, after crossing Interstate 5, they entered one of the least populated areas of California, the hills and low mountains of the Temblor Range and then the austere high grasslands of the Carrizo Plain. No towns, no gas stations, no houses, no traffic.

Here's where they'd use the cans of gas, the five gallons of water. And even all of that might not get them to the facilities along Highway 101.

"I haven't been keeping track of gas mileage," Charlie said after they had stopped to put in the last of the gasoline. "But we must have a leak, we shouldn't be going through this much fuel."

"It has to get us to the coast, is all."

"To the coast and then up to San Simeon."

"How's the radiator?"

Charlie said he'd check.

He took off his shirt and covered the radiator cap so he could get it off without being burned.

"When I was a teenager," John Brown Dog said, "I can't tell you how much time I spent with my head under the hood of a car."

"On the reservation, where I cut you down, most of the houses had old cars parked in the yards and fields. Not just one or two but sometimes a dozen or more around one house."

"Spare parts, Charlie. Poor people are resourceful. An engine or transmission might be blown but the belts and hoses are still usable, the alternator. A family will keep acquiring the same make or model so that parts are interchangeable. You go to one family for Chevy parts, another for Ford parts."

After filling the radiator, Charlie was putting his shirt back on when John Brown Dog said, "You are so Indian."

Charlie glanced down where he was buttoning the shirt. In the moonlight his skin showed a darkness fascinating to him. He touched his chest. The fork wound hurt a little but it was his skin he couldn't stop staring at.

Then he looked up at John Brown Dog and said, "Fucking white eyes give me any shit, and I'll slit their guts open."

"*Hoka hey*, motherfucker!" John Brown Dog said.

Charlie laughed. "I'm going to fill the water can from that irrigation ditch."

John Brown Dog went with him. "Watch for snakes."

Charlie stopped.

"This place is lousy with rattlers."

Charlie thought maybe the Indian was teasing and went on, walking carefully to the irrigation ditch, John Brown Dog right behind, saying, "If we were here centuries ago, the biggest danger to us wouldn't be snakes, it'd be grizzlies. This chaparral was perfect habitat. Tens of thousands of California grizzlies. The only one left today is on the state flag. The grizzly was the apex predator, had no fear of man, was more likely to attack than flee when encountering humans. Grizzlies used to saunter into Indian villages the way you or I might walk through a prairie dog village. Of course, it was the most aggressive grizzlies that were first killed off by the Europeans. The more cautious bears retreated into forests, and that's the dominant strain alive today. People call grizzlies ferocious, but they're timid compared to their ancestors. A five-hundred-pound grizzly would be considered big today. Back then they were three times that size. Roaming everywhere in California except the deserts. Grizzlies along Big Sur. And San Francisco and Berkeley. All along the coast. Feeding on sea lions, eating washed-up whales. That would be quite a sight, wouldn't it, Charlie, to see grizzly bears on California beaches?"

"From a distance, yes."

"When all the people die out, eventually the big aggressive strain will return. That strain will dominate and outbreed the cautious strain once the human factor is removed."

"And if Indians are around, grizzlies will be killing them."

"Yes. Grizzlies were the leading cause of death among California Indians, so that'll probably be the situation again. But the Indians will survive and so will the grizzlies. It won't be such a bad arrangement. It *wasn't* such a bad arrangement. It lasted thousands of years."

After Charlie finished filling the water can, they returned to the car. Elena was the same. Alive but barely. In some kind of coma, unresponsive to John Brown Dog's voice.

Leaving the rolling, treeless grasslands, they drove a landscape of deep valleys and blind turns.

At Highway 101, they found a station open and filled the tank with gas, the radiator with water. Charlie and John Brown Dog both thought that unless the Thunderbird's various leaks became worse, this would be the last stop before San Simeon. Twenty miles or so north on the interstate toward Paso Robles and then left on a tiny road, Route 46, and an hour later they would see the Pacific Ocean.

Charlie was driving when they reached that point. He thought the moonlit sea was sufficiently beautiful that Elena should be awakened to see it.

John Brown Dog agreed but couldn't rouse her.

"Is she dead?" Charlie asked.

John Brown Dog asked if he could stop.

Route 46 was steep here with a dangerous drop-off on the left and a close cliff on the right, but within a mile Charlie found a spot wide enough to pull most of the Thunderbird off the road.

"Put on the light."

Charlie did.

John Brown Dog began slowly unwrapping the sheet.

"What're you doing?"

He shook his head. "She suddenly went light."

"Went light?"

"The weight went out of her."

John Brown Dog had to keep lifting Elena, pulling the sheet out from under her, unwrapping it, lifting her again, her head lolling back and forth. "I know it sounds crazy, but she went from feeling like her normal weight on my lap and then there was nothing to her."

John Brown Dog lifted the last flap of wet white sheet from Elena but instantly put it back. Then lifted it again, because neither man believed what he'd seen the first time.

33

SHE HAD ROTTED. Or some combination of rot and mummification. For John Brown Dog and Charlie Hart it was like seeing something obscene that made them feel guilty just for having seen it. But the true horror of it was this: Elena still alive, turning her head, opening her mouth like a guppy desperate for air.

They were on a hill within sight of the moonlit Pacific. "Let's go," John Brown Dog said. "Take her to the water."

They both wondered what shape would she be in by the time they got there—would anything be left of her? But they both knew that's what had to be done.

Charlie turned north on old Highway 1 and drove slowly, looking for a place where they could carry Elena to the water.

"Pull up the road there and stop at that gas station," John Brown Dog said.

"It's closed."

"I want to use the phone."

"*Now?* Who the hell are you calling?"

"I have to call the grandfather. He said he'd be waiting for us, waiting with Elena's mother."

"And you didn't tell me this?"

John Brown Dog put Elena on the seat and went to the phone.

When he returned, Charlie repeated the question, "And you didn't see fit to tell me any of this?"

"Charlie, a lot of it I don't know myself."

"You obviously know the grandfather is supposed to be here."

"I checked in with him when we were in Vegas, when I went out for the ice."

"And never told me."

"A lot was happening in Vegas, remember?"

"I remember sticking with you, not trying to turn you in, keeping my word, I remember all that."

"Let's go down to the ocean, Charlie. The grandfather will meet us and explain everything."

Charlie doubted it.

John Brown Dog guided them to a place that the grandfather had just told him about.

They checked to make sure Elena was still alive. She looked vaguely fetal, her body parts blunt and unrealized. Her head, large by comparison, had not changed except to look all the more skeletal. The rifle wound to her skull was still evident but had crusted over completely. Everything from her neck down was in ruins, her breasts so empty that they lay flat against her ribby chest.

John Brown Dog and Charlie doubled the thin motel sheet and used it as a sling; she was easy to carry and moon and ocean made everything easy to see. They walked a hundred yards from the car, to where the land dropped off in a sheer dirt cliff that was only fifteen feet high but barrier enough when you're carrying someone in a sheet. Walking parallel to the shore, they found a pathway down with good footholds but each man had to grip the sheet tightly in one hand and use the other to steady himself.

It was beautiful and rugged here, the ocean and shore scattered with boulders and outcroppings, some stone plateaus as flat as a dance floor and, in the water, rock formations ranging in size from just big enough to stand on to larger than houses. Green-black sea-water surged over the rocks, creating white splash and soft sound.

Out just beyond the surf line, black shapes moved in the moonlight, sea lions or seals, sharks or porpoises.

Not a house or car or light or plane or boat could be seen. Except for the effects of natural erosion, this was how the coast must've looked a hundred years ago, a thousand years ago.

John Brown Dog and Charlie stepped into the water and then stopped. It was cold. They weren't sure how to proceed. Should they try to hold the sheet upright so she could see the ocean?

Charlie asked, "Is the grandfather bringing her mother?"

"I don't know. I hope so."

"Me, too."

Amazingly, against everything that seemed possible, Elena opened her eyes, which crossed and then uncrossed. "I smell it," she said softly. They could barely hear her above the sound of the ocean. "Put me in." They heard that.

Walking out until the water reached their thighs, they slowly lowered her until the seawater rushed onto the sheet and partially covered what was left of her body.

John Brown Dog and Charlie had expected that the touch of the cold ocean would shock Elena, cause her to cry out, but she immediately relaxed in the water, her thin empty limbs floating like tentacles. She flexed her fingers, her feet touching around the edge of the sheet and then extending over that edge into the ocean. John Brown Dog and Charlie watched, mesmerized.

"I remember the ocean," she said, "I remember now, I lived many years at the ocean. Lower me more."

They did, Charlie asking John Brown Dog, "I thought she said she'd never seen the ocean."

"She did."

"I forgot, was all," Elena said, smiling.

They allowed her to float in the water, one edge of the sheet keeping her face from going under.

"Seawater is alive," she told them. "And in this living seawater, the dream ends, comes true."

"Is the *ocean* her mother?" Charlie asked.

John Brown Dog said he didn't know.

A small wave rolled over her head, and Charlie and John Brown Dog quickly lifted that side of the sheet, so she wouldn't choke on water, but Elena only smiled more widely as the ocean covered her face. When they had lifted her head above the surface again she spoke happily, "I just tasted mozuka from Okinawa!"

They didn't know what that meant.

"Ah." She laughed a little. Her face had been washed clear of makeup and marks, her eyes uncrossed and no longer resembling fish. "I just felt a cold finger of water, Antarctic bottom water. It took a thousand years to get here. Oceans are—" She said a word that neither of the men recognized. "I can taste coral."

"She's happy," John Brown Dog said.

Charlie agreed.

"Put my head a little lower, until my ears are covered." They did. "There. Oh, listen to that." She listened to what they couldn't hear. "The blue whale is the largest animal that has ever lived; it is also the loudest creature on earth, louder than rock bands and jet engines. The song of a single blue whale can be heard by others throughout all the oceans of the world . . . and I hear one now . . . singing from his heart, a heart that weighs a thousand pounds, a heart with an aorta through which you could crawl . . . Do you want to hear?"

Of course they did.

She opened her smiling mouth, releasing a booming sound, like massively amplified electronic feedback, like kettledrums played by madmen. The song of the blue whale, transmitted or reproduced by Elena: it caused the hair to rise on John Brown Dog and Charlie Hart, and, all around them, the surface of the water was agitated.

Then she was quiet, both men solemn.

"*There* you are!"

They turned to see who had shouted at them from the shore.

34

"KATHY!"

Charlie Hart couldn't believe what he was seeing, the grandfather standing there on the rocky shore and next to him Charlie's daughter, holding his hand.

Charlie gave John Brown Dog the other end of the sheet and waded ashore.

"*Kathy.*" He was in tears when he reached the two of them and dropped to his knees in the sand.

It wasn't Kathy. Charlie should've known it wasn't his daughter, although this little Indian girl was about the same size and age as Kathy and Charlie so very much wanted it to be her.

He apologized to the girl, who wasn't frightened by Charlie and who had smiled at him even as he charged in from the ocean the way he did and knelt in the sand, weeping.

Ashamed of himself, Charlie wiped his face with hands wet and salty from the seawater. He could smell the fishy brine and taste it, too, as he stood to address the grandfather, who looked as calm and unruffled as he had when discussing those great white heads with Superintendent Leonards.

"I should've known it wasn't her," Charlie said. "They have different hair. I knew better."

"Wishful thinking," the grandfather replied. "Hopeful thinking."

Charlie shook the old man's hand. "Yes, I want to see my wife and daughter again. That's what I want most out of life right at this moment. Who is this?" Charlie put a soft hand on the little girl's shiny black hair, then looked out to the water where John Brown Dog held what was left of Elena in that folded sheet. "Is this Elena's daughter?"

"This," the grandfather said happily, "is the whore's mother."

Charlie smiled uncomfortably, waiting for a translation, a key to the riddle. The old man stood still smiling back at him. "What do you mean?" Charlie finally asked.

"I mean *this* is Elena's mother." The grandfather bent low to speak to the girl. "Do you want to see your daughter?"

The girl nodded eagerly.

The grandfather called to John Brown Dog, "Bring Elena in. Closer to shore. Her mother wants to see her."

As the girl walked to the water's edge, Charlie's smile faded.

"Look at you," the grandfather said, reaching for Charlie's hard-set face. "Listens to Indians has *become* an Indian. I think it flatters you—"

"Fuck you," Charlie said, knocking the old man's hand away. "I want an explanation. Not spiritual mumbo-jumbo shape shadow shit but an actual, understandable explanation of what's happening, of *how* it's happening. I want to know how my skin has been turned black or red or whatever you call it. I don't want the explanation to be couched in spiritual terms or some kind of racial-historical voodoo-hoodoo bullshit. I want to know how, pigmentally, how my skin has—"

"Pigmentally?"

"How the pigment of my skin has—"

"I know, Charlie, but *pigmentally?*"

Charlie lost his anger and the old man put a hand on his arm. "These things are very difficult to translate," the grandfather said. "What you consider deception is in fact confusion. It's not like translating from one language to another but from one *world* to another. The best I can do is try an analogy. I know you've studied the American Indian, so this should make sense to you. Imagine, Charlie, that you were sent to speak to Indian tribes in the 1800s and you had to explain to them what was heading their way over the next hundred years. Imagine that these tribes had had little contact with whites beyond a few fur traders and mountain men. So you tell them that millions of whites are coming. Whether or not they believed you, they could at least have understood that concept because they'd seen millions of buffalo on the Plains, and watched millions of passenger pigeons fly overhead in the Midwest. But then you have to explain other things, such as railroads. How would you do that?"

Charlie didn't know. "Indians called locomotives iron horses, didn't they?"

"So you're going to tell these Indians that a horse is coming their way that will be made of iron and so big that it can carry hundreds of people, and instead of legs it runs on wheels that have to stay on iron tracks and this big horse eats wood and coal and belches white smoke and has a whistle. Can you imagine, Charlie, what the Indians would think of your explanation? They're trying to picture a horse eating wood and making a whistle sound and carrying hundreds of people. They'll dismiss you as crazy in the head. Just like your people are dismissing me when I try to explain the new world that's coming.

"So let's say you persevere, as I'm trying to persevere in my explanations to you. You try to tell these Indians about telegraphs, the ability this new world has to communicate across hundreds of miles through a wire. Charlie, they don't even know what a wire is. So you say it's like a bowstring. People talk across hundreds of miles through a bowstring? With explanations like that, Charlie, they'll conclude you are not a serious man.

"But let's say that out of politeness they let you continue and ask you what will happen when this new world you speak of comes into contact with the current world in which these Indians live. And you tell them the sad truth. The Indians' world will pass away. No amount of fighting or negotiating or treaty signing will change the inevitability of the new world superseding the old. Of course they don't believe you. This crazy prediction comes from a man who speaks of horses with whistles and people talking through bowstrings and of something called dynamite, a few sticks of which can blow up a mountain. The Indians laugh at you and pick up oak sticks from the ground and shake them in your face and tell you that sticks cannot destroy mountains and this new world of which you speak cannot destroy the Indian world that has been in place for a thousand years. Speaking gently to you, because you are obviously simpleminded, the Indians might try to explain that something so long-lived and stable as their world is will not be thrown over in less than a hundred years by some new world that makes outlandish claims of horses eating wood and sticks blowing up mountains.

"Same deal with you and me right now, Charlie. Of course you don't believe when I tell you that in less than a hundred years your world will have passed away. You don't want to hear about spirits and opening doors to other worlds and shape shadows. You want a technological explanation. There is none. If I said that more powerful bombs or more virulent poisons were going to be used against you, you would understand that and prepare to fight against it. But you are ignorant of the spiritual world and mystified by claims I make on behalf of it.

"Charlie. I am not being evasive or deceptive. I simply can't get my explanations through your thick skull, just as you would not have gotten explanations of dynamite and telegraphs through the thick skulls of those nineteenth-century Indians.

"But it has always been the case that when a more powerful world comes into contact with a weaker world, the weaker world passes away. The world of technology from Europe was superior to the Indian spiritual world, which had been weakened by infighting, tribe against tribe. And now the spiritual world has been called back through ghost dancing, and your technological world is inferior because we have powerful allies and you have lost your way, lost your humanity."

Charlie shook his head. "I don't know any more than I knew before you began."

"Through ghost dancing and vision quests we have called on the spirit world, which includes the dead, which includes the good dead and the bad dead, and these allies are helping us bring about the promise of ghost dancing. There, does that explanation make any sense to you?"

"No."

"Elena was the daughter, the new world, an aging whore, profane and dying. Her mother is the old world, being reborn. How's about that for making sense?"

"More bullshit from an old Indian."

"Okay, try this. The dinosaurs were the dominant species on earth for millions of years and then one day at ten A.M. a meteorite hit the earth and the world of the dinosaurs became untenable, soon to pass away."

"Ten A.M.? How do you know that's when it hit?"

"Whenever it hit, it was ten A.M. somewhere on earth."

"You doubletalk, is all you do."

"You're right, Charlie Hart: we're no closer to understanding each other than when we began."

"You know what this calamity has accomplished? Making things worse for Indians. This country's *technology* will put your red asses back on reservations and under guard."

"Charlie, drop your trousers and turn around and look in a mirror, see whose ass is red."

Charlie laughed. "Sometimes I don't know whether to hit you or hug you."

"I'm rooting for you to make the right decision. But, truly, I am the last person in the world to deny the short-term power of technology," the grandfather said. "For example, in the short term, I think we could be in serious trouble from whatever technology is landing there on the highway behind you."

35

THREE HELICOPTERS were alighting on Highway 1, Charlie only just now hearing the thump-thump of their rotors. He looked to the grandfather, as if to say *What now?*

The old man didn't know. "The whore needs more time with her mother. They're negotiating."

The three of them—Elena, the girl, and John Brown Dog—were still in a couple feet of water, only John Brown Dog looking at the helicopters, Elena and the girl deep in conversation.

"If I buy some time," Charlie said, "will you give me your word that you'll go to the president and tell him as well as you can who you and your allies are, the powers you have? No mumbo-jumbo, no lectures about past transgressions, just the clearest explanation you can muster? Promise?"

"If I couldn't explain it to Listens to Indians, I doubt I can explain it to your president, but, yes, Charlie, buy us a few more minutes and I promise I'll do my best. We'll call to you when it's finished."

"When what's finished?"

"When the whore and her mother are finished negotiating, finished saying good-bye."

Charlie didn't understand, was past understanding.

The grandfather went to the sea, while Charlie walked toward the highway where those helicopters were unloading their cargo of federal agents armed with everything from electrified shields to riot guns. Some were dressed in white HAZMAT suits with full hoods.

When Charlie got to within fifty feet of them, their commander shouted clear orders for him to lie face down on the ground and clasp his hands behind his head. As these orders were issued, the agents dispersed in a semicircle around him, keeping their lights on Charlie Hart's dark face. These were not the excitable deputies and state cops from Rushmore and the Little Bighorn, these were precision-trained federal agents.

He held his hands high, palms facing them, but he did not lie down. "My name is Hart. I'm a special agent with the Federal Bureau of Investigation. I have my identification with me."

Get on the ground, the commander ordered him, and then we'll check your ID.

Hoping to buy more of that time he had promised to the grandfather, Charlie didn't comply. "Listen, I have a sidearm. I don't want someone to see it and go crazy, end up shooting me. I can take it out with two fingers of my left hand or one of you can come up here and—"

An older man stepped out from the line of other agents, contrasting with them dramatically because he wore no gear—in fact, was dressed in a simple black suit, dark shirt, red tie, shiny black shoes—and carried no weapon. He spoke quietly to the commander and then called out, "You're not Charlie Hart."

"I am. I've turned . . . I've become dark. Like those agents at the Little Bighorn."

"When did they turn you?"

"I don't know. A few days ago. I've lost track of time."

"Those men at Little Bighorn, they lost their blackness within 48 hours. How come you haven't?"

"I don't know."

"Maybe you're just pretending to be Charlie Hart. Maybe you're that Indian who kidnapped him. Maybe you killed Agent Hart."

"Take my prints."

"We will. We'll verify who you are. But first you have to get on the ground. Let these agents disarm you, check your identification."

Charlie hesitated, waiting to hear a signal from the grandfather or John Brown Dog behind him. Hearing nothing, he suddenly bent over and picked up a rock the size of a cantaloupe.

"Hold, hold," the older man in the black suit told the agents. Then to Charlie: "If you really are an FBI agent, you should know that a sudden movement like that can get you shot."

Charlie held up the rock. "This is that stuff, that black stuff that destroyed Rushmore, *shape shadows,* and if I throw this and break it open, all of your weapons will be rendered useless. Those helicopters will never fly again. And all of you will be turned black."

The agents took steps backward, even those wearing HAZMAT suits, until their commander told them to hold.

Charlie thought that the experience at Rushmore had made these men as superstitiously afraid of the spirit world as Indians had been of the new world of technology with its talking wires and iron horses.

But the man in the dark suit was not afraid. "It's just a rock, asshole."

"No, it's—"

"I saw you pick it up; we all did."

"I left it here just for this contingency and now—"

The man in the suit turned to the commander and said, "Take him down."

But when the commander gave the *go* signal, the agents hesitated because Charlie was lifting the rock higher, making motions as if he was about to throw it.

Then, from behind him, came John Brown Dog's booming voice, "It's done!"

Charlie threw the rock anyway, the agents crouching in anticipation—even the man in the dark suit and shiny black shoes wincing as the rock hit the highway. It sounded like a bowling ball dropped on tile.

There ensued one of those curious moments when nothing happens.

And then the agents swarmed Charlie. He tried to go limp and let them take him passively into custody but one agent kicked him in the ribs while another landed on his back with both knees—and he got pepper sprayed and punched and someone with a truncheon hit him across his lower back, his buttocks, and the backs of his legs, Charlie insisting all the while, "I'm not resisting, I'm not resisting!"

"Fucking Indian," one said.

Which made Charlie go hard and scream a war cry and call them white devils, throwing agents off even though his face burned with chemical spray and he could barely get a breath. Like a crazy Indian who has gone red behind the eyes, Charlie actually fought his way to his feet before the asshole with the truncheon started in on the back of his head.

Viewing all this with supreme indifference, the older man in the black suit turned to watch John Brown Dog, the grandfather, and the girl walking up from the sea. "These are the ones we want," the man said. "Take these three into custody!" he shouted.

The agents left Charlie bleeding red all over the ground and rushed to cuff the three Indians, even the little girl, whose wrists were too small for handcuffs so they had to use plastic ties on her.

Although the uniformed commander was now giving orders, the grandfather saw immediately who was in charge and told the man in the dark suit, "Let me see to your agent there, Charlie Hart."

"That's not Hart."

"It is. Let me see to him."

"Go to hell." Still, the man in the suit was impressed with the grandfather's audacity, cuffed and in custody yet making demands.

As the three of them in chains and plastic bindings were being led past Charlie Hart, the girl cried out, "Hun-hun-HE! Hun-hun-HE!"

The agent holding her thin upper arm shook her hard to be quiet but she continued the courage chant until John Brown Dog and the grandfather joined in that chant that announces the presence of a true warrior.

The agents became all the more agitated, worried where all this chanting might lead, but the man in the suit remained steady, ordering the men, "Drag those three onto the fucking helicopters *now.*"

As tightly as the little girl was being held, she wasn't being held tightly enough and got away and ran, hands behind her back, to where Charlie Hart lay and she danced around him like a small dervish before they could recapture her, and even then she danced furiously in their embrace and chanted, "This is Loon Heart! *Mahn-go-taysee!* This is Strong Heart! *Soan-ge-taha!*"

36

"WELCOME TO THE OVAL OFFICE."

The president behind his desk, several men and one woman in chairs nearby, the grandfather on a couch, two large men on either side of him, a plastic shield-wall separating the president from the grandfather.

"I welcome you on behalf of the American people," the president continued.

Each of the large men flanking the grandfather held a capture pole, a hollow pipe through which a rope was threaded. On one end of the pole, the capture end, the rope came out in a loop. On the handle end of the pole was a grip that a man could pull to tighten the noose. Capture poles are used by animal control officers to subdue vicious dogs, the rope preventing the dog from escaping while the pole prevents the animal from getting close to the officer. In this case, the capture pole nooses were around the grandfather's neck.

The president still speaking: "But more than that, sir, I offer you my personal welcome along with my sincere hope that we can work together to resolve our—"

"Fuck you—"

The ropes around the grandfather's neck tightened. He struggled a moment, then stopped—but they kept the ropes tight enough to cut off his air.

He'd thought he was too old to change, but they had changed him. No longer wry, ironic, sly. No longer amused by much of what he saw in the world. During the time—had it been weeks?—they had held him and interrogated him, the old man had lost his sense of humor, his patience, his mental balance. More shaming to him, the grandfather had lost his dignity.

Working with his allies, he had imagined presenting himself, on behalf of those allies, to the President of the United States. The grandfather intended to wear his ceremonial war shirt, embroidered with events of his life. He would carry several beaded leather belts representing tribes with ghost dancers. He would grease back his hair and carry himself with solemnity. The president would know he was a serious man. This had been the grandfather's plan.

He tried not to gasp for breath, not to give them the satisfaction. But when he realized he was about to foul himself, the grandfather closed his eyes from the shame of it and desperately sucked for air, which is when they eased off on the ropes around his neck.

They had dressed him in a hospital gown, open in the back. He had been incarcerated and hospitalized as a danger to himself and others, which meant they could do with him what they would. His hair was wild, eyes red from lack of sleep, but it was the awful gown that robbed him of the last of his dignity.

When the grandfather was breathing steadily, the president said, "I worked on the docks and probably have the foulest mouth of any man who's ever occupied this office but I think my advisers here were shocked to hear you curse me. You might be the first man to sit in the Oval Office, across from the president at his desk, and tell him to fuck off."

"I was interrupted before I could finish."

"Of course, go ahead."

"I was about to say, 'Fuck you, you fascist pig.'"

They tightened the ropes again, the president waiting a moment before instructing them to ease off.

"We can keep this up for as long as you want," the president said. "But it's not getting us anywhere. I've taken the extraordinary step of inviting you, a sworn enemy of the United States, a terrorist, inviting you into the Oval Office—"

"Dressed in this shameful thing . . . snares around my neck . . . this glass wall set up in front of me." The grandfather tried kicking at it with both feet but the clear, bulletproof, shatterproof panel was too far away to reach with his ankles shackled. "What's the thinking here?" he asked the president. "That I'm going to jump you, spit on you, piss on you—what are you being protected *from*?"

"The *thinking*, sir, is that you are in possession of some sort of toxin or transmissible agent that can do a great deal of damage. The sort of damage that caused the calamity that's gripped America with fear."

"Your Nazi doctors have probed and tested me for days; they know there's no toxin in me."

"Be that as it may, I was advised not to bring you here, regardless of what precautions we used. But I thought it was in the best interest of our people and of peace—"

"No, your scientists told you that the girl was doing something impossible, doing something your science said could not be done, doing something that buggered your technology. And for days I've been insisting that you bring me here before it's over. She's almost finished doing it, isn't she? And I told your fascist goon doctors who were torturing me in that fuck-fake hospital, I told them that if the mother finished what she was doing before I had a chance to come to the White House and talk to the president, then you people were going to be in a world of shit. And *that's* what finally convinced you to bring me here like I've been asking all along. Because of what the girl is doing. How old is she now?"

"I'm not going to discuss the details of—"

"She's a baby, isn't she?"

"I'm not accustomed to being constantly interrupted."

"Fuck you, you fascist pig. I know it's freaking your fucking fascist scientists out of their gourds because they're watching a child reverse time, getting younger and younger, which should be impossible, right? But heed me, Nazi—when she's young enough to be born, that's when your new world gets rolled up and the old world is revealed again."

"Yes, I know that's what you say. We've been reading reports on your statements."

"Soon you will be reading reports that women aren't getting pregnant."

"We doubt that claim. But in the interest of national security—"

"Let me ask you a question about national security. Could you order one of your Marines to fuck a baby if it was for national security?"

This genuinely offended the president. "I'll put you back in the hospital and wait for a call that you've come to your senses."

"Wait for that call long enough and there will be no one to answer it. Your people will be gone and my people, the tribe who will eventually live here, they will be grazing their horses on your lawn out there, you fucking fascist pig."

One of the men holding a capture pole simultaneously tightened the noose and shook the pole to make the old man shut his filthy mouth.

"Stop it," the president told the man and then started to get up from behind the desk. But several advisers signaled for him to stop and the president returned to his chair. "I was told you were an honorable man," the president said. "Obviously, I was misinformed."

"I once was an honorable man, but you have put me in this despicable gown." The hospital gown was more shaming to the grandfather than his shackles. When he walked and the gown opened in the back, showing his old red ass, men guarding him laughed. "You put a glass wall in front of me like I'm my ancestors' bones on display. . . . Treat me like a monster and I will by God act like one, I'll close my eyes and call down this White House into a pile of rubble."

He closed his eyes, everyone in the room tensing.

When the grandfather opened his eyes, he said, "But I promised my allies I would talk to you . . . even though you are a fucking Nazi."

The president waited a moment, then said, "Charlie Hart is waiting in the hallway, I'll ask him to come in."

The grandfather didn't believe Listens to Indians was alive, but an aide was dispatched to fetch him and here he is: Charlie Hart, still dark-skinned, dressed in a suit, very much alive.

"I thought they had killed you by the ocean," the grandfather said, his heart light for the first time since being in this office.

Charlie Hart smiled and nodded and took a designated seat.

"You don't greet me?" the grandfather asked.

Charlie looked away.

"What have they done to you?" the grandfather asked.

It was the president who answered. "We've done nothing to him. Agent Hart has agreed to become a kind of ambassador from his people to yours. I think he has a great deal of sympathy for you. At Little Bighorn, those officers whose skin was turned black? They returned to being white within a short time. As you can see, Agent Hart has stayed dark. Maybe that's an indication of his sympathies with his red brothers."

"Yeah, we'll smoke the peace pipe later, Great White Father—first I want to speak to Listens to Indians."

"Of course," the president said. "As soon as we conduct our business here. Let's talk about your allies."

"Let's talk about federal forests and state parks."

The president paused but then surprised the grandfather by agreeing. "All right, let's talk about them."

The grandfather wondered how far he could push his position. "I want to see John Brown Dog."

"I'm afraid that's impossible."

"You killed him?"

"No—"

"Charlie, did they kill John Brown Dog?" the grandfather asked.

Charlie Hart didn't answer; he had on an Indian face.

"If you haven't killed John Brown Dog," the grandfather said to the president, "then produce him. Right here, right now. After I see him I will tell you what must be done before the mother is young enough to be born because when that happens, there is no turning back."

"What exactly do you mean, there's no turning back?"

"Tell me, she's a baby now, isn't she? An infant? How young? How much time do we have?"

The president conferred with advisers before telling the grandfather, "Your John Brown Dog is in a facility far from here. It would take a whole day to bring him to Washington."

"Then fuck you."

They tightened the nooses and cut off his air again, until the president said, "I don't want either of you men to do that again, unless he tries to get away."

When the grandfather could speak, he said, "Fuck you. Let the mother be born and let your world roll away to reveal the old world as it once was, let it be done, fuck you, you fascist pig." The old man put on *his* Indian face.

The president and several advisers conferred, then the president and three aides left the Oval Office. The large men holding the capture poles occasionally tightened the nooses surreptitiously just to watch the effect on the grandfather, how he stiffened, how his dark face deepened toward purple—then they let him breathe again, then they started tightening the ropes again. In between these ordeals, the grandfather tried unsuccessfully to catch Charlie's eye.

Everyone returned in just short of an hour.

"John Brown Dog will be here in a few minutes," the president announced.

The old man said, "So he wasn't far from here after all. Is this how you intend to continue our negotiations, by lying at every turn, you fucking fascist lying pig?"

"It's childish for you to keep calling me names."

"Then let me dress in a man's clothes."

Before the president could respond, a door opened and John Brown Dog was brought in.

He shuffled the way the elderly shuffle or like a man in the final stages of tertiary syphilis, his eyes blank as if the lobotomist's blade had arced too widely; he'd lost weight and posture, hair and hope.

The grandfather was appalled and looked at Charlie Hart, who again looked away.

Although John Brown Dog was younger and stronger than the grandfather, he had been sufficiently weakened that capture poles were deemed unnecessary. His ankles were unshackled, his wrists cuffed in front, not behind his back.

"Here he is; now keep your word," the president said. "Tell us about your allies. Explain what happens after the girl's gone."

"Whatever you've done to this man," the grandfather asked, "is it reversible?"

The president heard from an adviser before speaking. "He was having psychotic episodes that made him a danger to himself and to those who were treating him. His treatment protocol was approved by licensed physicians."

The grandfather had a dozen things he wanted to say, but held his tongue.

"Now keep your word and tell us about your allies," the president insisted.

"Can these nooses be taken from around my neck? They remind me too much of earlier negotiations between Indians and Europeans."

After a quiet but animated conversation with several advisers, the president said, "Regrettably, the security devices stay in place."

"These *devices* are used on dogs, not men."

"You promised you'd speak to us frankly if we brought in this man, and now there he stands; will you keep your word or not?"

The grandfather closed his eyes, then opened them. "I promised you I would and I will. Even more important to me, I also promised Listens to Indians that I would tell you what must be done to prevent your world from being rolled up. Didn't I, Charlie?"

Hart said nothing.

"Who are your allies?" the president asked.

"Our allies are alien to you. Our allies are the dead, who are not without power. You were warned long ago not to mistreat the Indians or you would have to answer to our dead."

"Who's the girl and what happens when she's gone?"

"She is the old world, preparing to be reborn."

"And when you speak of our world, the new world, being rolled up, what does that mean?"

"It is the promise of ghost dancing, which we have been practicing for more than a hundred years—that the world of the whites would pass away without war, without anyone being killed. And that will be accomplished when none of your women ever become pregnant again and your world dies off naturally."

"And the significance of the girl reaching birth age, actually being 'born,' so to speak?"

"That's when it's too late for you to return our land."

The president was nodding as if he already knew everything the grandfather had just explained to him. "And Indians will continue having children, will eventually be reestablished?"

"So our allies tell us."

"Where will they be kept while the rest of us are dying off?"

"I don't know."

"How long will it be before Indian tribes are reestablished?"

"I don't know. The earth will require a long time to heal, hundreds of years."

"And then I suppose Indians will be good guardians of the earth—would these be the same Indians whose ancestors killed off hundreds of species when they first migrated to North America, who ran buffalo herds over cliffs to butcher a few individual animals, who set forests and prairies on fire to catch game that fled the fires in terror?"

The old man looked at the president and asked, "Where were you born?"

"I'm a New Yorker, born right in Manhattan."

"When your ancestors arrived in the 1600s, Manhattan was a tree-covered island of hills, full of game, drained by forty pristine streams. It was this way even though more than five hundred generations of Indians had lived on Manhattan for more than ten thousand years."

The president started to reply but shook his head and said, "I am signing an executive order this very day. Congress, with help from our friend Congressman Blaine, who has joined us here today, is passing legislation. And the Supreme Court is going into special session to review and, we trust, certify as constitutional both my executive order and the legislation. The bottom line of all this: you're getting the land."

The grandfather didn't believe him. "Every park, every forest?"

"Yes. It'll take time for the details to work out, for the federal government and all the states to remove our presence from those lands, but *as of today* it will be official. Now for your end of the bargain. You and your allies must reverse whatever you've done. You must not prevent our women from becoming pregnant."

"Charlie!" the grandfather called. "Are they telling the truth?"

"Of course we're telling the truth," the president said, turning to Charlie. "Tell him."

Hart nodded.

"I want him to say it to my face," the grandfather insisted, knowing how clever these people were with their words: *We will agree to this treaty,* and then the lands won't be given to us; or there will be court challenges that go on for a hundred years; or the parks will be bought back by giving the right amount of money to the right group of cooperating Indians. "If Listens to Indians says it to my face, I will believe it."

"Go on, Agent Hart. Stand up and tell him to his face."

Reluctantly Hart got to his feet and straightened his shoulders, while still refusing to look at the grandfather. He did, however, stare at John Brown Dog, who stood near the middle of the room, his head hanging down, mouth ajar, a string of drool dropping to his shirt.

"Agent Hart?" the president said. "Go ahead."

"It's too late," Charlie Hart said softly. "She's already gone, the mother has already been reborn."

Hearing this, John Brown Dog closed his mouth and lifted his head.

"The old world is here," Charlie said. "They already know . . . women aren't getting pregnant."

John Brown Dog began dancing, though weakly.

"It's done," Charlie said more loudly.

John Brown Dog lifting one foot, then the other, and then he began to chant.

The grandfather whooped. "One speaking the truth, the other dancing—how will you resist that, *Mr. President?"*

Secret Service agents swarmed John Brown Dog, the grandfather using this distraction to stand and begin dancing too, within the limits of his shackles. Before the handlers could choke him into submission, a window broke and plaster dust fell on everyone.

The Oval Office began cracking. Agents and Marines rushed to the president, covering him with their bodies while simultaneously moving him toward a door as the seal of the United States of America, sculpted in the ceiling of the Oval Office, fell like an arrow on the bull's-eye of the presidential seal that was woven into the Oval Office's oval rug.

Meanwhile, the big Indian danced on the edge of that oval rug, dancing as beams split throughout the White House, turning black.

37

PEOPLE WASTED THE FIRST twenty-five years trying to reverse the irreversible. A quixotic effort for babies was pursued throughout the world. Remote villages tried to entice fertility with prayer, chants, spells, and sacrifices. Researchers in technologically advanced nations were given unlimited funds to mount a war against sterility. Massive searches were conducted all over the globe to find native people still fecund, the idea being that maybe the natives' fertile wombs and motile sperm could be exploited by civilized society. The scientists of the First World and the shamans of the Third achieved equal degrees of success, which is to say none. People searched for but never found a native tribe still having babies.

Another common mistake made during this first twenty-five years was thinking that the world's end was imminent, so near that there was no point to working or making house payments. But the world went on. While the calamity devastated couples who wanted children and eventually wiped out the incomes of kindergarten teachers and pediatricians and baby food manufacturers, much of the world population was unaffected in the beginning. This was hard for people to accept, that all human life on earth was coming to an end with so little impact on how we lived our daily lives. No more babies, yet we still have to meet the necessities of food, clothing, housing. No more babies, yet we still have to take our heart medicine and deal with a monthly period and change the oil in the car. As the years passed, people who early on had quit work and walked away from responsibility were forced to walk right back and find jobs.

The last babies, whose mothers were pregnant during the origins of the calamity, were treasured, spoiled, protected more than any other generation of children, even those in America at the turn of the twenty-first century. *All* babies were prized, even those diseased, malformed, and of marginal intelligence.

Kidnappings became epidemic, but tapered off as the last children grew into teenagers and young adults.

A cult of youth spread throughout the world. Before the calamity, youth had been celebrated in western culture but that was nothing like what developed in the first twenty-five years of the humans' last century. People worshiped at the altar of youth. They paid enormous sums simply to be in the presence of a child. Some of this was tinged with sexuality but mainly it arose from a nostalgic desire to be near what was never again to be. And then it came to pass that the youngest person on earth was twenty-five years old.

During the next twenty-five years, societies accepted the inevitability of the calamity, and a renaissance began. Governments made plans for projects that would leave the earth better able to find its equilibrium once all humans were gone. Dams would be dismantled, river locks removed, nuclear waste entombed, animals freed from zoos and returned to the wild where possible, otherwise released in free-range parks where they would be cared for until they died of old age, presumably before the last of the humans.

During this inclination toward our better nature, people became spiritual and turned to philosophy. Although young people were gone, universities flourished to accommodate older adults seeking to make sense of the world. Ancient enemies shook hands to work on joint projects to, for example, reestablish the natural course of a border river that had been diverted to irrigate farmland and supply cities with potable water. Now that the previously largest age cohort on earth (those under twenty-five) no longer existed, pressure to produce the basics (agricultural products, drinking water, oil) eased off. Armies turned from studying warfare to practicing environmental restoration. Governments opened the spigots: whatever wealth, surpluses, reserves existed were given away. People turned to what they did before governments formed: neighbors and families took care of one another.

But the renaissance flourished for only a few years, followed by a period when the most brutish aspects of our nature came out for one last midnight show. Where national leadership had become soft and distracted, warlords took over. Battles were fought over land that would soon enough be occupied by no one. People on opposite sides of those ancient hatreds decided they couldn't wait for each other to die out naturally; their enemies needed to be killed now. National budgets that had been diverted to earth-restoration projects were diverted right back to war. The strong ruled the weak.

Alcohol and drug use became commonplace. As if some genetic core had been perverted by the idea of the species dying out, sexual promiscuity became the norm and rape was epidemic . . . a woman who had never cheated on her husband might fuck two or three different men a day, and a man who had never raised his voice to a woman might steal into a neighboring home and violently rape the old woman who lived there.

It was terrible—and by the end of it, the youngest person on earth was fifty.

During the third quarter of that last century, wars ended as warriors aged—old men being famous for conducting wars but lousy at fighting in them. The renaissance that had gotten under way and then been stopped a few decades before was given another, final chance. People were ashamed at having wasted so much time, so many resources. Dams that were going to be carefully dismantled were now simply blown up. Domestic and zoo animals that were supposed to be carefully reintroduced to the wild were simply turned loose or euthanized. People got too old and too few in number to do all of the work they had planned on earth's behalf.

Vast numbers left cities to walk the countryside. These wanderers abandoned their homes to join strangers in a migration—where, they did not know, and for reasons they could not articulate.

This wandering (also called the roaming) apparently rose from some ancient instinct to migrate in times of trouble. During the plague in the Middle Ages, entire towns emptied as people wandered across the land. The instinct to get up and go was what got our species out of Africa and prompted us to colonize the globe. It saved our asses when glaciers or droughts arrived and other species froze or died of thirst while we packed our things in bearskins and hit the trail.

During this third quarter, governments ceased to exist, society devolved toward the tribal, and people starved or thrived depending on their ability to live off the land.

At the end of this third quarter of the last century of humans, the youngest person on earth was seventy-five.

The final quarter was elegiac in a thousand ways. The last window was closed for the last time as the last occupied house went unoccupied. The last bicycle ever to be ridden was ridden and left on the ground. Catch was played for the last time, the last ball thrown by one person and caught by another. The last dog with a human companion got rubbed behind its ears for the last time. The last song was sung somewhere by someone; no one knows the tune, the singer, the venue. The last dance was danced, and then people were too old to dance.

This final generation had come to the end of its string. As children, they had been idolized. As young adults, they felt privileged and superior to their elders, who indulged them in all things. Even into their middle years, their forties and fifties, they felt and acted youthful—which, of course, they were in comparison to everyone else. But when they became the only elderly on earth, they had no one to care for them. And then at the end, at the very end, they paid the ultimate price for always being the youngest: they died alone.

The passenger pigeon had been the most numerous bird on earth, its flocks flying in multiple layers a mile wide and three hundred miles long, darkening the skies for days as they passed overhead. There were nearly as many passenger pigeons in North America (five billion or more) when the Europeans arrived as there were people on earth (six and a half billion) when the calamity struck. The passenger pigeon might be the only species for whom the moment of extinction is known to the hour: one P.M., September 1, 1914, when the female passenger pigeon Martha died in the Cincinnati Zoo.

Not so the last human on earth. Maybe an old man living near the coast in Japan, still able to catch fish and haul water, choked on a bone at age one hundred and one. Or an old woman in Appalachia, keeping chickens and still smoking a pipe, dying in her sleep at age one-oh-five. Whoever it was, wherever the last of us lived, by whatever name he or she was called, the passing, unlike that of the passenger pigeon, went unmarked.

At the end of the century following the calamity, give or take a decade or so, the modern human being, *Homo sapiens sapiens*—the wise, wise man—was extinct.

After that, time got old and forgot us. Nature sorted things out as she always does.

On an earth without humans, predators and prey thrived or perished according to the natural order. All over North America, deer flourished for a period of years, feeding on agricultural fields that had gone to grass and on overgrown suburban yards and city parks and the million miles of highway berms and medians. These deer presented a world of plenty for the major predators, which eventually spread across the whole of the United States, migrating from wilderness areas or breeding from seed animals that the last humans helped establish. The abundance of deer encouraged overbreeding of wolves and big cats and grizzlies so that when the deer populations crashed as lawns choked with weeds, and fields grew up in saplings, the predators died back also. Nature's balance is never static, never a benevolent Garden of Eden where all plants and animals live in harmony. Species that are winners in the natural order take over and dominate everything but then get killed off. Species that are losers lay low and die out or survive and seize their chances for takeover.

Nothing we did was any worse than what had happened before and would happen again. Man was natural. Everything we did was natural. Including dying off.

The human legacy to a place like Manhattan might seem immutable, those thousands of buildings and hundreds of miles of streets, subways and bridges, but Manhattan eventually went natural, too—with some interesting results for plant and animal life. One might think that the cockroach would take over New York City without humans to poison and trap the little bastards but, in fact, cockroaches are native to mild or tropical climates and when those New York buildings lost their heat not just for one winter but for a hundred years, forever, all the cucarachas died and New York City was cockroach-free for the first time since the insect was introduced from African slave ships in the 1600s.

New York City squirrels, who had for generations been living large, became easy meals for a dozen predator species moving to the city after we left. The squirrels that survived did so with humility, seldom seen or heard.

Rat populations, dependent on food stores of our garbage and living in places we provided, died back in this new-old world without people. Although *Rattus* ultimately survived, filling a niche in the natural order, it was a small one under heavy pressure from predators. Early in the first new century, a large number of cats and dogs, those resourceful and strong enough to survive at least temporarily without us, made rats their number one prey, as did the falcons and hawks and, eventually, eagles that filled the air over the canyons of Manhattan.

The dogs' case was a heartbreaker. One of the earliest pieces of archeological evidence of the dog-human connection was found in a twelve-thousand-year-old grave in Israel, where a woman was buried with her arms around a puppy. So close is this human-dog relationship that it seems to have left a genetic imprint that distinguishes the dog from all other canids, including the wolf. Behaviorists have done experiments in which they have given puppies and wolf cubs a perplexing problem to solve—a previously reliable source of food is suddenly made unavailable. The wolf cub will try to solve the problem in a number of ways and eventually give up and walk away. The puppy will also eventually decide he can't solve the problem but, instead of leaving, he will do a remarkable thing: he will turn his head and look to the human observer, clearly expecting help. Indians speak of the same phenomenon but in different terms, of the Great Creator making a divide between humans and all other animals: it is only the dog that jumps across that chasm to cast his lot with man. With his genetic and spiritual connection to humans severed, the dog did not survive long in the new-old world. But before they passed, outclassed by wolves and coyotes that would not breed with them in the wild, those last dogs trotted uncounted miles in a dead-earnest, perpetually hopeful search for the smell of you.

Some of the streams that once flowed across pre-Columbian Manhattan returned along remarkably similar routes as subways collapsed, caving in streets and creating waterways. Lightning set roofs on fire, opening the interior of buildings to the elements. Skyscrapers, without heat or maintenance, eventually cracked and collapsed, though some stood for centuries. Streets and sidewalks, heaved by tree roots, became seedbeds and eventually supported trees by the thousands, Central Park growing into a forest with canopy so thick that the perpetually shaded ground became empty of brush and briar, enabling creatures to amble freely among the massive tree trunks, making the forest a park. Although the mark of man would never be completely gone until the next glacier wiped everything clean, in a remarkably short geological time Manhattan came to look strikingly similar to the tree-covered island that supported five hundred generations of Indians.

Consider, then, a snowy winter's night hundreds of years after the last of us. The allies might still keep their word to return tribes to certain parts of the earth but that hadn't been done yet on Manhattan Island. A wolf has trotted across Hell Gate Bridge, the final New York City bridge still standing. Nearly two years old, the male has left his family to find an unattached female and begin his own pack as the alpha male. It is a story that was not unknown to our own Manhattan.

A thick, wet snow has made the night bright, all is quiet and all is white. Skyscraper debris blocks the trail here and there, the wolf scrambling over the rubble, catching no scent. He has to figure out if other wolves are in the vicinity. If there's a pack, he'll avoid it. If there's a female, he'll make his way to her. And there's one wolf way to find out. He yips a few times and then throws back his massive head and howls.

Hundreds of creatures hear that eerie ancient sound as it travels snow-softened, tree-filled Manhattan avenues. To the rabbit in his burrow, it means a new predator to avoid. To the fox in her den, it means the possibility of scavenging from a wolf's kill. To an unattached female of the species, the howl means a potential mate. But something important and something beautiful is missing, to the world's loss: the howl goes unnamed and its music undanced.

About the Author

DAVID LOZELL MARTIN'S previous novels include the international bestsellers *Lie to Me* and *Tap, Tap* and the critically acclaimed *The Crying Heart Tattoo, The Beginning of Sorrows,* and *Crazy Love. Facing Rushmore* is his eleventh book. Martin lives in the Washington, D.C., area.

Printed in the United States
By Bookmasters